Healing Heather

(Book 4 of the Ruadhán Sidhe "Shadows" Novels)

By Aiki Flinthart

2020

Thank you to the readers who have enjoyed my other books enough to leave nice reviews and to let me know. Because of you, I keep writing.

And...as always...thanks to my husband for his patience and encouragement. Seriously. Patient. Unbelievably patient. Even more so, recently. He is the love of my life and I'm deeply grateful to have met and married him so many wonderful years ago.

Healing Heather

Cover design by Lou Harper Design
Copyright © 2020 Aiki Flinthart

A Cataloging-in-Publications entry for this title is available from the National Library of Australia.

ISBN-13: 978-0-6487736-3-4 (Trade Paperback)
ISBN-13: 978-0-6487736-2-7 (e-book)
CAT Press
PO Box 3388, Darra
QLD 4076, Australia

Discover other titles by Aiki Flinthart

at: **www.aikiflinthart.com**

Including:

The Blackbirds Novels (Historical Fantasy)

Blackbirds Sing (#1)

The Ruadhan Sidhe Novels (YA Urban Fantasy)

Shadows Wake (#1)

Shadows Bane (#2)

Shadows Fate (#3)

The Kalima Chronicles (YA Adventure/Fantasy)

IRON (#1)

FIRE (#2)

STEEL (#3)

A Future, Forged (prequel)

The 80AD series (YA Adventure/Fantasy)

80AD Book 1: *The Jewel of Asgard*

80AD Book 2: *The Hammer of Thor*

80AD Book 3: *The Tekhen of Anuket*

80AD Book 4: *The Sudarshana*
80AD Book 5: *The Yu Dragon*

Sold! (Contemporary Romance/Adventure)

Short Story Anthologies
The Zookeeper's Tales of Interstellar Oddities
Return
Elemental
Rogues' Gallery

Healing Heather

Aiki Flinthart 2020

NOTE:
This book is written with AUSTRALIAN
SPELLING/ENGLISH,
not USA spelling/English.
Don't panic.

This is a side-story to the Shadows trilogy
Healing Heather is set a few days after *Shadows Fate*

CHAPTER ONE

TORIN O'CONNOR

'So, you'll take the case, I assume?'

The boarding-school accented voice made Torin O'Connor glance up from his perusal of the document. In his doorway stood a tall, swarthy man. Andrew Carleton's dark blue suit, though tailored, couldn't disguise a thickened middle. Nor could a gleaming Rolex and several large, gold rings distract from fingers swollen with rich living. Flanked by flat-eyed bodyguards, Carleton seated himself opposite Torin without awaiting an invitation. The chair's leather creaked beneath his bulk.

He pulled a cigar from his pocket, bit off the end and spat onto the polished timber floor. His dark eyes, calculating beneath thick brows, reviewed Torin. He pincered the cigar and pointed it at Torin. A guard produced a lighter and stepped forward.

Torin frowned. The guard seemed familiar, somehow. Big, light-footed, broken nose, blue eyes.

'Thank you, Baker,' Carleton said, bending forward to light the cigar.

Torin controlled his annoyance. 'Light that, Mr Carleton, and you can leave now.'

Carleton's lips thinned, then he rolled his wrist, inscribing a circle in the air with the cigar. 'As you wish. You read the file?'

Baker edged back, watching Torin narrowly.

Torin lifted one corner of the grey suede folder in front of him. 'I've read it.' He waited a moment to see if Carleton would speak and continued when he didn't. 'Why do you need to find her?'

Carleton stretched his mouth wide, his teeth white against tanned skin. He waved the cigar dismissively. 'I don't think that's relevant, is it?'

Torin allowed his heels to hit the wooden floor.

'Yes.' He clasped his hands together on the folder. 'With fifteen branches around the world, O'Connor Inc. has a reputation to maintain. We don't kidnap young women with no reason given.' He allowed ice into his expression, unintimidated by Carleton's sneer.

'So, I repeat,' he said, 'what do you need her for?'

Carleton shrugged. His expensive Armani jacket rucked up around his ears until his head appeared neckless.

'She's connected to the death of my youngest daughter, Amali. I want…information. I need to know how and why my daughter died, and where her husband is now.'

Torin stilled. 'Surely that's a matter for the police?' There was something more; something withheld. He was never wrong. That nose for lies was what made him good at being a private investigator.

'I do not want the authorities involved. This is a personal matter.'

'But if your daughter's dead—'

'They are aware of it. They believe it was natural causes. And my daughter, and her husband…' For a moment Carleton hardened and his jaw worked. '…are *my* affair.' He regained control and relaxed into a thin imitation of amusement. 'I simply wish to ask the lady whose details are in that folder you hold, what Amali's last words and wishes were. And to extend my condolences to my daughter's husband. I'm hoping this woman can tell me where to find him.' He heaved a sigh. 'Please. Indulge a grieving father and find her? Surely, you understand how important family is.' He indicated the picture Torin kept on his desk: a twenty year old photo of Torin, his father, mother and sister.

Torin laid the photo face down. His family were long-dead but he disliked Carleton even mentioning them, for some reason.

'I will pay well,' Carleton said.

Torin hesitated, still not liking the feel of this interview. He'd learned to trust his feelings over the last thirty-three years and something about Carleton didn't sit right. Still…. He considered the file on his desk. The young woman in question, if the information was true, was dangerous. Someone needed to rein her in before she killed anyone else.

'I'll put my best man on it,' he conceded, rising and extending a hand.

'I trust so.' Carleton ignored the offer to shake. 'When he finds her, have them meet me here, in New York. Here's my card.' He tossed a gold-embossed business card onto Torin's desk and swept from the office.

The guard, Baker, saluted with a hint of a smirk on his lips.

Torin texted his partner.

#

Twenty minutes later Kade Miller sauntered into the room, energetic, careless, throwing a laughing rejoinder to Torin's secretary over his shoulder as he flicked the door shut. He strolled to the desk, his sneakers soundless, hands jammed into the pockets of faded jeans, plain grey tshirt hanging loose across his lean shoulders. He seemed comfortable. Relaxed. A lopsided smile was echoed by ironic humour in his grey eyes.

Torin examined him speculatively. Was it wise to give him this case? It had taken years for the bitter withdrawal to fade into acceptance and for Kade's natural humour to resurface. Was Kade ready to take on something that hit so close to the bone? There was no-one else available. Besides, something about the case made Torin determined to give it to someone he trusted.

Settling into a chair, Kade rested his feet on the desk and stifled a yawn. 'What's up, oh great leader?'

With an eye-roll, Torin sat. 'We're equal partners.'
p14

Kade's grin twisted into smugness. 'But you *like* the leader thing. I much prefer the road.' He gestured at the leather-and-timber office with its dark wooden furniture and earth-tone colours. 'You get off on running this place. And you're good at it. Let me do what I'm good at.'

'And that is?' Torin tapped his fingertips on the folder. He knew what the answer would be.

'Finding people for money,' Kade replied. 'Isn't that why you called me? What've you got?'

'Not sure it's a good idea to give you this one. But I don't have anyone else available.'

Kade grabbed the folder and opened it. 'Reverse psychology? Bit obvious for you. What's so…' He flipped a page. 'Ah. Not reverse psychology. You were serious. Shit, Tor. You know how I feel about people like this woman.'

The humour slipped from his mobile face, leaving it blank. He finished skimming the written file. The eyes he raised to Torin's were haunted by old pain and Torin cursed his own stupidity. He should have turned the job down rather than inflict it on Kade.

'No one else at all?' Kade's voice was flat.

'Sorry. I should have told him to get lost. It's just…' Torin spun the grainy photo and flicked it across the desk. 'There's something about this girl. And something about the client. I think we need to take this job. I don't know why.'

Kade picked up the photo and stilled. Slowly, he lowered the image, then examined it again. Nodding, he stood. There was a hint of bewilderment in his expression when he tucked the photo into the folder and patted it.

'Alright,' he said, 'I'll do it. You've always had good instincts about people. It's how we're still alive, after all. Get me a meeting with this Carleton. I have a few questions.'

Taken aback by his ready acquiescence, Torin could do no more than agree. Kade left, the folder under one arm.

Torin noted the lack of spring in his step, and swore. Hopefully he wasn't putting Kade in danger.

Again.

CHAPTER TWO

TORIN

Ten minutes after Kade left Cathy admitted Torin's next clients. He got to his feet and assessed the two strangers when they entered. Both young, late teens perhaps; early twenties by the confidence with which they carried themselves. The girl was slender and graceful with blonde hair that seemed subtly wrong against her olive skin. Her brown eyes flicked about his office, touching on his gun cabinet.

She winced when sunlight, reflected off a window opposite, flashed across her eyes. She ignored Torin's offer to shake hands, instead seating herself in the chair vacated by Carleton. She shifted so her back was to the wall, both exits from the office in sight.

The man also walked with the lithe confidence of someone with body-training; movements under control; aware of his surroundings. He shook Torin's hand and inclined his head at his partner.

'Thankyou for seeing us. I'm sorry about Rowan.' He smiled at her and she returned cool resignation. 'She's never liked shaking hands. I'm Logan.' His accent was neutral but with hints of British. Interesting.

Torin studied them both. Why did they seem familiar? Had he met them somewhere before?

Waving Logan toward the second chair, Torin seated himself behind the desk.

'What can I do for you folks?' He steepled his fingertips and waited.

Logan angled forward, intense, all humour gone. 'We need you to find someone.' He pulled a thin, yellow folder out of a knapsack and slid it across the desk. A usb device was clipped to it. 'This is everything we have on him. Last we saw him was in Florence, Italy, about two weeks ago. His jet's flight plan was logged as coming to New York but we can't find a record of his landing.'

Spinning the folder, Torin flipped it open and perused the front page. 'Finn Andvarisson. Why are you trying to find him?'

Rowan, who'd slouched in silence, sat up. 'He's wanted for murder. Of Logan's mother.'

'Shouldn't you be talking to the police?'

'No. He'll run if he finds we've spoken to the police, or that we're following him.' She stood, wiping her palms down the front of her jeans and green tshirt.

Torin plugged the USB into his laptop and skimmed the files. 'Impressive military training history. But why does it stop over a decade ago? Where's he been in that time?'

'Not important,' Logan said.

'How about you let me decide that? Knowing his work contacts from the last decade will give us a place to start.'

Logan exchanged a look with Rowan, who shrugged and strode to the window.

'He's been working for an organisation called the Mors Ferrum,' Logan said. His jaw clenched and his fingers whitened where they rested on his chair arms. 'We…closed their branch in Italy, but someone here in the US must have offered Finn a place to hide.'

Tapping at his keyboard, Torin frowned. 'Nothing on a Mors Ferrum but a few crackpot sites on conspiracy theories. Who are they?'

Logan raised flat eyes, his lips pressed thin. 'People the conspiracy theorists were right about. There's a file on that usb listing as many known members in the US as we could find. But it's unlikely he'll contact them. He knows we have the list. Try the dark web.'

'Twisty kind of place,' Torin replied. What would these two kids know about the dark web? 'Hard to find what you're after without the right contacts. Not giving me much to go on, are you? Even a photo?' Torin spotted an image file and opened it. Surprised, he inspected Logan, who was pale but returned only steady calm. 'A relative?' Torin asked. The similarities were unmissable.

'My father,' Logan replied, his voice harsh.

'Ah.' Torin knew better than to make any other response.

Rowan moved to stand behind Logan's chair, her hands on his shoulders. 'Let your people know he'll wear a disguise, but a photo will show his real image.'

'Some sort of holographic projection?'

'Something like that,' she said. 'But if they find him, do *not* let them engage. He will show your people no mercy.

Make sure they observe and report only. Find him and we'll take over.'

Torin folded his arms, quashing a flare of irritation that this girl-child presumed to take such a tone of command to someone a decade older than herself.

Logan cast her a resigned eyeroll. 'Rowan. Behave.'

She shot Torin a small, half-smile. 'Sorry. Logan keeps telling me I don't play well with others. I apologise for telling you how to do your job. I know how dangerous Finn can be and I don't want your people to get hurt.'

Logan rose. 'I might not agree with Rowan's diplomacy, Mr O'Connor, but she is right. Find him, but be careful. Money isn't an issue. Here's my number.' He passed over a card with nothing but a phone number and a generic, numeric email address.

Torin looked up at them. He accepted the card. 'Alright, but if you're intending something illegal I can't be an accessory.' Something about this couple pulled at him. He'd met a lot of distraught relatives but few as composed as this pair.

'*We* aren't intending anything illegal,' Logan's reply was wry. 'He usually is, though. We just want to bring him to justice.' He glanced at Rowan. 'Be aware, though, even working outside the Mors Ferrum, he's got…connections. He won't be easy to find.'

'Mob? Russian? Yakuza?' Torin asked. 'What kind of connections? Where should I start?'

'A little less mainstream.' Rowan pursed her lips. 'Think in terms of human trafficking, perhaps. Medical experiments.'

Torin ground his teeth. 'Unpleasant. I'll see what I can do.'

'He'll have money and resources,' Logan warned.

'Understood,' Torin agreed. 'I have several ex-military who'd jump at the chance to do something other than insurance claims and unfaithful spouses.'

Logan offered a hand and Torin shook it, impressed with the boy's level-headed calm.

Torin held out a hand to Rowan, keeping it there even when she resisted. Sighing, she gripped it, ignoring Logan's abortive negatory gesture.

'Thank y—' She broke off, then gasped and wrenched free of Torin. Her cheek was pale, her eyes shadowed. She sagged against Logan and he held her close.

'Mr O'Connor,' Logan said, ushering Rowan to the door, 'we appreciate your help and discretion. Call if you have any questions about the file.'

Rowan paused at the exit. Her expression was grave when she addressed Torin.

'Mr O'Connor.' Her jaw sharpened.

'Rowan, don't,' Logan said.

She ignored him and continued, 'When your partner finds that woman, he's going to need your help. Keep your chopper on standby.'

'How—'

She spoke over Torin's query. 'But *she's* going to need your help, too. She's…important. To both of you. Take care of her. She's in great danger.' Rowan spoke in a rush. 'If you don't, she'll die.'

'But how—'

She cut him off with a sharp gesture. 'And I think our cases might…possibly…be connected.' She made a frustrated noise. 'I'm not sure. I can't see—'

'Rowan!' Logan's low-voiced warning stopped her mid-sentence.

Sending Torin a piercing look, she added, 'When he finds her, if she survives, call us. She'll need us.'

After they left, Torin drummed on the desk phone, debating whether to call Kade. But what could he say? "A teenager has predicted some weird shit would happen when you find Carleton's target?" He uttered a mirthless laugh and left the phone unused.

CHAPTER THREE

HEATHER

The sensation of being watched tingled at the nape of Heather's neck, overriding her pleasure in a warm autumn day and a decent cup of coffee. The feeling was too strong to ignore any longer. She sipped her coffee, brushed aside a strand of straight blonde hair and eyed the other café patrons with feigned casualness.

An elderly couple bickering over the price of breakfast; a pretty young college student texting while her impatient boyfriend watched on; the waiter, yawning already at eight in the morning. No one special. She made a show of rubbing her neck as if to ease sore muscles, then twisted her head to look around.

There. Leaning against a pole near the counter. A tall man, observing her with covert interest and admiration. Sunglasses on his head framed a strong, angular face and light grey eyes, narrowed against the morning glare. Auburn highlights glinted in dark brown hair. He exuded an aura of strength, sexual potency and leashed energy that matched his muscular frame. One hand was jammed casually into the rear pocket of his jeans, the other held his phone.

Accidentally catching his gaze, Heather looked away in polite disinterest, hiding her relief. She sipped her coffee. Admirers she could ignore. She was jumpy today, that was all.

Sensing danger where there should be none. Her skin prickled with anticipation of…something. Perhaps Angela or Carmelita would call today. They were both due to. Then she would have something to do other than sit around and wait and worry. It would be better if this weren't her day off work. At least at work she was too busy to worry.

She swiped a page of the online news and tried to ignore the miserable headlines. War, famine, death. Why did she bother? What difference did she make in this stupid, self-destructive world anyway?

Sighing, she tilted her head to catch the warm sunshine, to draw a breath of soft air that hinted at mown grass and flowers, letting the end-of-summer's bounty of life restore her own. She couldn't afford to think like that. She did what she could and made a tiny difference to a few people. That's all she could ask of herself. All anyone could ask.

A shadow fell across the table.

Her handsome admirer from the counter blocked the sun. She squinted to better study his light-haloed face.

'Can I help you?' she asked, shading her eyes. My lord, but he was handsome. Tanned, dark-haired with the most intelligent, grey eyes she'd ever seen. His lips curved in a quirky smile that invited trust.

He gripped the back of the chair opposite, his strong hands wrapped around the gleaming metal. Broad shoulders, lean hips, long legs. Casually dressed in jeans, sneakers and a grey sports shirt. Radiating confidence and humour. Her heartrate jumped.

'I was standing over there. Noticed you.' His voice was deep and slightly rough—like he'd spent too long yelling at a football game the night before.

Heather shivered, feeling the hairs on the back of her neck rise. Tension coiled in her stomach and her feet moved to gain purchase on the rough, brick-paved ground beneath her chair. This *was* what she had been anticipating.

Him.

But the sense of him wasn't only the red-gold of sexual attraction; it held the darker blood tinge of potential anger as well. She repressed her instinctive reaction to run. It never helped. Instead, she opted for flirty, knowing it to be expected.

Flicking him coyness from beneath her lashes, she said, 'I noticed.'

The man shifted his position. He crossed one arm over his chest and rested an elbow on it, stroking his jaw with long fingers.

'You remind me of someone. Do I know you?'

Heather gathered her handbag into one fist beneath the table. 'That has to be the oldest pickup line in the book.' She tried to recall the area around the café. Alleys. Little hidden shops. Somewhere to disappear.

'Sorry.' He raised both palms, submissive. 'Not trying to be stalkerey. Let me start again.' He grinned and, in spite of her distraction, Heather noted the sheer force of his charm— and refused to succumb to it. He stuck out a hand. 'I'm Kade Miller.'

Heather froze. Touching was risky. Something she rarely did with anyone. She stayed still. Surely he would get the message? He kept his arm extended, apparently oblivious to the idiocy of his position.

Reluctantly, Heather touched the tips of her fingers to his. He grasped her entire palm in a warm, tight grip that rocked her senses. A sharp tingling coursed through her arm, shooting from the centre of her body, sucking resistance from her.

She jumped to her feet, trying to pull free. He didn't let go. Her knees weakened and she tugged harder. Glancing up, she made the mistake of meeting his eyes and saw her nemesis in their cool grey depths.

He knew.

The tingling sensation grew stronger. Her knees weakened and his eyes widened. She clutched at the chair, head swimming. He was stronger than she. Needy. Hurting. Angry. Wanting her on many levels. Taking more and more when she couldn't afford to take back.

She had to break this contact.

Wrenching free, she scooped up her sunglasses. 'Nice meeting you. Running late. Sorry. Have my table. Bye.'

She spun on one heel, striding as rapidly as her shaking legs would permit, out of the café. Once outside the planter-box border, she turned left without hesitation. She knew he followed at a distance. It didn't worry her. He would be easy to lose. She'd had a lot of practice.

The taste of him, though, that lingered in her mind. That would be harder to shake.

Settling into her little car, she paused. Unexpected tears formed. One of her contacts shifted, tinging the world a weird brown. She blotted the tears away before the darned thing came out altogether.

This just wasn't *fair*. When did she get a break? Or was she destined to die young, like her mother? Giving too much. Never finding love. Worn out at 30.

Heather clenched her teeth and jammed the car into gear. Wallowing was for idiots. Time to run.

Again.

Driving at a smart pace, she checked for tails several times; taking odd and devious turns before feeling certain she was no longer being followed. He was good. She was better. She'd been doing this a long, long time.

Then she found a mechanic who'd been recommended by a friend of a client. At his tiny, oily shop she did some sharp haggling before catching a taxi into the middle of town. Nothing like a mall to shake any remaining tagalongs.

At the mall she mingled with the mindless masses, shopping with apparent randomness but with serious intent— hopefully belied by her vague smile and blonde, doll-perfect looks. Finally, after once more checking for unwelcome tails, she ducked into a high-traffic bathroom and, to all intents and purposes, disappeared.

KADE MILLER

Kade smacked a tiled wall in frustration. She'd given him the slip—again. Damn!

He'd lost her in the maze of back streets behind the café, and had almost abandoned hope when a phone call from Luke, who was staking out the mall, had sent him hightailing it over to that end of town. She was good. Too good.

He suspected the reason he'd been able to follow her around the mall was that she thought she'd lost any tails in the car. Even then, she'd almost tricked him three times in the busy shopping centre. Luckily, some sixth sense kept drawing his attention, wherever she went. Then that had failed him.

Now she was gone.

It didn't make sense.

He reviewed the situation.

He'd spotted Meagan O'Hara sitting at the café, as she did each morning. For three days previously, her morning routine had been unvaried. She rose at six am, did some strenuous yoga and martial arts exercises in her living room, showered, and went to the café for a breakfast of fruit, yoghurt and coffee. Then she went to her day job as a midwife in an obstetrics clinic. Nothing unusual.

It was her other activities that interested both Kade and Andrew Carleton. The ones that put young women in danger. The clandestine, illegal ones. Life threatening ones. But he couldn't kidnap her in broad daylight, and was reluctant to move on her without proof of criminal activity.

Meeting Carleton had inspired Kade with loathing and an inclination to protect anyone the man's lascivious gaze fell on.

So far, Meagan O'Hara had done nothing illegal. He'd followed her on ten legitimate house calls to pregnant women. But that was all.

Finally, frustration had got to him. Or perhaps he had given in to the stupid, insane desire to talk to her that had fizzed in him since seeing her photo. One examination of those big brown eyes haunting him from a fuzzy photo, and he'd taken a job he'd already decided to reject. He still didn't know why.

She seemed to be somewhere in her late twenties, tall, ordinary, and too-slender. Lush mouth, but a face easy to miss in a crowd. Hard to believe she was a killer; even harder to believe he was attracted to a woman who was quite possibly a murderer.

He'd expected the job to take only a few days to complete. Andrew Carleton's information had been sketchy at best: two known aliases and addresses with only that one candid, slightly blurry, photograph. But he'd dealt with less.

Of course, the job was made harder when she'd dyed her hair from brown to blonde, even if that did make her delicate features and creamy skin more obvious. But he'd picked up her last known trail in Phoenix and followed her fairly easily to Oklahoma City, where he'd spoken to several of her bewildered legitimate clients after she left town. No leads.

They all agreed: one day, she'd vanished.

She was good at hiding, Kade had to give her that. Professional-level good. It made her seemingly-innocuous daytime activities all the more suspicious in his book. He'd tracked her to a medical centre in Nashville, figuring her work as a midwife would be the link in each city, even if her name and appearance changed.

Now, after only a measly three days of surveillance, he'd given in to his libidinous desires and spoken to her. Stupid. Unprofessional. Unnecessary.

And look what it had got him. She was gone. And he had to start all over again. Neither Torin nor Carleton would be impressed with him. Hell, *he* wasn't impressed with himself.

With absent habit, Kade flexed a stiff shoulder but a lingering ache of the old injury was gone for once. He went to find a quiet place to report his blunder and plan his next move. At least he'd managed to get a decent photo of her.

Studying the brown-eyed blonde who smiled out of the image in his phone, Kade grinned. She had that effect on him.

He dialled Tor's number. 'You're not going to believe this,' he said, not even bothering with a greeting. 'I lost her.'

'Shit,' Tor's deep voice ground out. 'Carleton is already breathing down my neck. We're out of retainer money and he wasn't thrilled when I asked for more last time.'

Kade glared at a random woman who bumped him as she passed by in the mall. She flipped the bird at him and he chuckled.

'I'll do this next find for free, Tor. This woman is too damned good to be an amateur. I don't like Carleton any more than you, but I think he's right to be suspicious. She's hiding something.'

Tor paused then groaned. 'Fine. You're on your own, then. I'll have to take out Luke and Allison to put them onto the Finn Andvarisson case. Those clients need him found asap.'

'Fair call,' Kade replied. 'I'll keep you posted.'

HEATHER

'It's ok Juanita. You're doing great.' Heather checked on the woman. Woman—what a joke. Juanita was barely sixteen, her beautiful, brown face twisted in pain and fear; her skin sheened with perspiration. Her thin hands twisted the colourful blanket draped across her distended stomach.

The smell of blood on the bed mingled with the rich scent of spicy cooking that drifted in from the kitchen next door in the tiny, two-room flat. Juanita gave a screaming sob and overhead someone thumped three times on the ceiling, cursing audibly through the thin boards.

Heather refocussed on her job. It wasn't her place to condemn a frightened sixteen year old for having sex, for getting pregnant, for being too poor to go to hospital. It was her job to help with the birth.

The baby's head crowned and Heather nodded at Juanita's mother.

'Get ready.' She spoke in Spanish, since the soon-to-be-grandmother didn't speak English. 'Juanita, I've got the baby. Don't push for a minute while I position him for the shoulders to come out.' Damn. Her fingers encountered the umbilical cord, wrapped around the baby's little neck. It wasn't tight yet, but it would be once the shoulders were clear. She'd have to work fast to make sure the baby didn't lose circulation and die.

Not again, please. She sent a silent plea to whatever deity happened to be listening. After fifteen years of this, it was hard to believe in any at all.

'Ok. His shoulders are almost clear. One more big push and we'll be done.'

Juanita, sobbed, tears smearing her cheeks. 'I can't. I can't.'

Heather wavered, torn between comforting and encouraging the mother, and forcing her to squeeze again for fear of the baby's life. She cast a pleading look at the grandmother, who set her jaw. A sharp smack echoed as the plump Mexican woman brought the flat of her palm across her daughter's cheek and told her not to be lazy.

In a less dire situation, Heather would have laughed at the shock from the young girl. Crying and snuffling, Juanita took a deep breath and grunted once more. The baby slid into Heather's gloved hands, his face beginning to blue.

She unwound the cord, her actions steady in spite of the adrenalin spiking through her gut. There was no time to wait for the cord to stop pulsing. She clamped and cut it. Wrapping the baby in swaddling, she shielded him with her body; the two women mustn't see what she was going to try next.

Would it work, though?

CHAPTER FOUR

HEATHER

She stripped off a glove and felt the baby's chest, concentrating as she pressed with more than just her fingers. A tiny cough from newly opened lungs. A thin wail echoed through the apartment, then a delighted sob from the new mother when she heard her baby's first cry. The tiny boy was perfectly ok.

Heather returned to the girl, hiding the weakness in her legs as she placed the baby on his mother's breast. And there it was: that look of awe, of unbelieving wonder, of pride and humility. Fresh tears streaked both Juanita's and her mother's cheeks and they examined the baby. Juanita's mother murmured praise and reassurance, stroking her daughter's sweat-soaked hair.

Heather applied herself to the job of checking the placenta was intact, and cleaning up.

An hour later, mother and baby asleep, Heather emerged into the cool midnight air and dragged in a deep, relieved breath. Her shoulders slumped and she stumbled the few steps to her car and climbed in. A light autumn rain soaked the asphalt into a blurry, dark mirror, reflecting streetlights. The streets were almost empty at this hour, which was good. She was so tired she wasn't sure she could cope with traffic.

Each difficult birth took more of a toll than it used to. The drain to her energy levels outweighed the renewals three to one. Maybe it was time she took a break. Didn't she deserve one? Hadn't she sworn never to become like her mother—grey and broken by the age of thirty-five; dead of exhaustion by thirty-seven?

Here she was, twenty-seven and life hadn't changed since she was eleven. The only difference was that now the responsibility was on her shoulders, instead of her mother's. The job of midwifery was hers to carry on. Could she really quit, knowing how many women needed her?

She sighed, switched on the ignition, and drove to her apartment. After parking, Heather pulled her coat close and hurried through the sleeting wind to the barred glass of her shabby apartment block. Toeing aside a little pile of plastic wrappers and drink cans, she tried the door handle. Locked.

A cold wind slipped between buildings and twisted around her body and she shivered. She fumbled amongst her keys for the one to the grille, her fingers made clumsy by fatigue and cold.

A shadow detached itself from the wall and imposed on her space. It was a measure of her exhaustion that she didn't register a threat.

'Meagan O'Hara?'

Heather jumped. Panic sheeted through her system and she raised both arms in automatic self-defence. But the man stayed half-hidden in the darkened corner of the doorway and some of her initial fear dissipated. Finally, the words he'd spoken triggered a response. Sense reasserted itself and she shaped a denial.

'No.' She feigned regret, fiddling with brown curls that escaped her ponytail. 'I'm sorry. You've got the wrong person and I don't think there's a Meagan living in this complex.'

He emerged from the darkness. The door light cast deep shadows under his brows and cheekbones, lending him a menacing air that set her heart racing again. She struggled to keep her face impassively inquiring. Struggled not to show recognition.

It was the man from the café, two months ago. Kade something. How had he found her?

A car swooshed along the wet street, sending a light mist of water into the air to settle on both of them. Droplets glistened on his dark hair.

For a moment, he reviewed her, his grey eyes narrowed. Then he smiled.

'Sorry if I scared you. You do look a bit like Meagan, but...' His grin became rueful.

Heather was not in the least bit fooled. He knew who she was. He'd found her and now she had to move again. Tears pricked the corners of her eyes. She squeezed them away and managed a wan chuckle.

'No problem. I have one of those faces, I guess. Good luck finding her.'

Deliberately, she turned away and steadied herself long enough to fit the key into the door. No sound of retreating footsteps behind her.

'You shouldn't do that, you know,' he cautioned.

'What?' she asked, all innocence, the door half open.

'Turn your back on a stranger in the middle of the night. Open your door while an unknown man is standing right beside you.'

Heather should have felt threatened, but she didn't. For several reasons. Not the least of which was that she got no sense of violence from this man. At least, not toward her. There was a strength, a capability, the aura of leashed passion with a hint of anger. But true violence, no.

'Am I in danger from you?' She dared him to come clean. A loaded question and they both knew it, even if neither would admit it.

A glint of admiration shadowed the grey of his gaze. 'Not from me.'

'I didn't think so.' She turned away again, almost regretting they were on opposite sides. It would have been nice to borrow some of his strength. Lord knew she needed it.

She hesitated. That interchange wouldn't be enough. She needed to throw him off the scent. Looking over her shoulder as she entered through the door, Heather played her best card.

'I'm Fiona MacDonald.' She tipped her head to one side, letting a flirtatious smile play. 'I know it's forward of me, but there's something about you...do you want to have lunch tomorrow?'

There it was: a combination of startled admiration and naked desire. Swiftly masked and replaced with flattered interest.

'Sure. Why not.' He spread his arms wide. 'Name the time and place. I'm free tomorrow.'

'There's a great Indian restaurant on Main street. Two o'clock?' A late lunch would give her time to pack and be ready to disappear.

He nodded. 'Done.'

Just before she closed the door on his handsome face, she snapped her fingers. 'Oh! I forgot to ask your name.'

'Kade. Kade Miller.' A slight, wry smile flickered over his sexy mouth.

'Good night, Kade.' Heather murmured, closing and locking the door. Though she suspected a lock wouldn't keep him out if he decided to pay her a midnight visit.

KADE

Kade grinned in dumbfounded admiration. She was good. Either that woman truly wasn't Meagan O'Hara, or she was the best actress he'd ever seen. But she had to be. Her MO fit exactly, even if her appearance had changed. Midwife again. Where the hell did she get the false paperwork every time she moved? It spoke of a lot of practice and an intimate knowledge of the criminal networks in each city. What was her real name?

This time she had long brown curly hair and dark blue eyes, instead of straight blonde hair and brown eyes. But he'd never forget that mouth. Perfectly shaped, soft, a little wistful in repose. Sexy. Even up close, it was only the shape of her lips, a tiny scar on her temple, and the hint of *wariness* that betrayed her. Otherwise, Meagan O'Hara and Fiona MacDonald were two different women.

Meagan had been described to him as a petite, quiet, efficient blonde. People here described Fiona as a tall, fun, outgoing brunette. Meagan dressed in shapeless, dark, unflattering clothes and walked with hunched shoulders and head bent; Fiona wore bright shades, striding with her chin high.

Kade retreated from the filthy glass door of her apartment block and inspected the front of the building. A cold, neon light flickered on behind a thin curtain on the third floor. A female shadow passed to and fro a couple times, then the window next door—small and frosted—lit up. The bathroom.

He paced around to the alley running beside the building, examining the layout. The fire exit, a set of rusted, unsteady-looking ancient ladders clinging to the side of the building, was in plain sight, but too high to reach. The five-storey building was isolated from its neighbours and only an Olympic pole-vaulter would be able to cross the gaps.

He scratched his beard stubble, grinning in anticipation. If he went away now, he'd be abandoned for lunch tomorrow. Fiona/Meagan would disappear tonight. That meant playing the game a little more cleverly and letting her know he was here for the long haul.

Finding a door recess across the road, he settled into it, his collar raised against the cold drizzle that drifted from a lowering sky. She wasn't going anywhere tonight. Or any time.

Not if he could help it.

HEATHER

Heather, alias Fiona MacDonald, alias Meagan O'Hara and several other names she'd almost forgotten now, walked slowly into her bathroom and examined her wan reflection in the cracked, spotted mirror. Dragging the long brown wig off, she ran stiff fingers through her own short, jet curls, feeling the oiliness of a stressful day.

After washing her hands, she extracted and stored the blue contacts, undressed and stepped into the shower. Hot water soothed her aches but nothing so simple would restore her flagging energy, or her freedom.

Twenty minutes later, dressed in shades of ebony and grey, she peered out the unlit bedroom window at the street below. Two a.m. and he was still there. Hard to see, hidden in a dark doorway, but slight, occasional movements betrayed his presence—and his impatience.

He was getting smarter. She'd have to be even better.

Was he police? Federal? Something else, entirely? He held himself upright and moved smoothly, like someone with martial or military training. So perhaps ex-military and now in law of some sort? No way of knowing.

Might as well get some sleep.

Heather laid out her outfit for the morning next to the oversized floral handbag that contained her medical kit and a few other essentials—new identity papers being the most important. The rest of her scant belongings she could leave behind without remorse. She'd done it often enough.

Indeed, it had been so long since she'd lived in a real house and owned anything of worth the memory of such comforts were nothing more than dim, warm dreams. Someone else's life. Someone loved and valued, secure and treasured.

Before the nightmare. Before the onset of…everything. Before the anger, her father's raised voice, the fear in him that segued into resentment and thence into hatred. The midnight flight with her mother, leaving everything behind.

Inured to the old pain, she lay on the narrow, creaking bed and willed herself to sleep with meditation techniques. Her last coherent thought was that the time between discovery was getting shorter. Kade Miller was the cause of it. Perhaps the moment had come to quit, after all.

#

At six a.m., her body clock woke her into instant awareness. She gazed absently at the dirty, stuccoed-plaster ceiling. She'd wanted to make sure Juanita and the baby were alright, but couldn't risk it now. Couldn't lead Miller to the home of an illegal family. Undoubtedly Kade Miller would be still watching, unless he'd fallen asleep. Unlikely.

No, today she had to act as carefree as Fiona MacDonald would.

Rising stiffly, she completed her morning routine, though her body ached and her thoughts drifted toward melancholy vagueness. At seven-thirty she showered, washing off the sweat of a tough workout. She planned her escape route while warm water stung her skin and mingled with unwanted tears of self-pity.

Shortly after, Fiona MacDonald emerged forth from her apartment block, apparently without a care in the world. Wearing a white longsleeved top under a long black jacket, with black jeans and frivolous, red low-heeled boots, she approached her car then pretended to reconsider. Overhead, a pale blue sky showed clear and the morning crispness spoke of a fine day.

With a deep breath of sharp winter air, Heather strode along the sidewalk, imitating a woman determined to make the most of a beautiful day. She tucked her large, red and white flowered shoulder bag against her hip, swung her free arm, and ignored the car following half a block behind.

Good. If Kade was in a car, it meant she had a slight advantage. It would take him time to find somewhere to park if she ducked into a shopping centre. There was a chance she could lose herself long enough to switch identities and disappear again. Did he have accomplices? A shaft of anxiety speared her chest and she almost tripped over an unevenness in the pavement.

She couldn't risk a glance at the car to see if he was alone. She'd have to chance it. Damn him for catching her off guard and unready. She'd only been in this town a couple of weeks. Not long enough to establish the contacts she needed to make a total disappearance easy. She had new papers but not the untraceable transport needed to get her out of town. She'd have to count on a total makeover and book plane or bus tickets in her new name. What was it this time? Oh yes. Katherine Douglas: blue-eyed brunette. The long, black wig was already tucked into her bag.

Heather grimaced. Her finances couldn't stand many more of these identity changes. It was time to take a holiday. Get a normal job. Maybe something in an office. Somewhere people weren't hurting—physically, anyway; just long enough to recuperate her strength and her cash.

Difficult decision made, Heather caught a bus into the middle of town and did her level best to lose Kade Miller in the busiest shopping centre she could find. She sensed, at the end, that it hadn't worked. He was still close by; observing, waiting.

A bare half hour before their appointed lunch date, she feigned a surprised reaction to the time on her watch and bolted to the taxi rank. Climbing in the third cab, she directed the driver to the café and gave him certain other instructions at the same time, plus a handsome tip.

CHAPTER FIVE

'So,' Heather said, smiling winsomely across at Kade, 'what do you do for a living?'

He'd been waiting for her at the café. How had he arrived there first when she *knew* he'd been following her only minutes before? He was good. Oh yes, he was good.

Now they sat opposite each other in a cosy booth in the Indian restaurant she'd recommended. It was a crowded, untidy sort of place with at least three exits. There were no chairs, only low couches with scattered, brilliantly-coloured cushions and various thick-timbered tables at shin-height. Incense and Indian music drifted through the air along with the sound of laughter, and rich spices from the kitchen.

The restaurant was cluttered and full enough that it might make standing and rushing out difficult for a tall man like Miller. Difficult enough, perhaps, to give Heather a running start.

The waiter deposited a huge mug of black coffee in front of Kade, who grinned his thanks. He had a sexy, unfairly bewitching smile.

After stirring half a teaspoon of sugar into his drink, Kade said, 'I'm a private investigator.'

Heather gasped at his sheer gall. He arched an eyebrow and she changed the gasp into a squeak of delight.

'Wow, what an exciting job.' She whispered the next question, 'And are you trying to find that woman you were searching for last night? What was her name?'

Kade chuckled and revealed a brief, knowing gleam in his eye. That involuntarily made her smile. He was enjoying playing this game and, in a weird way, she was, too. Even though she was in serious trouble, there was something fascinating about Kade Miller that made it hard to *feel* like she was in danger.

'Her name was Meagan O'Hara.'

'Has she done something wrong?' Heather couldn't quite disguise the undertone of worry in her voice.

He cocked his head. 'Why would you assume that?'

She paused, considering. She had to be careful here. Lifting her tiny gilded coffee cup, she relaxed into the soft cushions. 'Too much Netflix, I guess. You never see shows about a PI tracking someone down for a huge inheritance. It's only if they've done something bad.'

He guffawed, the sound rolling over the top of conversations and music. Several women sent him admiring looks. Heather glared at them.

'You're right,' he said.

She gulped. Right about what?

He continued, 'You do watch too much Netflix. It's nothing so interesting, I'm afraid.'

A tiny knot of tension eased in her shoulders. Then she clenched her fists below the table. No. Just because she *wanted* to believe him, didn't make it the smart thing to do. Nobody spent this much time and money on a PI to find someone and tell them something good.

'So what is it, then?' she managed to ask.

'Oh, I've been hired by a father to find his lost daughter.' Kade sent her more sharp shrewdness. 'The father thinks Meagan was the last person to see her alive.'

Heather started. She hid confusion behind her cup, sipping the hot, sweet coffee. In her years doing this work, she had only lost three young mothers, both to complications she couldn't heal and they wouldn't go to hospital for. Had one of her clients' parents gone to the police? Was she under suspicion of murder?

She struggled to show only a cool, inquiring expression; to pretend she was curious but unconnected to his story. But all she could think was that she had to get out; to escape; to go somewhere so far away he wouldn't find her again. But how? He examined her like a hawk, waiting for her to either reveal her secrets or to make a run for it.

Time to execute Plan A.

The waiter delivered their lunches and Heather used the diversion to change the conversation.

'How did you get into the PI business?'

He shrugged. 'Not a lot of interesting jobs for ex-military. When my business partner and I got out of the Special Forces we pooled our cash and started the company. He runs it. I do legwork.'

Heather peeked at his left hand. No ring, but that didn't mean much. 'Does all the travelling affect your family?'

His knuckles showed tense and white beneath thin skin. He chewed and ate a bite of rogan josh, leaving enough silence that Heather shifted uncomfortably on her seat.

'No,' he finally said. 'Not married.'

'Oh.' She tried to seem uninterested. Being attracted to him was sheer madness. She couldn't afford to be interested in anyone, least of all this man.

'What about you?' Kade relaxed. 'Married? Kids?'

'No time. Maybe one day.' She applied herself to the excellent butter chicken on her plate. Marriage and family was something she'd never let herself think about. Too painful. Too difficult. Impossible, in fact. She couldn't ask anyone to take on this life.

Forcing a light smile, she offered him a piece of butter chicken. His fingers brushed the back of her hand as he steadied the fork. The same connection she'd felt last time fizzed along her arm. He made a show of tasting the cuisine. She withdrew and focussed on taking another bite. She'd need the strength, if that touch was any indication.

'What's your job?' he asked, casually.

Heather sipped at her glass of water. Did she lie or tell the truth? Would he call her on it if she lied?

'I'm a nurse. Working with an obstetrics clinic.' Half a truth, anyway. If he queried her she could say she'd hedged because people tended to be uneasy with midwives, like they were some layover from medieval times.

But he merely cocked his head. 'Huh. Must be tiring. Working so late at night.'

She shrugged. 'Sometimes. But rewarding, too. Who doesn't like babies? And saving lives, bringing new life into the world. Nothing better.'

He pushed meat around on his plate. 'Of course.' His tone was neutral. 'And where are you from, originally?' He waved a fork in a circle.

'New York,' she said, 'but I move around a lot.' Her throat tightened. She hadn't thought about home in a long time. It didn't exist any more, anyway. There was no returning.

'And next? Where to?' He eyed her narrowly.

'Who knows? Wherever the job takes me. That's the fun part of being unattached. Maybe Florida? I hate the cold.'

He shot her a quick, speculative look. Would the delicate bit of misdirection work when she left town? Would he drive south when he lost her this time?

They talked as they ate, dancing around difficult topics and backstories; a delicate game of cat and mouse in which Heather wasn't sure who was who. In the end she was obliged to acknowledge she had met her match as an actor. Kade was simply biding his time, willing to play along; giving her enough rope to hang herself. Part of her regretted that she had to give him the slip. He was the first man in a very long time to pique her interest in any way.

Finally, Heather patted her stomach. 'I'm so full.' What she would give to be able to go to her flat and sleep for hours.

Kade sipped from a glass of rich, red wine. 'Good food.'

She sighed and collected her bag. 'I do have some work to do this afternoon, though, so I can't stay any longer. Here's cash for my half. I'll go to the bathroom and meet you at the front counter. OK?'

Kade nodded agreeably, waving aside her offer of payment. 'My treat. You can pay next time if it's an issue.'

'Next time…yes.' She tucked the money into her purse, not loath to keep it; strangely attracted to the idea of a 'next time', insane though that was.

She made her way toward the rear of the cafe, uneasy. He was letting her go? That didn't make sense at all. He had to be suspicious. Surely she wouldn't be able to walk out the bathroom exit without being intercepted.

Glancing over her shoulder, Heather couldn't see him anywhere. She extended an arm to palm the exit door open. Her hand landed squarely in the middle of warm, muscular chest.

Kade smiled, arms behind and feet apart like a soldier at ease. Affable. Uncompromising.

'Going somewhere?'

She recovered and sent him her best *duh*. 'The bathroom, of course.'

He jerked a thumb to his left. 'I think you'll find *that's* the bathroom. This one leads to a back alley.'

Heather laughed but it was a poor attempt. 'Oops. Well, if you'll excuse me.' She shoved open the bathroom door and shot a cheeky smile over her shoulder.

A quick check showed the tiny room and its three cubicles to be empty. Ornate tiles blanketed the floor and walls in eye-aching colours. Led bulbs overhead poured down harsh, white light, making her skin sallow in the unflattering mirrors over the three sinks. A narrow window above the cubicles offered a possible escape route. She was thin enough to slide through. Maybe.

For lack of any other ideas, she went to the toilet and examined the window. Yes, she should be able to get through if she used the next cubicle, which had a steel bar she could use to pull herself up.

When she came out of the cubicle, Kade was there, waiting *inside* the women's bathroom, leaning against the door with his arms folded across his chest.

Stunned, Heather could only gape at him. 'What...?'

Fear flickered. She was trapped here. What if her instincts about him were wrong? What if he did mean her harm. No. She'd never been wrong like that. He wasn't a bad person. He was angry, confused and holding tightly onto both those and desire, but he wasn't about to lose control and attack her.

She recovered her poise. If she played the righteous, outraged woman card he could very well overpower and arrest her here. Could he do that? Could a PI arrest someone? She had no idea. It wasn't worth the risk.

Still, the temptation to make sure she was safe…to incapacitate him…

No! She'd sworn. Never again. There were other ways.

Time for Plan B. She needed to convert his persistence to her advantage. Men were stupid when it came to sex.

'How nice of you to wait for me,' she murmured, flashing him a heavy-lidded look. She swayed toward the sink, inwardly cursing his dedication to his job. She had to distract him long enough to get out of this place. He snicked the lock on the door and shifted across to the sink next to her. She washed her hands slowly, studying Kade's cool, amused expression in the mirror. Reaching past him, she tugged out a paper towel, allowing her breasts to brush his chest.

There. His breathing changed, ever so slightly. Now she had him.

Leaning over further, she threw the screwed-up towel into the wastepaper basket with a deft flick and sent Kade a quirky smile. He didn't return it, merely continued to stand propped against the sink with his hands placed behind, watching her.

'So.' She stood before him, her feet on either side so his thighs were between hers. Slowly and deliberately, she leaned the length of her body against his. By the time her breasts were pressed against his chest, she could feel his heartrate accelerate; feel the first stirrings of arousal below his belt, feel the change in his aura and the red-gold of desire deepen.

'I hope you've followed me in here for a really good reason,' she purred.

'Yes.' His hands came to rest heavily on her shoulders.

p50

Would he shove her away? Resist her? She dialled up the lustful feelings, driving them through his fingers on her skin. Heather looked into his grey eyes. Outright hunger warred with cool intelligence, there.

Good. A little more and she'd have him where she wanted him.

Determinedly ignoring her own self-loathing at what she did, she unbuttoned the front of her blouse. The back she left tucked into her skirt, and let the cloth fall from her shoulders.

With a shuddering groan, Kade took his hands out from under the bright cloth and placed them gently on her bare waist. Heather bit her lip against the faint surge of power when he drew strength from her again. Her head spun. She stiffened her knees and concentrated on blocking him out; on letting him only see desire. It wasn't easy. He was so needy and she was scared.

She fumbled at his belt, keeping her attention on his face. He kissed her neck, sending unexpected shivers down her spine. His arms slid around her waist and Kade pulled her closer, burying his face in her neck with a groan and drawing in her scent. His fingertips trailed along the chain that held her locket, following its path between her breasts.

Against her will, Heather felt the first stirrings of her own arousal. Desperately, she worked at his buckle, buttons and zip. She had to get out of here before things went horribly wrong.

The heat of his lips on her skin was unbearably enticing. Oh…what she would give to reciprocate and abandon herself.

He kissed his way up her neck. His mouth covered hers, took hers, possessed hers with single-minded intent. Her agenda temporarily forgotten, she glided her arms around him and pressed herself closer to his firm body.

She drowned in him, merging with him; melting into his arms, his mouth, his mind. The gold of desire and lust flared hot in both of them. Heather yanked open Kade's shirt. Buttons flew across the tiny room, pinging off metal and glass. With a moan of pleasure, she stroked his bare skin.

He tugged the straps to her bra off her shoulders, exposing her breasts. Heather bit back a groan, trying to stay focussed. But her breasts peaked beneath his touch and his strong hands cupped and caressed them with surprising gentleness.

Finally, she managed to get his pants undone. She shoved them down, past his hips, fighting the irrational desire to do exactly what they both obviously wanted. It stunned her to realise how much she wanted to have sex with this man right now, right here.

She had never done or felt anything like this in her life. It was liberating to feel so sexually powerful, so thoroughly aroused that nothing else mattered but the feel and taste of his skin, the touch of his hand, the scent of his hair.

Kade slid his palms up her thighs, lifting her skirt and hooking his fingers into her underwear. Heather allowed her head to fall back and he suckled at one taut nipple.

A knock and rattle on the doorhandle startled both of them. She gasped. He swore softly. Yanking her skirt down, Heather pointed to one of the empty cubicles. He hauled his pants up far enough so he could walk.

Heather fixed her clothes and unlocked the door.

Outside, a bitter older woman with a young girl waited. Berating Heather, the woman brushed past and ushered the child into one of the other toilet cubicles. A second woman breezed in and occupied the third. Another pair entered, chattering, complaining at the need to wait for a free cubicle.

Panting and heated, Heather seized the moment and escaped from the bathroom, the restaurant and, hopefully, from Kade Miller.

CHAPTER SIX

KADE

Two hours later, Kade admired the swaying rear view of a classy brunette. He was still furious at her deception and his own stupidity at the cafe. His attraction to this woman had almost cost him the job.

He couldn't believe how easily he'd succumbed to her transparent little seduction routine. He'd never lost control like that before. Ever. She wasn't even that *good* at it. At least, he amended fairly, she wasn't *deliberately* good at it. There was just something about her; something about the catch in her breath; the scent of her skin; the flush in her cheeks; something that had beaten through his careful walls and laid siege to his very core.

He could still remember the feel of her skin, the tentative eagerness of her full mouth; the taste of her breast. He *still* wanted her. She lingered in his mind and her scent lingered on his hands.

Damn her!

He'd had to wait until the bathroom emptied, which took a good fifteen minutes. She was long gone when he emerged. So it had taken a little ingenuity and a lot of luck to find Meagan/Fiona before she left town. Working on a guess, he'd made his way to the nearest, biggest shopping centre, staked out the cheapest chain-store clothes shop and hoped for the best.

Half an hour later, she'd appeared. He'd been unable to resist a soft chortle. This time she'd slipped and he had her.

He hid and waited. Careful to stay out of her line of sight and out of mirrors and windows. Even after she obviously thought him long gone with her little lunch time vanishing act, she still led him a fine dance and checked for tails. Force of long habit, probably. It took every surveillance skill at his disposal to see without being seen; to follow without being spotted while Meagan/Fiona dodged in and out of stores in an apparent orgy of shopping.

When he was beginning to think that shopping really was all she was going to do, she ducked into the busy ladies room and he knew she was about to undergo a transformation.

So he scanned every woman that emerged, comparing the sharp jawline to each face. Ah! There she was. The flirty, colourful outfit and brown curly hair gone, Meagan/Fiona emerged as a cool brunette. Long, straight black hair tied in a low ponytail, ice blue eyes behind small, wire-rimmed glasses, slim body disguised in a conservative dark blue trouser suit and sensible-heeled black shoes.

Even her walk was different—purposeful. She strode to the exit; a woman late for an important business meeting. She'd done something with her makeup; her eyes seemed bigger, more exotic and her nose and cheekbones sharper. If it weren't for that fantastic mouth and the red fingernails she'd forgotten to change, Kade would have doubted himself. But it was her and now he had the advantage.

He chuckled in admiration and sauntered off in generally the same direction, careful to keep out of sight.

What was it with this woman? No matter how she dressed, she turned him on fast and hard. When she'd had him in the bathroom, he'd thrown sense to the wind. It was so out of character that he was bewildered. Within O'Connor Inc, he was famous for his even temper; his ability to put aside emotion and see through the most confused situations with humour and logic. Where Torin worried and took every relationship failure to heart, Kade had always been able to shrug women off—at least, since Amanda. What the hell was happening to him?

This woman was a murderer; a negligent medic who could walk from the deathbed of a young woman and a baby without a second thought; responsible for the death of Amali Carleton and who knew how many others.

How could he feel anything but utter contempt for her? And yet he did. He felt a powerful sexual attraction, and a reluctant admiration for her intelligence and skills as an illusionist.

When Meagan O'Hara had given him the slip two months before, he'd spent a fruitless month trying to find her before admitting defeat. He'd gone to Torin and Andrew Carleton and given his apologies with polite regret externally and seething resentment internally. Carleton had been scathing and Torin disappointed, but Kade had borne it with stoicism. He'd moved on to the next case, but hadn't stopped trawling through leads in his spare time, hopeful of catching a thread connected to her, somewhere.

Unfortunately, Meagan O'Hara's wide eyes and sad, soft pink mouth had shown a tendency to hover at the edges of his consciousness and invade his dreams with astonishing regularity.

Then he had, during a brainstorming session with Torin and Luke, come across a stunning photograph. One of their staff, in Charlotte, had been hired to track and photograph the pregnant wife of a jealous man and had snapped a few shots of her meeting with her midwife, Fiona MacDonald. And there she was. Smiling, drinking coffee with the soon-to-be-mother, living in Charlotte. Unbelievable. Unforgettable.

With minimum explanations and maximum apologies, Kade packed and left town.

Now here he was, watching Meagan O'Hara/Fiona MacDonald transform herself into someone different, yet again.

And wishing they'd had a few minutes more in that damned bathroom.

He shook his head irritably, pushing the persistent thought aside again. He couldn't risk losing her this time. He might never get another chance.

The question was, how to get her back to meet with Carleton in New York without causing an almighty uproar in this very public place. Short of dart-gunning her—impossible since he didn't have a dartgun on him—he couldn't think of any way that wouldn't lead to a very loud altercation. He wasn't fond of guns and rarely carried one, ordinary or otherwise. Could he try the old 'I've got a gun in my jacket pocket' finger routine? No. She was too smart for that.

Snorting at his own stupidity, he followed her at a discreet distance.

#

Twenty-four hours later, following a bus along Highway Eighty-five, he was still at a loss and practically asleep behind the wheel. He had no idea how where she was going and if he stopped to sleep he would lose her. He couldn't stalk her at the next bus-stop, knock her out and drag her onto a plane.

These things were always easy on television. But they had access to the latest gadgets, drugs and a whole host of accomplices to pull off smooth kidnappings. Kade had only himself this time. Torin was too far away to help and too busy with the company.

The thought of his partner triggered a memory. Yes. If he was right and his target was headed north. If she went to ground anywhere in New York state, then he might have a way of digging her out. If the mountain won't come to Mohammed... He swiped savagely at his cell screen. Right now, he needed help tailing her and help hounding her to the right location for this to work.

Tor answered after the second ring.

Kade confirmed his position on the gps before speaking. 'I'm tailing her but she's in a bus and I haven't slept in two days. Get a team on her ass. Get someone obvious at every bus stop so she has to keep travelling. Send her to Syracuse.' He paused and listening a moment. 'She's too good at staying in public places. I have to separate her somewhere isolated. Yep. That's the idea. I'll get her there, you get us out when I call. Thanks.' He thumbed the End button and tossed the phone onto the passenger seat.

Grinning, he rubbed at burning eyes and renewed his grasp on the wheel. Only a couple more hours and he could sleep.

HEATHER

'Where are you?' Heather listened to the frightened, accented voice and nodded, momentarily forgetting the girl on the other end of the phone couldn't see her. 'Si, si. I can help. But you'll have to give me directions, I'm new to town.' She listened for a moment, jotting street names onto a notepad.

Finally she broke into the agitated spiel and gave soothing reassurances. 'It'll be ok, Maria. If your contractions are ten minutes apart then we've still got some time. Are you sure there's no one who can come and stay with you? No, no. That's fine. I'll be there quick as I can, just relax.'

Sighing, she ended the call and stared blankly at the white wall of her tiny bedsit for a while. How quickly word got around. She'd only been here a week and that was the third call from a scared, illegal, underage girl wanting help with delivery of her unwanted baby. The underground network was certainly strong in this town.

She wished it wasn't, and yet she needed it to be. Finding work when she had no other skills proved almost impossible. She'd been obliged to fall back on midwifery in spite her best intentions to take time off.

Heather pursed her lips and packed her medical equipment. At the last minute, she threw a couple of changes of clothes and a few other items into a backpack. The girl, Maria, had given directions to a remote cottage in the hills near Hall Island State Forest. It would take awhile to get there and, if this were a long labour, she'd probably have to stay a day or two.

Finally, she called her boss at the medical centre and told him she'd be gone for a couple of days. He was understandably annoyed. She sat quietly through a verbal rake down and threat to her job. But good midwives were hard to keep. He wouldn't let her go in a hurry, no matter how many days she took.

#

Two hours later, she was deep in the forested hills and concerned that she'd taken a wrong turn. Her cellphone showed no reception and nothing looked like the final turnoff Maria had described. Ominous clouds gathered, threatening the first big snowfall of winter. Gritting her teeth in frustration, she faltered, studying the lonely, narrow road in trepidation. No, she'd drive on for another two miles before asking for directions. Only the thought of the poor girl, struggling with her first pregnancy, scared and alone, made her keep going at all.

Two minutes later, she spotted the large boulder and gnarled tree that marked a dusty side road. Relieved, she turned the tiny Volkswagen into a rutted driveway. The first flakes of snow drifted from a heavy sky. Switching the headlamps on in the dusk gloom, she slowed to a crawl. The road wound up the side of a hill, beneath a double row of overhanging pines. Snow flurried in front of the car, turning the dirt road white.

Heather shivered. It wouldn't pay to end up snowed into this lonely place with a young mother and brand new baby. Hopefully there would be no complications.

The snowfall eased and the headlamps picked out a house, but it was hardly the cottage she'd expected. More like the holiday home of someone with a lot of money. The house nestled comfortably into rocky terraces, surrounded by what was obviously an extensive and lush garden in the summer. Now, with trees stripped bare and the lawn a sad brown dusted with white, it seemed bleak and unloved. It overlooked a large lake that, too, would be breathtaking in summer but today seemed threatening, black and wind-ruffled. Off to one side was what must be a helipad—broad, bare, and with a giant circle picked out in the centre.

The house stood two stories and must have at least five bedrooms. It was painted a welcoming honey colour with cheerful red window frames and white shutters. A single light glowed in the bottom storey and one in the upper. Probably the kitchen and a bedroom. What on Earth was an illegal immigrant girl doing alone in a huge place like this? Maybe hired to look after the house during winter when the owners were gone? The owners mustn't know the poor thing was pregnant and alone here.

Heather manoeuvred the struggling Volkswagen onto flat ground in front of the garage and doused the lights and engine. Wishing again she'd been able to afford a car with a better heater, she clambered stiffly out of the seat and shouldered her medical bag and duffle.

Sharpening winds plucked at her coat and long wig. Flurries of snow chilled her exposed cheeks. Head bent, she mounted the front porch and knocked on the white door.

No response.

She knocked again and still got no answer.

She tried the handle and found it unlocked. Not surprising, this far out of town. Torn between getting out of the cold and the fear of entering the wrong house uninvited, Heather opened the door a fraction and called out.

'Maria? Are you there? It's Katherine, the midwife.'

Still no voice in reply.

Now she was concerned. What if, in the two hours or so it took her to get here, the girl's labour had progressed faster than expected. What if…

Cutting off her runaway thoughts, Heather stepped inside and shut the door.

Warmth and the faint smell of Italian food spices greeted her, seducing her, easing her fears. A fire burned low in the grate of the cosy lounge room to her left, throwing dancing yellow lights across timber-panelled walls and thick, soft-looking navy suede couches. To her right, a kitchen was brightly lit and beautifully decorated in a classic country theme, complete with blue and white cupboards, polished timber bench tops and a massive wooden centre island. A large, lidded pot sat on the stove, steam rising faintly from it.

Straight ahead, along a wide hall, were several closed doors.

Calling out the girl's name, Heather dropped her duffle and opened each door in sequence, finding an empty bedroom, a study-library lined with books, a laundry, a large bathroom, and a mudroom/woodstore room, full of chopped wood and the heady smell of pine.

Winter preparations were in place. That was a relief.

She closed the door and headed for the nearby stairs.

With one foot on the bottom riser, Heather delayed. Something was amiss. Each step she took upward increased the sensation. Vague uneasiness gelled into a sharp awareness of wrongness. Not danger, exactly, more like a certainty that something was just not right.

She reached the top of the stairs but hesitated. At the front bedroom door she paused again, trying to shake off the feeling she was in a bad horror movie; that a ghost or something equally ridiculous was about to appear. Her grandmother had had the Sight, but even she hadn't believed in ghosts.

Hardening her resolve, Heather flung open the door and stepped into…

An empty, warm, lit bedroom.

What?

There were no other exits. The ensuite lay open for inspection, empty. She checked the three other bedrooms and bathrooms on the upper level. All empty and dark. Where could the girl be?

She re-read the directions. Yes, she'd found each road correctly and this house had to be the one. It matched the description of the external appearance.

So where was Maria?

No. There was something wrong. She needed to get out. Get back to the town. Hurrying down the stairs, Heather concentrated on where her feet went on the slippery timber risers...

…and careened headlong into a large man standing squarely between herself and the front door. Gasping, she tried to shove free and encountered broad, muscular chest clothed in blue wool.

A familiar smell. A familiar power.

No!

Kade Miller.

He'd found her.

CHAPTER SEVEN

HEATHER

Stunned, Heather made the fatal mistake of meeting his amused gaze. His hand latched onto hers. She reeled beneath a welter of his uncontrolled feelings—grim triumph, relief, a hint of anger and, underlying them all, the strong red-gold of desire.

Yanking free, Heather retreated back, cradling her hand. Her heart raced. Was it worth trying to play dumb again? No, pointless. The triumph and relief in his feelings showed he knew who she wasn't: Katherine Douglas.

Did he know who she *was?* That was the next question. Why was he here? And where was the girl, Maria?

Nope. Of course there was no Maria.

This was an elaborate setup that meant serious trouble.

Heather gathered every ounce of mental strength at her disposal and struggled to calm her nerves; to think clearly. She had to get out. No matter what it took. Looking at him down the length of her nose, she raised a supercilious brow.

'Can I help you, Mr Miller?'

To her surprise, his handsome face lit with a broad, wry smile.

'At least you're not going to pretend you don't know me this time, Katherine.' He cocked his head. 'Or is it Fiona? Or Meagan? Or Margaret? Or, what was the other one?' He snapped his fingers. 'Oh yes, Alanna. That was my favourite, by the way. Alanna Donnelly.'

He flicked on a light in the lounge room and walked to a bar tucked into the far corner. Pouring himself a nip of brandy, he offered the balloon glass to her.

'Want one?'

Heather pulled herself together. How did he know so many of her past aliases? She swiftly surveyed the room, searching for ideas, tools, exits. With him out of the way, a clear path lay to the front door. She bolted for her car, fumbling to keep her footing on the now-snowy front stairs. Snow fell so thickly that she could barely make out the outline of her little bug.

With the key in the car door, she checked the house. Kade Miller leaned against the doorframe, backlit by the golden glow from inside, sipping his brandy.

What the…?

Heather spotted the reason for his lack of concern. A large, black SUV was now parked behind her car, blocking the narrow exit from the property. No way could she drive out. The fences on either side of the driveway were solid stone and there was no other exit.

How far was the next house? Several miles, from memory. Too far to walk in this weather. It was almost dark, and extremely cold now. She wore clothes suitable for indoors. Her coat and boots were not heavy enough to keep her warm in a snowstorm. Only a desperate fool went out unprepared in this sort of snow. She might be desperate but she wasn't a fool.

Shivering, Heather glanced at the house. He still hadn't come after her. She didn't have much choice but to go inside.

But what did he want with her?

Four times she'd met him now and each time she'd got strong overtones of desire, anger and strength from him. That episode in the cafe bathroom had almost knocked her over with the mutual inflammation of their desires. He'd never given her a sense of potential for abusive violence, though. Somehow she knew that, whatever he had planned for her, it didn't involve anything physically hurtful.

But no man went to this much trouble to track a woman just because he wanted to chat, PI or not.

She stood in the cold and snow for a long time, uncertain. He stayed where he was, smiling, waiting, certain.

With a growl, she went back.

Stomping the wet snow off her boots she ignored his fake sympathy and brushed past into the warmth. She held out her chilled hands to the fire and kept her back to her captor. That's what he was. She was stuck here until he decided to let her out—or she could steal his car keys. Even if her phone had reception, or the phone in the house worked, who could she call? No-one. She was alone, as she had been since her mother died ten years ago.

'Warm enough?' His deep, rough voice sent curls of heat through her, which she tried hard to ignore.

'Yes.' Her reply was as cool as the snow outside.

'Want that drink?' He seemed undaunted.

'No.'

'Hungry?' Now he sounded like the perfect, polite host.

'No!' Heather whirled on him. He was closer than she expected and she had to step aside to avoid colliding with him again.

He yanked the eyeglasses off her nose. 'Do you need these? Ah.' He peered through them. 'Thought not. Plain glass.' He tossed them aside and they landed on the coffee table with a metallic tinkle.

Heather retreated to the warm wall next to the fire. he wind whistled outside, howling. The storm battered the house, echoing her fear and reinforcing her sense of isolation.

'What do you want?' Her voice sounded more shaky than she wanted it to.

Kade sent her irony. 'Probably not what you're thinking.'

Heather returned the haughtiest indignation she could muster. 'Why are you keeping me here?' T

He stalked across the room, and slammed his empty glass on the bar. 'Oh please. Spare me the dramatics. I thought we were past these stupid games, Katherine. No.' He glanced over his shoulder, amused again. 'That's not your real name, is it? What shall I call you then? Alanna?'

Heather raised a shoulder. What he called her was a matter of indifference. She scanned the room, assessing its masculine, heavy timber furniture and minimal ornamentation. Not much in the way of potential weapons. The fire pokers that ought to be in the stand next to her were missing. Had he removed them? Was he that forward-thinking?

Kade folded his arms and mimicked her pose, resting against the wall nearby.

'Can I ask you why you always choose names of Irish or Scottish origin?'

Heather said nothing.

'Maybe…' He tilted his head. 'Maybe it's because your *real* name is something Irish or Scottish.'

Heather tried not to let surprise show. It was the truth. She'd gotten careless; habitual. She wasn't wearing contacts over her ice-blue irises this time and, although her real hair was shorter and wavier than the long wig she wore, it was Celtic black. Common enough in Ireland. As was her real name.

He hitched himself off the wall, striding toward her with long, panther-like steps that made her shrink against the brickwork. He placed a hand either side of her on the wall and searched her face. Heather battled to keep her mind blank and her expression calm.

'It's a common mistake people make when they're trying to hide,' he murmured, his gaze dropping to her mouth. 'They either take names with initials the same as their own, or they use their first name and change their last, or they have some sort of theme running through their choice of name.'

Heather froze, caught by the hunger in those stormy eyes; unable to move even though a part of her mind screamed at her.

His first kiss fell softly on her lips and, much to her surprise, she swayed into it. The second was harder,

Healing Heather p71

demanding, taking, controlling, giving passion and drawing it from her. She had no chance to guard herself. This time she was swept into the desire that billowed from his core and overwhelmed his innate sense of right and wrong. She knew that he knew he shouldn't be doing this. She also knew he couldn't help himself, and that was her fault. Neither could she.

Was she being carried along by his emotions? It was hard to tell. It had been so long since she'd been held, kissed; made love. She couldn't tell where his lust began and her own ended. She was too emotionally wound up, tired and aroused to keep her mental walls intact. Her mind merged with his, egos and emotions swirling in a thickening cloud between them; bodies pressed tightly together; rapidly submerging in a tide of white hot desire.

A log cracked in the fire and Heather jumped, smacking her head on the bricks behind.

'Ow!' Grateful for the brief pain, she rubbed her skull and Kade retreated, wide-eyed.

'What the hell did you do to me?' he demanded, his voice rough.

Heather glared at him. 'Do to *you?* You're the one holding me prisoner. You're the one who lured me here with a fake call out. You're the one who came on to me like some sort of won't-take-no-for-an-answer jerk. What do you want with me?'

Kade turned from her, running a hand through his thick, dark hair. He cast her a look full of irritation that spoke volumes.

'I felt, no...*you* felt...' He hesitated. 'Afraid. Confused. Turned on. How do I know that?' For a moment he frowned at her. Touching his lips, he added softly, 'I felt it last time, too. I just didn't realise it...'

'How do you know?' she snapped. 'Maybe you're just growing up and realising you're being a jerk. Realising that you're scaring an unarmed, unprotected woman who's trapped on her own in the middle of nowhere.'

With a short laugh, Kade replied, 'You knew you weren't in any physical danger and I've seen you do a martial arts workout that would shame most in the military.'

Heather narrowed her eyes. 'Stalking *and* spying. Nice.'

'Stop trying to change the subject. I *am* a PI, remember. Besides, I've never hurt a woman like that in my life.' Pain fleetingly darkened his expression and his jaw worked. 'No. There's something else going on...'

She stayed silent, mouth tightly closed. Could he really feel her emotions? Her heart stuttered.

He frowned, stared at her, swore under his breath and pointed to the large, wooden dining table nearby. 'Sit.' Reaching for her elbow, he stopped at the last second and growled, throwing his hands up. 'You don't have anything to fear from me. I won't touch you again. I'm going to finish making dinner.' He strode purposefully to the kitchen.

Heather followed him more slowly, sank into a straight-backed wooden chair and watched him move around the kitchen. He added seasoning to the bubbling pot and produced a tray of breadrolls out of the oven, sliding them onto the countertop. All like nothing untoward had occurred.

But he'd felt her. He felt what she felt. She tried to come to grips with this development, to fit it into a scheme for escape but it was too new and incredible. She'd had a total of four lovers in her past and not one of them had ever shown any sign of knowing what she felt when they were intimate—or at any other time.

Sex had always been a trying duty. A time when she was drained; when her partners fed off the strong emotions, battering her with theirs and sucking her emotional energy dry without giving any in return. The cause of all her relationship breakdowns had been her partner's complaint that she didn't want to have sex often enough. Explaining why was impossible, so she'd resigned herself to a single life.

Now, here, with this inexplicable stranger in this inescapable place, she'd finally experienced a hint of something more: a duality; a two-way connection with another human. It was as unexpected as it was terrifying; as incredible as it was impossible.

She still didn't know why he'd been sent to find her. What had she done to someone's daughter that warranted sending a PI after her?

KADE

Kade inspected her profile, chin propped in her hand, those incredible black-circled ice-blue irises focussed blank past him, toward the white-darkness outside. What colour was her real hair, and how long? The dark locks she wore as Katherine MacDonald suited her, as did the startlingly light blue eyes with dark rims. Were they contacts? What did the rest of her look like? Was she smoothly creamy, ivory and rose all over that stunning body?

A rush of heat to his skin and various other parts of his anatomy brought him to his senses. He growled and ladled out two bowls of thick beef stew with fierce concentration. Dammit. What had she done to him? Was she inside his head? He was losing control; losing focus on his job; being drowned in the intoxicating emotion of being near her.

No woman had ever rattled him this much. Not even Amanda.

This was ridiculous. He had to remember what he was paid to do and who she was.

She was a midwife practicing obstetrics on illegal immigrants who couldn't afford to take her to court for malpractice. She had to be stopped. Yet Kade had the distinct impression that Andrew Carleton wanted to do more than simply talk to this woman about his daughter's death, and the thought made his palms sweat. The last thing he wanted to do was give his prisoner over—to anyone.

Annoyed at his own lack of control, he stalked to the dining table and plonked a bowl in front of the woman

Healing Heather p75

responsible. She flinched, her expression showing clearly that her situation was sinking in. She was his prisoner. The realisation was tinged with savage glee. Stuck here, in his power, until he could get them to the airport and onto Torin's helicopter, to New York.

He finished laying out stew, bread and butter, a good red wine and tableware without comment. Seating himself opposite, he poured two glasses of wine and began to eat with methodical hunger.

She sat opposite, watching him but not eating—though her attention slid to the bowl over and over and she swallowed.

'It's perfectly safe,' he said calmly. 'If I wanted to drug you or poison you I wouldn't need to use any subtlety. You're not going anywhere for awhile. Eat.' He waved a spoon at her, ignoring her half-frightened, half-defiance. She selected a spoon and took a tentative mouthful.

'You cook well,' she said, though her tone was grudging.

Kade laughed. 'I do a lot of things well.'

'Including humility,' she shot back.

He shrugged. 'No point. I'm confident I can cope with pretty much anything.'

'Must be nice to have an easy life.' Bitterness and a hint of longing edged her throaty voice. She directed her attention to her food, blowing on a spoonful as though it were the most important thing in the room.

'I never said I had an easy life,' he responded mildly. If he told her even half the things he'd done in the Special Forces with Tor, or even in O'Connor Inc over these last few years, she'd... He cut off the line of thought. What was it about this woman that had him even contemplating telling his maudlin backstories? He had to be insane. She was a job, nothing more.

'Oh?' She gestured around the room with her spoon. 'This house must have cost a fortune. The kidnapping industry must be lucrative.'

Kade bit down on a hasty, angry reply and let his shoulders relax. She really knew how to push his buttons. Instead, he took another bite and swallowed. There was no point in letting her know she got to him. She was smart enough to find a way to use his anger against him, as she had used his desire before. So he simply shrugged again.

'One, I don't own this house. It belongs to my business partner, Torin O'Connor. And two—' He glanced up to find her open-mouthed. 'What?' he asked.

'Your partner's name is Torin...O'Connor?' she asked. One hand stole to the side of her head and stroked the small, white scar on her left temple.

'Yes. Do you know him?' Surely Tor would have said if he'd recognised this girl from her photograph. He couldn't know her, or he wouldn't have sanctioned this job in the first place. Would he?

CHAPTER EIGHT

HEATHER

Heather collected her wits, scattered to the wind by another in a long line of shocks she'd endured tonight. Torin O'Connor. That was a name she hadn't heard in a very, very long time. She released a shaky breath.

'No. I don't know him. The name sounded...familiar.' She picked at a breadroll, tearing it to pieces and squishing it into tiny, doughy balls. When she had four perfect little white spheres, she felt calm enough to take him on again. If she humanised herself enough and showed him the craziness of what he was doing, he might let her go.

'You were about to tell me how lucrative the kidnapping game is nowadays.' She pasted on a look of polite enquiry and had the satisfaction of seeing Kade's jaw clench. At least she'd distracted him from asking about her reaction to Torin's name.

'I'm *not* kidnapping you,' he said.

'Oh? What do you call luring me out here under false pretences and keeping me prisoner, then?' She sipped her wine, determined not to lose herself in an alcoholic daze. 'A new kind of second date?'

His glower cleared and he chuckled. Heather had to stop herself from smiling. Even when she wasn't touching him, his emotions were contagious. But she had to hold herself aloof if she was to think her way out of this.

'Well, you did disappear on me at lunch…Fiona.' He sent her that annoyingly sexy, lopsided grin again.

'I had somewhere—and some*one*—else to be.'

'Mmmm. Katherine Douglas in yet another town. I know. I followed you.' He selected another rough chunk of buttered breadroll to dip in the dregs of his stew.

'You followed me?' Heather gaped at him. 'But I was on buses for days. I mean, it couldn't have been safe, driving that far alone.' She glanced around apprehensively. 'You are alone, aren't you?' If he had a team of people lurking somewhere to help then she had no chance of escape.

'Yep. Don't need anyone else here.' He cocked his head. 'Took me a while to track you down. After I lost you in the café—neatly done, by the way. Worthy of Mata Hari herself.'

His eyes held scorn, anger and a hint of admiration. She flushed.

'I made sure to keep an eye on the mall,' he continued. 'Sure enough, you went on a shopping spree and lo, into the bathroom went flirty Fiona MacDonald. Out came the mistress of cool, Katherine Douglas.' He screwed up his nose. 'I didn't know your new name, so when the bus company wouldn't tell me who you were or where you were going, I had to tag along behind. My office sent a team to help. Then I set this up.' He gestured at the room, full of ironic pride as he studied her from beneath his lashes.

'So how…why…?' Heather spread her hands. 'Why here. Why a week later? Why me?'

Kade tossed back the last of his wine before replying.

'I have to get you to New York without causing a major scene in public.'

'New York!' Heather shot to her feet. Her chair tipped and crashed to the ground, loud in the silence of the vast house. 'Why do you have to get me to New York? Who sent you after me?'

Kade walked around the table to tower over her. Heather, who stood five foot eight, felt dwarfed by his six foot of muscle. She shrank away before regrouping. There was a hardness in him she hadn't seen before and didn't like.

'The *who* is not relevant right now.' He raked her with a contemptuously cold gaze that almost physically hurt. 'The why should be obvious.' With a slight sneer, he collected her plate and cutlery before striding into the kitchen. Dishes clattered and he swore.

Heather drew a deep, shaky breath. The strength of the man; the power of his emotional field shattered her each time he came near. If he'd touched her, feeling that kind of anger, she couldn't have coped with the onslaught. What was happening to her? No-one had ever had such a huge influence on her before.

Not since her father.

After leaving home, she'd learned how to block people rather than fight their feelings. She was able to shield herself from most people but it took energy, so she tried to avoid being touched. Right from the start, Kade had been different.

It shook her to the core; kept her offbalance.

'No,' she managed, calmly as she could, 'it's *not* obvious. What have I done that warrants this kind of treatment and…animosity…from you? I don't even know you.'

He spun back and stalked close, his face rigid. 'No. You don't know me. But I know what you do and I don't *want* to know you, believe me. You make me *sick.*'

Heather retreated before the waves of his conflicting emotions, genuinely frightened for the first time. Desire, confusion, and frustrated anger emanating from him, battering at her self-control, threatening to consume her.

'What have I done that's so awful?' she whispered.

He reached out and she flinched. Instead, he dropped his hands and spoke through gritted teeth.

'You're responsible for the deaths of at least one young woman and baby—and that's only the ones we know about.' He grabbed her wrist.

Energy poured from her into him. Anger flowed back, overwhelming the small measure of calm she'd held onto. She cried out.

His dark brows snapped together. He released her and stared at his hand, then at her face, searching. 'God! You're terrified of me. I should loathe the sight of you…so why do I feel…?' His voice trailed away.

In the long silence that followed, the houselights dimmed to yellow, sputtered and restarted in full strength.

He swore. 'I'm going out to fix the generator. It was low on fuel before and I don't want to lose power in the middle of the night.' He pointed at the kitchen. 'Help yourself to coffee or tea. I'll be back in a minute.'

When he left through the rear door, Heather stayed where she was for a minute. Then she righted the chair, sank onto it and covered her face.

Oh God.

Her mother had warned her this day might come. That one day she'd be called to justice for her decisions. If only he knew how hard each death had been; how difficult the decision had been to let them go; how each departing life had ripped out a tiny part of her own soul; how she ached with the pain of each loss even now.

He couldn't possibly understand. No-one could. Kade Miller only saw her as everyone else in the world did: a midwife operating outside the system, thereby endangering the lives of innocent young women and babies.

She uttered a short, mirthless laugh and rose. She had to get out of here. Before he returned. Even if she had to walk through the storm to town. No way was she going to New York with him. Not to see Andrew Carleton. That name had bled through the connection and she knew who he was. What he really wanted.

Her.

She strode for the hall. There must be cold-weather clothes stored in a closet somewhere. Glancing quickly at the kitchen window, she knew a moment's apprehension. The wind had strengthened. It screamed through the trees outside and battered the windows with sleet and snow flurries. Maybe it wasn't as bad as it sounded.

She flung open the coat-closet. There. A thick down-filled coat. Perfect.

A sharp crack and a loud crash echoed behind the house. Agony sliced into her left thigh. Pain billowed behind her ear and in her chest and arm. Bent double, she almost succumbed to it and drowned in the wave of blackness that followed. Dizzy and weak, she staggered along the hall, aiming for the rear door. Unable to resist.

Something had happened to Kade Miller.

#

Snow lashed her in an icy torrent as Heather wrested open the door and squinted into a white-black night. Wind whipped through trees that sighed, shrilled, and creaked in protest. Snow and sleet stung her cheeks. Cold seeped through her jeans and boots, numbing her toes. She tucked ungloved fingers under her armpits and jogged on the spot.

'Kade!' Her voice was snatched away, stolen by wind, muffled by snow. She quivered, listening. No reply. She called again, louder. Her words were sucked into nothingness.

She stepped out into ankle-deep snow that now piled into drifts around the house. A dark, square shape off to her right was probably the generator shed. But where was Kade? The house platform was carved out of the hillside. Only a few feet of flat ground lay between the house and a retaining wall, behind, just visible through the blurring snow. There was nowhere else for him to go.

There! Next to the generator shed. A brief hiatus in the snowfall showed a large, bare tree branch lying across the yard and a dark, motionless form huddled beside it, already half-covered in snow.

Cautious of the slippery, unknown surface, Heather picked her way over. Her extremeties were numb, the cold eating into her flesh, stealing what little warmth and energy she'd regained with food. She hurried on.

Dropping to her knees in the snow, she brushed the white stuff off his face and pried open one eyelid. No response. Then a tiny puff of breath from his lips gave her hope. He lived. A slow, steady pulse throbbed in his neck. But how much damage had the branch done? Calling his name did nothing. If he'd been hit on the skull he could be in serious trouble.

She inspected every inch of his body, using all her senses to gauge his injuries. There: a long, shallow gash over his ribs on the left side; two ribs fractured by the feel of it. And the left forearm he'd used to fend off the falling branch: both bones broken but not compounded.

Another deep wound that ran the length of his left leg from thigh to knee, bleeding heavily. That was a worry. Finally, she felt his skull, dismayed to find her fingers again sticky with blood that oozed from a wound behind his right ear. At least his neck and spine were unbroken—she got no sense of injury there.

Ripping off strips from his shirt and hers, she put a rough pressure bandage on the worst leg injury.

He'd managed to avoid being trapped beneath the branch. That gave her some hope of getting him into the house. Now she had to get him inside before they both froze to death and he bled out. The distance to the door may as well be a mile.

Despair gripped her harder than the cold. Tears formed and froze to ice on her cheeks.

'Damn you. I wish I could leave you here, you stupid bastard!' Cursing her own sense of responsibility, Heather reached under his arms and hefted him. Her feet slipped on the icy ground and she sat, hard, on her ass in the wet snow.

She tried again. This time she stayed up and dragged his heavy, inert body—step by shuffling step—across the seeming-acres of space to the house. The thick trail of dark blood left behind was rapidly covered by more snow.

Twice more she fell, bruising her thigh on the sharp corner of the stairs the second time. Screaming her anger gave her the strength to haul him up the last few steps to get inside the door. Once in, she slammed the heavy timber shut, resting her head on it weakly, sobbing.

It had taken far too long. He was pale, his pulse slower and skin clammy, fingers and lips blue. Being inside the house wasn't enough. He would bleed to death in a few minutes. She had to heal the worst wounds, stop the bleeding and get him warm so his body would repair what she couldn't.

Her frozen fingers struggled first with boots then buttons until finally she simply ripped off his shirt, sending buttons flying. The fastener and zip on his jeans defeated her and she swore again. Staggering to the kitchen she snatched a knife and made short work of the tattered remains of his jeans, slicing them from ankle to hip and peeling them off.

Finally, in the half-lit hall, she saw him in all his battered, naked glory and almost quit. Covered in gore, his leg once again sluggishly oozing, the sight of his injuries revealed her worst fear.

Too much to fix. Too much damage.

He might survive, but she probably wouldn't.

There wasn't enough time, or even a chance, of getting out through the deepening storm. Even if the phones worked, no-one could get to them here, in this wind and snow. His life lay in her reluctant hands.

Saving him could mean sacrificing herself. Was she prepared to do that? Prepared to give everything for a man who knew nothing about her and feared and hated what little he thought he understood? And if she saved him, and somehow survived, he would still pass her over to Carleton.

Heather stared down at him and bit her lip. She could let him bleed out, clean the house of her trace, take his car in the morning and run.

She would be free again.

But Torin. He was Kade's partner and this was his house. Torin would come after her. Relentless, because that's the sort of person he was: loyal, fierce. He'd lost enough. He didn't deserve to lose his friend.

And, from her connection with Kade, she knew Kade was a good person. Someone joyful, reliable, loving, caring beneath the superficial veneer of anger and the scars of his own past traumas. Someone deeply thoughtful and self-aware.

Someone worth saving. Maybe more so than she was.

She studied the strong planes of his face, softened by sleep and smeared with blood.

Then she examined her own scarlet-streaked hands.

'Shit.'

CHAPTER NINE

KADE

Kade surfaced slowly from a bizarre dream involving snow and blood and pain. As wakefulness pried its way into the fuzzy depths of his brain, with it came self-castigation.

How stupid was he? He'd practically run out of the house, angry and confused after talking to the woman, Katherine/Fiona/Alanna—whatever. In his blind rage, he'd filled the generator's tank and stalked toward the house without watching his path.

He'd lost his footing and fallen to the icy ground. No. That wasn't right. He concentrated, focussing on each action taken, until memory returned. A tree branch. That's what it was. He remembered pain in his…leg, his arm and …head? Then cold blackness.

No. That must have been a dream. Because he now lay, warm and pain-free, on the…where was he? Gingerly lifting his head, Kade felt a twinge of warning from his body—as though he'd overdone it at the gym. But he hadn't been to the gym for a month.

He squinted in the pale half-light that seeped around thick curtains. Only one place had such revolting green and gold striped wallpaper. How had he come to be snugly tucked in bed in the downstairs bedroom of Torin's holiday house?

Tentatively, he touched the back of his scalp and felt a slight, tender bump. Tossing the covers aside, he inspected his left thigh. How odd. Somehow he'd expected to find a nasty fracture, or a dislocated kneecap or even a cut of some sort.

But all he could see was a purple and green bruised area on his thigh, centred around a thin, white line that appeared almost like an old scar. The same went for his arm, he realised, spotting the heavier area of purple-blue bruising on his forearm. He touched it and grunted at the stab of pain. Pressing his ribs revealed more large, tender areas of bruising.

Not a dream, then, But not as drastic as he thought. He must have fallen hard to be this banged up, though.

Swinging his leg over the edge, he put some weight on it. There, a slight twinge of pain, but nothing unbearable. Hmmm. Maybe he'd twisted his knee and received a good thump from the tree branch when it fell. Lucky.

Obviously the woman had found him and brought him inside.

A soft chime from the bedside clock, brought a new source of astonishment. Ten a.m. He'd been out for over seventeen hours!

He looked at his nakedness. She'd undressed him, too. Which meant she'd have found his carkeys…

Damn damn damn damn! Of all the stupid, idiotic, unprofessional, dimwitted…She would be long gone. Maybe Tor could track the car's gps, if she hadn't ditched it or sold it to a chop shop.

A robe lay across the foot of the bed and he draped the terrycloth over his shoulders. He headed for the door, staggering a few steps. His head swam and his knees sagged. Steadying himself on the door he waited until the dizzy spell passed.

His hand lay on the doorknob when a soft sigh revealed the presence of a second person in the room. He squinted into the shadowed corner beside the window. There she was, tucked in an overstuffed armchair, asleep.

What the hell? He crouched beside her. She wore the same jeans and blue tshirt she'd had on last night, but they were covered in some dark stains he couldn't identify in the grey morning light. Her hands were pushed into her armpits and her bare toes were curled under. She shivered and moaned in her sleep.

Why did she seem so...fragile and cold. The room was warm, thanks to the house's excellent heating system. A whimper emanated from her. That drew his attention to her face.

What the...? Deep bruises circled her eyes and her skin was ashen pale; her lush lips thin and almost white.

Tentatively, Kade stroked her cheek, then pressed his palm there. Why was her skin so cold and clammy? She shivered again, coughing.

Damn, she must have caught some sort of flu dragging him in out of the snow last night. Stupid girl! She could have just woken him up. He could have walked. The thought was savage but he slipped gentle arms beneath her too-thin body.

An unpleasant, familiar smell rose from her clothes. What on earth had she spilled on herself? The very familiarity of the scent nagged at him as he placed her in the still-warm bed he'd left. What was it?

After a moment's hesitation, he repaid her services by stripping off the filthy clothes. Left in only her underwear and bra, she seemed vulnerable and a lot less robust than he remembered. She moaned in her sleep. He yanked the covers over her shoulders.

The image of her helplessness stirred something in Kade that he was at a loss to identify for a moment. Then he cursed himself for being soft. So, she appeared sweet and fragile. She wasn't. She was a murderer and he had to remember that. If he let her deceptive innocence fool him he'd be thrice an idiot and he'd deserve to lose the hefty fee Carleton was prepared to pay for her handover.

At the thought of Carleton's heavy face, Kade shuddered. He didn't trust that man. Looking again at the drawn, delicate features of the young woman in his care, Kade was revolted at the idea of giving her over to Carleton.

She moaned, louder, and shifted restlessly under the covers. 'No! No. Please don't. Not him... I didn't...I didn't...I couldn't help...please?' The jumbled, blurred words were torn from her throat and she fought the feather quilt, kicking.

Kade sat on the edge of the bed and stroked her thick, damp hair.

It came off and he gasped.

Then the knot in his gut unwound. A wig. He tossed it aside. Her own hair was dark, short and sweat-soaked, clinging to her skull. She looked even younger and more fragile.

Tears leaked from beneath her closed lids.

'Shhhh,' he murmured, 'it's alright. You're safe. Sleep. You're safe.' The words were automatic, but they seemed to soothe her a little. She relaxed and a smile brightened the corner of her mouth. A faint surge of something tingled his arm; a mild, warm electric current passing through his bones.

'Kade...' she breathed and sank into a deeper slumber.

He stood abruptly. Cautiously, he touched her cheek. It was a little warmer. She slept, even if it seemed to be an unnaturally deep sleep. He trod into the dim hall and made his way to the bathroom, intending to have a long, hot shower.

He almost tripped over a pile of rags. No, that was his shirt and jeans. They were torn. Not a small rip, but great ragged tears. Dark stains covered huge areas of his jeans and the remains of his shirt. Everything was still damp with water and...

Blood? That was the smell on her.

He flicked on the hall light. The floor was slick and sticky with blood; great red-brown smears and a drying puddle of pinkish water showing where *something* had been dragged in the back door. There were bloody handprints on the door and the door to the bedroom. Small footprints tracked blood along the hall to the kitchen and back again.

Her footprints.

Her handprints.

Her blood?

No. He'd seen her almost naked. No injuries, no bruises but a large black one on her backside. Certainly no cuts that would result in this much blood.

Whose, then?

Kade snatched up the bundle of clothing, stepped into the bathroom and shucked the robe. Sliding the sticky-damp sleeves of his once-grey shirt over his arms, he flipped it onto his shoulders and examined himself in the mirror. All the buttons were gone, so he held the front together while he tried to reconcile the reflection with reality.

Both legs of his jeans were slashed from waistband to ankle. The left leg had a massive tear over the thigh. The cloth was damp and black with blood. He touched his bruised thigh and ran a thumb along the length of the thin, ragged white scar. Holding his jeans up to his hips, he matched the position of the torn material with the marks on his body.

It had to be his blood. There was no other explanation. But how?

Dropping the clothes, he checked his watch—only to find it missing. Damn! He hurried along the hall, slipping on the wet floor, and picked up his cellphone from the kitchen bench. The time and date confirmed his suspicion. The bedroom clock was right. Only about seventeen hours had passed since the accident. Not days, not weeks, certainly not the months it would take to heal wounds that bled so much.

He had to be going insane. This wasn't possible. Was it? This made no sense at all. It wasn't happening.

He needed that shower. And time to think. A lot of time. Kade shoved the destroyed clothing into a bin.

#

Half an hour later, showered, dressed and feeling less like he'd been stomped by a herd of horses, Kade was no closer to an explanation. He fixed himself an enormous breakfast of eggs, bacon, toast, coffee and orange juice before finally directing his thoughts to the woman in the guest bedroom.

Something was totally out of place here. Something he didn't feel qualified to understand. There had to be a rational explanation. Several years in Special forces, and another five in O'Connor Inc Private Investigators and Security had exposed him to a lot of bizarre things, but this had to top the list.

By rights, judging by the amount of blood around the house, in his clothes and on the back porch, he should have bled to death last night. Or at least be semi-comatose in a hospital, hooked up to beeping machines and an IV.

Instead, he was sitting over the remains of breakfast, staring out the window while the storm blew in fits and gusts against the hillside. Hell. There's no way anyone could have got to the house last night; or got him to a hospital and back.

What was it Sherlock Holmes used to say? Kade searched his memory of teenage under-the-covers-reading stints. Oh yes. *Once you've eliminated the impossible, whatever is left— however improbable—must be the truth.*

The only unaccounted factor left here was…her.

Damn. He thumped a fist on the table. He still didn't even know her name.

A quick search of her duffle bag and handbag left him no better off. She was a professional identity-changer. Every piece of paper and information on her was in the name of Katherine Douglas. Undoubtedly she had her real papers stored somewhere else. He needed to find that out, at least.

Carleton would want to know, too. Especially if she was connected to his daughter's death. It was obvious that Carleton didn't want this girl just to chat about his daughter's last wishes, as he'd told Torin. He wasn't a sentimental fool. He wanted the woman he suspected of letting his daughter die. Kade understood that feeling. He empathised. He'd wanted justice, too.

But what if there was more to this than just catching a murderer? What did Carleton *really* want from this woman?

A soft cry of despair whispered from the bedroom. Kade flung open her door, expecting to find her awake and upset. She slept on, but restlessly; moaning and crying out in her dreams. Her fingers scrabbled at the bedclothes.

Kade frowned. Her skin was again clammy and cold to touch, so she wasn't feverish. It had taken on an almost translucence. Blue veins were starkly visible. The pulse at her neck beat erratically. A tear trickled from beneath those long, dark lashes. She released an anguished whimper.

This wasn't right. Whatever she'd done last night had obviously taken too much out of her. She needed to get to a hospital. One quick glance out the window at the unleavened, heavy grey and white outside showed that idea to be impossible. The storm had deepened again, throwing its rage full force against the house until the solid, double-glazed windows rattled in protest.

He had to *do* something.

Acting on impulse, Kade scooped the featherweight of her out of the bed, complete with quilt, and carried her along the hall. She huddled into him, trembling.

In the bathroom, he lay her on the tiles, the quilt wrapped around her. Then he turned the taps on full and fast, filling the bath with warm water. He added some of the aromatherapy oils Tor kept for his female friends, just for good measure. Next he retrieved apple juice, water and a chocolate bar from the kitchen and placed them handily beside the tub. Finally he shucked all but his underwear, unwrapped the girl and carried her into the enormous bath.

As her body submerged, she cried out and twisted. Her eyelids flickered and half-opened before drooping shut again. Kade held her firmly against his body and murmured soothing nothingsayings. He sank down until both of them were under cocooned in warmth.

Cradling her like a baby, he sponged off her face and even managed to awkwardly wash her damp hair. Eventually, the worst of her shivers slowed and her lashes lifted.

Those ice-blue eyes stared at him without recognition for a moment. She released a long, heavy sigh. The soft flutter of her breathing stopped. Her slender body loosened. Her head lolled, attention focussed on nothing but the emptiness of death.

CHAPTER TEN

KADE

Panic and fear froze Kade's rational thought. He could *feel* the life slipping out of her; *feel* her relief at it all being over; *feel* her spirit drifting. No! He'd lost too many people to lose another. This was *not* happening. He hauled her higher in the water, shaking her and calling the only name he thought truly fit her.

'Alanna! Alanna! Goddammit, don't do this to me. Stay!' Hastily, he tested the pulse in her neck. Thready, but there. Hope surged. She wasn't gone yet. There was time. Holding her tightly, he pressed her body against his chest.

'Dammit, fight!' he yelled. 'Don't you *dare* quit on me! You hear?!' With all that was in him, he willed her to live, to stay. For some reason, beyond comprehending, he *needed* her to stay. 'Live, Alanna,' he whispered against the soft skin of her neck.

A strange surge of almost-sensation passed through his body; a visceral connection that sucked energy from his bones and flesh. Dizzy, he had to push against the end of the bath with his feet to prevent them both from slipping under. Water sloshed around them, splashing into his eyes, stinging.

She drew a deep, shuddering breath and coughed. Another breath. He felt her pulse again. Stronger than before, surely.

Now those eyelids opened again and this time showed a hint of recognition.

'Kade,' she whispered. 'I'm so thirsty.'

Suppressing a surge of elation, he snatched a premixed glass of half-water, half-applejuice. She lifted a hand but it dropped back into the bath with a splash. He held the glass to her lips. She gulped at it, swallowing the whole before giving a little, sobbing exhalation. Her head lolled once more on his shoulder. He boosted her upright again, this time to force a tiny piece of chocolate between her teeth. She objected faintly but he insisted. Obediently, she ate.

It took fifteen minutes, but he managed to cajole her into eating half the block of chocolate and another glass of juice. Not much, but hopefully enough fuel for her body to repair itself.

Finally, exhausted himself and with the water cooling, Kade hauled her out of the bath. Gravity dragged at his limbs and his knees buckled as he crouched to lay her on the quilt. Cradling her, he absorbed the impact on his shoulder, grunting when pain shot through his ribs. He lowered her onto the cloth and paused, panting. Man. He hadn't felt so weak since the surgery to remove two bullets lodged in his gut. She weighed nothing but he could hardly carry her.

Water beaded on her skin and she shivered. Kade yanked a towel from the rack and dried them both. With the last of his strength, he wrapped her and carried her to bed. It was barely after twelve thirty, but he felt like he'd run a marathon. His arm, leg and ribs ached. His brain pounded worse than any hangover.

Fetching a dry quilt, he rolled her onto the bed and covered her. Now to get himself up those damned stairs and find another bed. The prospect of climbing the steep risers was daunting. Kade braced himself against the wall.

Heather's thready voice drifted through the dark room. 'Please, stay.'

He vacillated. Was she dreaming—perhaps repeating what he'd said to her in the bath?

'I'm s-so c-cold,' she said, her lips blue again. 'Please?'

Utterly spent, Kade stumbled to the bed and wriggled beneath the covers. Her skin was still chilly, so he hauled her close, ignoring her faint protest. With his last waking thought, he noticed an essential *rightness* to the way her body fitted against his, the way she exhaled and snuggled languidly closer.

#

'Kade?'

Her soft, wondering question roused him from a light sleep. Only darkness showed around the curtains so the entire day had passed but he had no idea how much of the night. Neither of them had moved. She still lay snugly in his embrace, fitted along his length, her legs entwined with his. It was the deepest sleep he'd had for many years and his body was heavy, relaxed.

For a moment he didn't reply, wondering if he'd dreamed her word. No. Something had changed. He could feel it in her. Her skin was warm, the rise and fall of her chest even. Then she spoke again and shifted a little against him.

'Are you awake?' She sounded hesitant, wary, unsure.

He *knew* she was wondering how she'd ended up naked, in his bed. He could *feel* the beginnings of fear mounting in her and spoke quickly to allay it.

'You were sick. I didn't know what to do, so I held you and tried to *think* you better.' He shrugged and felt her relax under his arm; the tips of her breasts brushed the thin skin there.

He had to clamp down on some very unprofessional urges that tried to take control of his body. Now was not the time to think of making love to her, but at least it showed he felt better, too.

She stiffened again, shifted from under his touch, and covered her breasts. By the hall light filtering around the doorframe, he saw her look at the door.

Kade kept still. He pretended to yawn, deliberately relaxing every aching muscle. Her quick, shallow breaths eased a little.

'It's ok, Alanna,' he murmured. 'You're safe. Go to sleep.' Now what had possessed him to say that?

After a few moments, she released a sigh and faced him. She tucked the sheet between them, but laid her head on his shoulder. He could tell she was smiling even as her body pressed against his.

'I know. Thank you.' She relaxed.

Kade waited to see if she said more, but silence followed. Had she fallen asleep?

She spoke again, dreamily, her words blurred. 'My name's Heather. But my grandad used to call me Alanna. He was Irish.'

Unaccountably moved, Kade brushed his lips against her forehead and whispered her real name, inexplicably certain it was true. She had given him a gift.

Together they drifted into sleep.

HEATHER

When she awoke, Heather felt an odd sense of loss. She swept a hand languidly across the bed, feeling for....? Vague memories skipped across her brain and confirmed that her captor had indeed shared her bed—and...a bath? Had anything else happened? Surely she'd remember sex?

The bed was empty beside her now, cotton sheets rumpled and still warm, his scent lingering faintly. She briefly dwelt in contentment; the memory of his arms around her, his shared strength, the giddy feeling of safety.

Then the midnight conversation blossomed in her mind. She'd told him her real name. Only half of it, admittedly, but still her real name. What on earth had come over her?

And safety? She was mad to think herself safe with him. He might have nursed her but only out of duty and because he was being paid, undoubtedly very well, to bring her in alive.

She couldn't afford to trust or like him. After all, he intended to take her to New York and give her over to Andrew Carleton—a man she knew by reputation to be calculating and ruthless in the extreme. Regardless of how well Kade had cared for her, she had to get away.

Heather threw aside the covers and spotted her duffel bag. Hauling a change of clothes out, she threw them on, ignoring the trembling weakness in her legs. She shoved the rest of her gear into the bag, hefted it and gently eased the bedroom door open.

The sound of running water in the bathroom assured her of Kade's whereabouts.

On the kitchen bench lay Kade's wallet and, glory be, his carkeys.

Snatching them up, she padded to the front door and flung it open. Only to be greeted by air so cold it stole the breath from her lungs. Snow lay piled in drifts of six feet or more. Both cars were no more than white lumps in the driveway. The sky was still leaden, although snowfall had eased off to a few dainty flakes. Icicle teeth glittered along the eaves. The world slept under a thick, white blanket.

Heather stood, staring blindly at the featureless front garden, her hopes of escape falling about her.

'Going somewhere?' Kade's deep voice startled her and she spun to face him.

Bad move. The house kept spinning even after she stopped and she staggered. He was by her side in a flash, supporting her with a strong arm around her waist. All his concern, his confusion of mixed feelings for her, the slight twinges of pain from his healing wounds, engulfed her and she sank to her knees in the middle of the cold doorway.

He dropped to one knee beside her, stroking her hair, urging her to rise and come into the warmth.

'Don't touch me,' she whispered, struggling to separate herself from him both physically and mentally. Afraid of what she might do, unintentionally, if he didn't let go soon. If he triggered that response, she might not be able to control it. 'Please!'

In reaction to her final, agonised plea, he withdrew his hands and body, taking his tumult of emotions with him. Relative calm returned to her mind and Heather climbed stiffly to her feet. Cold air crept into the gaps of her inadequate clothing. She shuffled inside and leaned on the wall, resting.

What now? She was trapped here. By him. What would he do?

Kade closed the door, stepping carefully around her. A mixture of anger and worry flashed in his fine grey eyes. Worry? What over? Her? Anger, why? Because he felt rejected. Normally she could deal with that by removing herself. Here she couldn't. Would he take it out on her?

She studied him closer. Confusion, too, lurked in him, tinged with glimmers of fear.

Fear was more familiar. Fear she'd seen more often than she could count. Fear was an old companion and antagonist.

How to diffuse it, though? He was intelligent enough to have worked out *something* had happened last night, even if he didn't understand what. He wanted an explanation. She'd tasted that in his touch. But what could she possibly say that would make any sense? It was too hard to explain and he wouldn't believe it anyway.

So she simply struggled to a chair at the kitchen table and dropped her forehead onto her arm. Within a few minutes, a mountain of food appeared before her, along with a huge, steaming mug of milky coffee. Heather wasn't sure if she was hungry until she tasted the first forkful of scrambled egg. After that she didn't stop until the plate was empty. It had to be the largest meal she'd had for years, but it barely touched the void in her belly and made no dent in the emptiness in her heart.

'Better?' Kade's inquiry reminded her of his presence and she slipped behind a calm mask, feeling too exposed without any disguise paraphernalia for the first time in many years. She touched her blue-black wavy hair. Clean and soft. The bath?

He pointed, seeming calm again. 'I like your own hair and your own eye colour. They suit you.' He sipped his coffee and added conversationally. 'Your eyes are quite extraordinary. I can see why you change their colour. Far too memorable.' His words sounded reasonable but even now she could sense the anger and frustration radiating off him, battering her weakened defences. His calm was a mask.

'Don't.' Heather held out a hand to stop the words, the emotion, both. Her voice broke and she hated herself for that betrayal of fear. What was it about this man that affected her so much?

'Don't what?' His tone sharpened and he set his cup down so hard that coffee sloshed onto the timber. With arms folded, he glared at her. 'Don't speak, don't touch, don't find out what's going on here? Why the hell not?'

Heather flinched from the pent up anger and frustration bubbling under the thin lid of his self-control. She dug some of her own anger out of storage in an effort to fight the weakness that caused her to shake and her ears to sing.

Gritting her teeth, she tried to match his intensity. 'Don't pretend to be nice to me when you're going to sell me to someone who'll have me killed or tortured the minute you walk out the door! Andrew Carleton is one of the most vile—' She broke off, disconcerted by the look of shock he turned on her.

'How did you know that?' Kade shot to his feet, expression fierce and bewildered at the same time. He loomed over her, hands flat on the table.

'What?' What was he on about now?

'I never told you Carleton was the person who hired me. Never.' His scowl deepened.

'I don't…surely you said…didn't you?' She stammered to a halt, unable to remember what had been spoken and what she had plucked from his thoughts.

'No.' His voice dropped, as dangerously soft and cold as the snow outside.

'Oh.' Heather fiddled with her coffee cup, draining its bitter dregs with a grimace.

He stalked around to her side of the table, standing over her. She tried to sit still and raised her chin.

'What are you, Heather. How did you do this?' He revealed the still-blue bruises on his arm.

She touched them, briefly, lightly, snatching her finger back when his feelings surged through with renewed intensity. She shuddered.

'Do you really want to know?' This was a now-or-never moment. If she were to convince him that she was not the badguy, it had to be right now.

'Yes, dammit!' He clenched a fist and thumped it on the table, making her cup jump. 'By the amount of blood on my clothes and the floor, I should be in hospital. Or dead.' He sank onto the chair next to her, his tone softening to bewilderment. 'Why am I alive?'

Heather hesitated. Was she about to dig her own grave? She'd never let anyone into her secret life before. It was frightening to think how much power he would have with this knowledge. But what choice did she have?

'OK, I'll show you.' She grabbed his bruised flesh. He twitched, but she tightened her hold. 'This won't hurt *you.*'

She hesitated. Was that true? Her body was so low in energy she had to be careful. Emotions weren't the only thing in danger of bleeding from him.

Did she have enough for even this small task? The rich food weighed heavily in her stomach, its energy not yet available to her body. Her weakness frightened her, but she had to do this. It was the only way to get him onside. Her only chance to be left alone again.

He nodded once but there was tension in his arm; in his clenched fist and stiff body.

The welter of his angry, confused thoughts blurred hers, threatening to overwhelm her feeble attempts to concentrate. Normally she could block but she was too tired and he was too strong. She dug her fingernails into his arm, feeling the sharp pain reflected in his surprised thoughts.

'Would you *please* stop *thinking* for a moment?' Her voice sounded strained, even to herself.

CHAPTER ELEVEN

KADE

Startled, Kade hesitated. How did you stop thinking? He tried, though; tried to put a damper on his wildly careening thoughts.

'Thank you.' She closed her eyes, still and composed, free of fear at last, almost ethereal. An odd rush of not-quite-warmth surged through his arm. A strange ache twisted in his head. Her breath caught on a half-sob. The bruising on his arm faded from blue to greenish to yellow to nothing.

Heather released him. She uttered a low moan and slumped, her lips white and tight-pressed.

Kade gaped at his arm. It was one thing to suspect, but another entirely to watch it happen. He delayed, not sure what to say. Belief opened the doors to clarity and his thoughts tumbled into the future.

What the hell did he do with her, now?

'Does that answer your question? That was a double-fracture last night.' Her voice was a thread, dull and careless. 'I'm a freak.'

Pulled from his thoughts, Kade took in her pale face and shivering body and felt a surge of protectiveness that astonished him. He gathered her into his lap, trying not to think, willing his energy into her as he had done yesterday. She resisted feebly but he tucked her against his chest and rocked her gently as he would an upset child. Slowly, her shivering abated, her fear faded and colour returned to her skin.

'I don't think you're a freak, but I do think you're stupid to have done that unnecessary demonstration and wasted all your strength again.'

To his surprise, she chuckled. It was an encouraging sound. She had a nice laugh.

She slid off his lap and broke all contact with him. Then she reclaimed her empty cup and held it between them. Kade examined her, strangely bereft, alone in a way he'd never felt before.

He scowled and forced himself back on track. This was no time to go all mushy. He still had a job to do.

Beside him, Heather flinched, wiping at her eyes.

'So tell me how you do this…healing thing,' he demanded.

She said nothing for a while, merely refilling her coffee cup from the pot on the table. 'I just do it. I did nursing and midwifery at college so I'd have enough medical knowledge to know what was wrong with someone. Then I *will* it to be the way it should be. The ability's been in my family for generations – at least six that I know of. My great-great-great-grandmother left Ireland when she was sixteen to escape being tried as a witch.'

Kade gaped at her. 'A witch? No-one believes in that crap.'

She flicked him a quick glance full of ironic humour. 'Not now, but a hundred plus years ago, yes. In the backwoods of Ireland where people still very much suspected witches and faery folk might really be true. I grew up on stories of the Sidhe—the faeries.' She smiled wistfully. 'My grandmother swore we were part sidhe. I used to dream it was true, hoping I could have a huge family that all understood me. That didn't fear me.'

Kade interlaced his fingers behind his neck. 'So your great-something-grannie came to America,' he prompted. If she was willing to talk, he should listen. All the better for getting the truth about Carleton's daughter from her.

Heather rested her head on one fist. Her eyelids drooped.

'Mmmm. And at least one daughter in each generation has inherited the gift—if you can call it that—of healing. Sometimes stronger, sometimes weaker.' She focussed far past him, into memory.

Kade observed her, fascinated by the play of emotion, not so much across her face, but beneath. He could almost feel the sadness, the pang of loss as she remembered.

'Someone close to you?' he guessed, wanting to snap her out of the past.

Heather closed her eyes. 'Yes. My mother.'

As much as he wanted to soothe her, Kade had to keep his task in mind—and that meant knowing more about her so he could work out how to get her safely to New York. He kept prodding. 'What happened?'

Her mouth thinned and her eyes opened to focus on the fire. 'She died ten years ago.' Her voice was flat with old, suppressed pain.

Kade could almost feel her struggle not to break; not to burst into tears. This time he waited, so she could fill in the silence with truths. After several minutes, his patience was rewarded.

She looked at her own thin hands twisting together on the table. 'She wore herself out trying to help every helpless, illegal, pregnant girl who crossed her path. I couldn't bring her back. She was too tired. I tried but…she said I would drain myself and we'd both die. She made me let her go.'

Kade caught his breath at the break in her voice, wanting to hold her but afraid to at the same time lest they both be overwhelmed by emotion again. He was used to being in control. This emotional rollercoaster she generated in him was too hard to handle. His own fear of what she could do to his customary equanimity made his next words harsher than he intended.

'Is that what you call what you do? Helping them?'

Heather gulped. 'I try, but I can't always save everyone.'

Kade needed to put distance between them. If he wasn't careful he'd start believing in her and he couldn't afford to do that. All the evidence he had seen proved her to be a reckless, careless, feckless bitch who played with people's lives. How many women and babies had died in home-births through her negligence? The practice needed to stop.

He, at least, shouldn't need to be reminded of that.

He surged up from the table and paced into the kitchen. Turning to lean on the counter, he threw his next words at her like a knife.

'What right do you have to play God with people's lives?'

HEATHER

Heather had had enough. Enough of the accusations and the misinformation; enough of the anger, pain and confusion pouring off him. She thrust herself upright, struggling to stand against the weakness of her knees. Glaring at him, she put all her remaining energy into her words.

'Do you think it's easy?' She moved around the table, pinning him with an icy stare. 'You think I decide who lives on some sort of whim? I have to make tough decisions. I can only save babies and mothers that can live without medical support after I go. I have limits, too. If they need a major operation or ongoing medical attention I can't fix, then I can't bring them back.

'Each time it's like dying myself. Each time it rips a piece of me away forever. Each baby that dies because their family is illegal and can't afford fake papers. Because they can't afford medical insurance. Because they're too scared to go to hospital.'

She jabbed a finger at him. 'Every single time I let one go that I *just can't save,* I lose part of myself.' She was only inches away now, but could hardly see him through the tears that blurred her vision.

He gripped her arms and she cried out against the flood of anger that flowed from him.

'Why? It's not your responsibility!' He yelled and she wasn't sure if he was angry *at* her or on her behalf.

Bracing her shaking knees, she tried to stay upright, but her strength was rapidly fading again. He sucked it from her through sheer force of personality, trying to assuage an ancient pain he'd somehow connected to her. His energy and passion was a flame and she the moth, burning.

She couldn't stand against him. But if he didn't let go she'd have no choice and she wouldn't be able to control what happened next.

Gasping, she pushed feebly at his chest. 'It *is* my responsibility. If I call an ambulance the family will disappear, or the mother will walk out of hospital and abandon the baby anyway, or the police and social services will get involved and deport them. Then they'll try to return and maybe not make it this time. Or get sold into prostitution or worse.'

His touch gentled. Instead of shaking her, he led her toward the couch in front of the fire. She went in blind obedience, too tired to worry about trying to hide anything any longer. Kade knelt in front of her, rubbing her arms as she shivered.

'Why do you do it?' he asked roughly.

Finally, she faced him and saw reluctant belief. 'Because it's the only way I can make a difference. Because I can save most of them. In the last ten years I've helped almost a thousand babies born outside the system. I've only lost five, and three mothers. I think those are pretty good odds, considering.'

Kade released her and their connection was severed, scalpeled, lost.

'What about Amali Carleton?' he demanded.

'Who?' She was too exhausted to invent any stories, even if she knew who he was talking about. The room took on a faint sepia tinge and everything sounded distant and muffled.

Striding swiftly away, Kade reappeared with a small photograph and shoved it at her. Heather managed to focus on the image of a dark-haired girl.

She blinked, feeling drunk. 'Oh. Amy. Yes. I didn't know her real name.'

Again Kade grabbed her, this time stopping her from collapsing sideways to lie on the beckoning couch. 'What was your excuse for letting her and her baby die?'

Heather chuckled weakly. His touch sucked more strength from her. Sleep called and she couldn't fight it off any longer no matter how much he wanted her to.

'I didn't let her die. She had a difficult birth and I had to heal both her and the baby, but she was alive and so was her baby when I left them a year ago.'

KADE

'What?' Kade rocked on his heels. But it was impossible to doubt her. The truth of her statement bled through his touch—somehow. He scrubbed a hand through his hair, feeling thick-headed. 'But her father sent me to find you. He said the birth had been mishandled. That his daughter and grandson were dead because of you. I've been tracking you for the last few months on his behalf.'

Heather sat straighter, her expression clouded with pain and weariness. Kade repressed a spurt of concern. He had to know the full story; had to get this sorted out now. He put space between them, needing some distance.

'He lied.' Her eyelids drooped and she visibly fought to stay awake. 'Amy, her baby and her husband, David, were all perfectly healthy when I dropped in to see them three months ago.'

'Three months ago? Where?'

She didn't reply so he crouched in front of her again and shook her gently, trying to ignore the wave of weariness that oozed into his arms from her thin frame.

'I can't tell you,' she finally said. 'I promised. Amy's father is hunting for her. The stupid thing is that he didn't care when she left home. He only got angry when she married David. He hates David for some reason neither of them understand. If Amy wants Carleton to think she's dead then she has a good reason.'

Heather covered Kade's hands with hers. 'Kade, she's happy. She has a beautiful son. She loves her husband. He's a good man. He left his career as a surgeon to keep her safe from Carleton. Let them be.'

Against his will, belief and agreement flowered in his mind. She was right. He should forget about Amali. She was happy.

Kade frowned. Why should he believe her word? He wrenched free from her touch. His mind cleared.

'What?' He jeered, trying to claw back his scepticism. 'She wants to be out of her father's life as a wealthy businessman? What's so awful about that?'

'A wealthy businessman. That's rich.' Heather sneered. 'Maybe you need to spend more time doing background research on your clients and less time chasing me around the country. Frankly, I'm tired of changing identities and running. Leave Amy alone. Stay away from me. Let me do what I do best.'

He hesitated, torn between divided wants. 'I've been paid to bring you to Carleton.'

She smiled faintly at him, sagging. 'You only need to bring me to New York if Amy's dead, right? Here.' She fumbled in her purse and pulled out her phone. Angling it so he could see the screen, she pointed at the photo displayed there.

'Look. Amy and her baby and her husband. Taken only three months ago. See? The baby's about eight months old, so no-one can possibly say he died in childbirth.' Her eyes drifted closed and she slumped onto the white cushions.

Kade roused her lightly, then let go when her exhaustion all but smothered his own energies. Dammit. How did she *do* that?

'Don't you fall asleep now, Heather,' he warned, worried by the pale cast to her skin. 'We have to sort this out.'

She yawned, her head listing to one side. 'Tell him you couldn't find me. Show him the photo.'

Kade held her upright and snorted at her naivety. 'He won't believe me and he'll say the photo's a fake.'

'Make him believe! Make him leave me alone. I'm too tired to run any more. Please?'

Her pleading almost broke him. If Carleton thought Heather was dead, he'd leave both women alone. Maybe that was the best thing for everyone. What harm would it do if he let her go? He didn't need to take her to New York.

Kade rubbed at the base of his skull. No, that was stupid-thinking. Plain dumb. He scrutinised Heather, unable to hide astonished realisation. She was influencing his thoughts? Could that be it? He let go of her arm and the feelings diminished.

She was! Somehow she had the ability to project her emotions into his head when he touched her. That explained his fuzzy thinking. What else did it explain? His attraction to her? It would account for the strength of his desire, his crazy behaviour in that café bathroom.

He climbed jerkily to his feet, and glared at her, his anger fuelled partly by fear, partly by annoyance at her ability to manipulate his emotions.

'Stop messing with my mind. You're going to New York. You can explain it to Carleton yourself.'

CHAPTER TWELVE

HEATHER

She blinked at him. 'Sorry. I've never met anyone as sensitive to my feelings as you are. Normally I can feel people and have some small effect on their emotions, but they don't know it. It helps me calm a frightened mother. I wasn't doing it to you on purpose.' Tiredness loosened the guards on her tongue. She hadn't meant to tell him that part of her abilities. Manipulating people's feelings had saved her several times. Kade was more difficult. He seemed to be aware of it in a way that no-one else had been.

He took a step away, glowering. 'That's what this is all about, isn't it? You've been playing me, haven't you? The stories you've spun. That seduction scene in the bathroom. That was all *you* inside my thoughts, making me believe you; making me want you, wasn't it? None of it was real! None of what you've said is real.'

Heather faltered. He wouldn't believe her. But she had to try anyway. 'No. You wanted me from the first moment you saw me. I felt it in the café when we touched hands.' She caught his confused, angry gaze with her own strait one. 'You know that's true. I just…' She made a helpless little gesture. '…fuelled it a bit.'

'Well.' He moved further away. His handsome face turned cold, bleak. 'You can try your influence on Carleton and see how you go with him. From now on, don't come near me.'

'No! Please? He'll…' She shuddered.

Kade propped himself against the mantelpiece, folding his arms. 'He won't do anything to you. I'll be there the whole time.'

Heather bit her lip. How could he be so blind to Carleton's nature and so judgemental of her own?

Fear. He judged her because he was afraid of her abilities, afraid what he felt for her might be real, afraid it might not be.

She tried again. 'And afterward?' she said softly, studying his lean, tensed shoulders. 'When you're gone? He'll hound me for the rest of my life if he thinks I know where Amy is. Don't you understand? It's bad enough running from each town when local people start to suspect I'm doing something odd. If you add the people working for Carleton then I'll never be free. I'll never be able to relax. I'll spend the rest of my life running. And I can't do it anymore. I'm so tired.' Her voice broke because she couldn't help it, but he must have seen it as more manipulations. The look he sent her was colder than the air outside.

He shrugged carelessly. 'So lead me to Amali and let her face her father.'

Heather flushed with anger that gave false energy. 'Now you're being naïve. She married David against her father's wishes. If she contacts her father, he'll find a way to destroy her marriage.'

Kade shrugged again. 'Marriages fail all the time. People divorce, run away, die.' Bitterness flickered in his eyes.

The last of her energy drained away, leaving her limp. She curled up on the couch, clutching a fluffy cushion to her belly and pillowing her aching head on another. She sighed heavily, lost in the crackling, spitting fire.

'Kade, just leave me alone. Go and tell him I died here. I'll disappear again and we'll all be happy.' She finally let her eyes close, welcoming the bliss of unconsciousness.

A stinging pain on her cheek brought her blearily back.

'Heather!' Kade called her name from a vast distance.

'I'm awake,' she muttered crossly. 'But I want to sleep. Please. I'm so tired.'

'No!'

She opened her eyes to see his handsome face inches from hers, clouded with a welter of emotions.

'You have to stay awake, Heather.' Anger and fright faded, replaced by concern. 'You almost slipped away again, like you did last night in the bath.'

'What?' She didn't understand. 'Slipped away?'

'You almost died then,' he said tersely. 'And you will now if you go to sleep.'

Heather yawned. 'That might not be so bad. I am very tired. It would solve everything, too, wouldn't it?' She wanted to thrust him aside, but her arms were too heavy.

Darkness claimed her and she went willingly.

KADE

Kade saw her slide into unconsciousness again, and was helpless to stop it. What could he do? If he touched her she would have so much power over his mind he wouldn't be in control. The thought filled him with apprehension. How could he save her—without touching her—when she had clearly given all her strength to save him? Surely he owed her his life, at least.

Even as he argued with himself, her breathing slowed and her hold on the pillow relaxed. She appeared peaceful, innocent, angelically lovely.

'Dammit!' Kade swore fiercely. Unable to think of anything else to do, he laid a hand on hers and willed his own energies into her. The surge of transference was feeble at best. It did no more than cause her lashes to flicker. Not enough. She had drained herself proving her abilities to him, fighting him, convincing him. He had to give more. Maybe the energy transference had something to do with the amount of skin contact?

Half-reluctantly, he gathered her fragile figure into his arms. Still no response. She weighed almost nothing, barely a burden as he carried her along the hall to the bed they shared last night.

Dragging off her clothes and his own, he bundled her once more under the covers. Then, gritting his teeth, he hauled her slight body against his. She lay limp and unresponsive, though he knew she still lived. Not for long if he didn't do something.

He rolled her onto her back. Long, dark eyelashes fringed her ridiculous eyes. In the mellow lamplight, the creamy skin of her long neck seemed a rich gold. Shadows emphasised the clean lines of her jaw and the gentle double-curve of her lips. A tiny, faint pulse in her neck jumped erratically.

All his reactive anger faded at the sight of her slender, helpless form, relaxed in his arms. This time, he knew it was his own feelings, not hers. She was too sunk in lethargy to project any thoughts into his mind. There were no excuses. No way he could blame her for the chaos of fear, anxiety, admiration, and desire that pulsed through him now.

Never in his life had he been so affected by a woman. Lovers came and went. He stayed detached. No amount of feminine tears, recriminations, pleas and declarations cracked his shield after Amanda. Yet, somehow, this defensive, elusive, unusual girl had snuck right through his walls and cracked him open, exposing his soul for her pleasure.

No. He let that bitter thought go. He knew enough…he'd *felt* enough of her to know that she wasn't trying to manipulate his feelings out of any sort of vindictiveness or spite. She was simply trying to survive as best she could with the skills she had.

He looked at her again. The pulse in her neck slowed, jumped, stopped and started again, fainter than before.

He willed his energy into her; willed her to live, as he had before.

Nothing.

Why wasn't it working this time?

'Come on, Heather,' Kade whispered. 'Come back.'

#

'No, Tor, do it now or she's going to die! I don't give a shit who hired the damned thing. It's your helicopter. Get it out here or get me a paramedic helicopter. The local emergency services is, literally, snowed under with calls already.' Kade tromped on the snow in the driveway, crushing on the white stuff restlessly. His breath frosted and his nose had lost feeling about three minutes after he'd left the house.

When Heather's response to his plea had been to sink further into stupor, he'd had to act. Dressing in the warmest outdoor gear he could find in Tor's closet, he'd pocketed his phone and strapped on snowshoes. Tor had warned him cell reception was patchy at best, and only possible from halfway down the driveway.

So Kade now flattened the small area where the phone received signal and swore at the delays. The sun, high and brilliant in a crisp blue sky, glittered off the blanket of snow. He'd forgotten sunglasses so his eyes ached and watered in the dry air. His fingers were numb because he'd had to strip off the gloves to use the phone keypad. Hopefully the phone would keep operating in these temperatures.

Torin came back on the line, his voice crackly and tinny. 'They're firing her up now, Kae. I've had someone call a doctor and he said you're doing the right things. Keep her warm. Get more juice into her. The chopper'll be there asap. Is the pad clear?'

'Jeez, Tor!' Kade reviewed the terraced area where, in the summer, a helipad allowed easy access to the property. 'It's four feet under. I can't clear it. I'd be leaving her alone for too long. Tell them to bring the winch. I'll be waiting. Make it quick.'

'That bad?'

'You have no idea.' Kade glanced at the house. Did she still live? 'This girl is…no, I can't explain it. I'll tell you when we get there—if she survives.'

There was a long pause. Had the line dropped out again?

'The day you took this job, someone told me,' Tor said, his voice low and thoughtful, 'the woman we were searching for would be important to you. Is she?'

Kade hauled his thick wool hat off and thwacked it against his thigh.

'Yes. No.' He swore. 'I don't know, Tor. All I know is that there's something weird going on and she's part of it. I don't think Carleton told us everything, either. Do me a favour and get a deeper background done on him – and on his daughter. She evidently married a surgeon named David something. See if you can find him, too. More than the usual. Dig.'

'What am I looking for?'

'I don't know,' Kade repeated. 'That's the problem. It's a… gut feeling. There's something not right here.'

'I'll get someone on it.'

'No.' He stamped in the snow. 'I think it's one we need to keep between us. You do it.'

In another long pause Kade could almost hear Tor totting up his time and the cost to the business if he took his focus off running it for long enough to do a deep background search on Carleton.

'Alright.' Tor ended the call.

Used to his abrupt ways, Kade pocketed the phone and regarded the silent house for a long time. Was it Heather's influence that made him doubt Carleton's veracity? He'd forgotten, now, what he thought of the man at their first meeting. All his memories were coloured by feelings of uneasiness and distaste. But were they his or hers? Why was she so afraid of a man she'd never even met?

He trudged to the house and inspected Heather. She still breathed, but shallow and soft, barely audible even in the silence of the darkened bedroom.

Swearing, he raced through the lockdown preparations. One of the upstairs windows, left unshuttered in the storm last night, had blown in and the floors were a mess of water and leaves. Cleaning it wasn't high on his list of priorities so he threw a towel over the water and made mental note to send a cleaner in when the roads were clear.

He tidied the kitchen, at least, then packed her clothing and his own. At the last minute he bagged his torn, bloodied clothing and stuffed it into his haversack. It might be useful.

Arriving back in the bedroom with juice and chocolate, Kade managed to rouse Heather enough to force the liquid into her, though much of it dribbled down her chin, onto her throat.

Her eyelids opened briefly and drifted closed again. Despairing and helplessly angry, he dressed her, scooped her up, wrapped in the quilt, and carried her to the front room.

Peering out the front window, a faint, dark speck high in the blue sky brought a grim smile to him. The distant tick-tick-tick became a deeper note that thrummed through his chest.

The helicopter neared and dropped lower. Lower, still, and the noise drowned the peaceful silence. A cloud of snow surged up from the landing pad. The helicopter hovered, waiting.

Kade studied the pale, sleeping figure in his arms and kissed her white lips gently.

'Hang in there, Alanna.'

CHAPTER THIRTEEN

KADE

Kade paused in his pacing when Torin re-entered the room with a beer bottle in each hand. He passed one to Kade, who threw down a mouthful. Tor sipped his and sank onto the red leather couch, shoving aside a pile of unread junkmail. It cascaded to the floor, joining a welter of others.

'You do know you could afford a bookkeeper or PA to do your private accounts, don't you?' Tor said. 'The business does, actually make a profit.'

Kade threw him a half-hearted grin. 'I have a lower care-factor about these things than you do.'

'I noticed,' Tor said drily. 'But your care-factor about this girl Katherine-Meghan-whatever seems to be pretty high.' He hooked one arm over the back of the couch and took another swig of beer. 'Want to tell me what's going on? Have you heard from the hospital?'

'Yes.' Kade strode to the window and stared out over the busy streets of the Tribeca without seeing them. 'They have her on a drip. She's still unconscious but they think she'll be alright with a few days rest and food. Exhaustion and exposure, they said.'

He laughed bitterly. 'You should have seen the way they looked at me. Like it was my fault she almost died.' He leaned on the window frame and hung his head, hearing the truth of it again.

Leather creaked on the couch behind. A heavy hand fell on his shoulder.

'It wasn't this time and it wasn't last time, either, Kae. She made her own choices, as did Amanda.'

Kade made a noise of frustration and shoved Torin's touch off, gritting his teeth against the upwelling of pain. 'Easy to say,' he spat, 'but it was my choice to hound this poor girl until she couldn't run any more. *My* fault I pushed her too hard; that I got injured and wasn't there to protect her.'

'Injured?' Tor's deep voice cut through the darkness and Kade clenched his jaw, trying to master his spiralling guilt.

Tor asked, 'Are we still talking about this girl? Because you couldn't have got out of hospital in time to get home to Amanda, we both know that. You had two bulletholes plugged for God's sake. What does that have to do with this? I don't see the connection.'

Collecting his discarded haversack, Kade tipped it out on the floor and snatched up the plastic bag containing his clothes. He thrust it at Torin and turned again to the window. Plastic crinkled behind him and Tor made a noise of disgust.

'Is that blood?'

'Yes.' Kade held himself tightly in control again. 'I want at least two good men on her door and two in the room, Tor. We need to get to the truth behind this girl before we give her over to Carleton.'

After one, quick, searching inspection of Kade's face, Tor produced his phone and barked the orders. Tucking it away he brandished the clothing, wrinkling his nose.

'So explain.'

'I can't. Not yet, anyway. Let them dry and put them into the evidence locker at work.'

'Kade, what is going on?' Tor tied the bag shut and threw it at the door.

'We need to wait until she's well enough to get out of hospital.' Kade clutched his partner's arm, half-surprised not to feel what Tor was thinking. 'Trust me. It's important. And I'll take over the investigation into Carleton. I think I know what I'm looking for now.'

Tor frowned, his dark-rimmed storm-blue eyes heavy with doubt. 'Fine. Three days. No more. After that, if you've found nothing and she's well enough, we arrange the meeting with Carleton.' He swallowed the rest of his beer and headed for the door. There, he paused. 'So, when she's released from hospital, what do we do with her? Where's she going to stay and what's to stop her running?'

Kade directed a furious glare to his partner. 'She'll stay here, with me. I'll keep her from running.'

Tor grinned and glanced around the room with its welter of unread mail, clothes, and random sports equipment. 'I'll send the cleaner over, shall I?'

HEATHER

Heather woke to a familiar, yet unfamiliar environment. She recognised the antiseptic smell and the background hum of voices and machines before she even opened her eyes. She'd spent many hours in hospitals over the years—but never as a patient. But which hospital?

She braved the world, opening her eyes. High-rise buildings dominated the view outside.

He'd brought her to New York after all.

'Ah!' An over-cheerful face appeared and Heather flinched. The female nurse checked Heather's pulse and blood-oxygen content. She nodded. 'Nice and strong now.' She patted Heather's arm and tugged the heavy white sheets unnecessarily into place. 'You'll be fine in a couple of days. Buzz if you need anything.' She pointed to the button dangling by the headrest. 'We'll take the catheter out a little later, when you're stronger. You can rest now.'

'Wait.' Heather's voice cracked. 'The man who brought me in. Where is he?'

'Mr Miller?' The nurse dimpled. 'He went home to get some sleep. But he left two of his people outside your door and two inside, behind the curtain. He said you were worried about a stalker. Don't be worried. You're safe here.'

Heather turned aside to hide the tears. The door closed and a lock snicked in the silence.

#

The first two days she spent doing little more than sleeping, eating and trying to resist self-pitying misery. It wasn't easy. She didn't have the energy for any other sort of emotion and no-one to vent it on, anyway. No-one visited except medical staff. Kade had installed round-the-clock security who never spoke to her. Straight-faced and unflinching they basically ignored her, though their eyes followed her and their bodies tensed every time she left the bed.

So she was alone, yet not alone at the same time. The only time she had any privacy was in the bathroom. It was humiliating but also strangely comforting. Yes, she was basically imprisoned, but she was also safe from Andrew Carleton. But for how long?

After two days recuperating, she felt well enough to confront Kade and ask the question. She asked one of her stoic bodyguards to request Kade's presence.

'Sorry ma'am,' the woman replied stoically. 'You're not to have visitors. Including him. Mr Miller's own instructions. When the doc releases you, we're to take you straight to Mr Miller's office. You can speak with him then.'

Heather looked at the woman, then at herself. She sat in bed, dressed in nothing more than a hospital gown, with a drip still attached to her arm. The security guard and her clone sat near the door, dressed in jeans and longsleeved business shirts, carrying pistols in holsters under their arms. They also wore gloves. She needed skin contact to influence someone.

Kade had taken precautions. No way could she escape the room.

Lethargy and misery overcame her and she lay on her side, facing the window, staring out at the blue sky. Tears dampened her cheeks and dripped off her nose. She wrapped around her fear and cried herself to sleep for the first time in many years.

When she awoke the next day, it was to a cheerful doctor and his professional assessment that she was ready to go home. He admonished her to take better care of herself and recommended she see a dietician. When she cautiously asked about the bill, he beamed and told her it was all handled and not to worry about it.

Subdued, she dressed and came out of the bathroom as ready as she could be. Her bodyguards carried her bag and escorted her in close formation—careful not to touch her—to a waiting car. Not a car; a limousine.

She climbed in. Before she could slide out the other door, it opened and one of her guards ducked inside, giving her a quick nod.

Heather ground her teeth, humiliation mounting and rapidly becoming anger. What *right* did Kade have to hold her against her will? What right did he have to pass her over to Carleton, like she was some sort of commodity, a slave, a…thing to be bought and sold?

How could he do it after she'd saved his life, and after what she'd revealed? She'd trusted him to make the right choice, the humane choice, and he'd chosen to throw her aside.

Well, she folded her arms and smiled grimly, she had one last card to play. Hopefully it wouldn't backfire on her.

KADE

'She's on her way.' Torin restored his office-phone in its cradle and grimaced at Kade. 'Emma says she's pretty angry, too.'

Kade supported himself on the dark timber desk, his head lowered. He'd spent the better part of four days digging into Andrew Carleton's background and what he'd found, frankly, scared him.

Heather had been right. Carleton had a reputation as a ruthless businessman, but that wasn't the worst of it. There were hints, buried deep in his activities, of things a whole lot more unsavoury than just dodgy business practices. But nothing concrete. Nothing that could be directly linked and proven.

But more than enough to make Kade doubt the wisdom of giving Carleton any access to someone as vulnerable and unique as Heather.

The question was: how did they prevent it? Torin, unaware of the events in the mountains at the time they unfolded, had already informed Carleton of their success in finding her. So now there was no choice but to follow this thing through. But there had to be some way to give Carleton what he wanted, whatever that was, and still keep Heather safe.

Kade glowered. 'What does he really want with her?'

'Not sure.' Tor tapped on the grey suede folder that contained all the information provided by Carleton. 'All he'll say is that he wants to know what his daughter's last words were, and speak to her husband. Obviously there's more to it, but no way of knowing what. Possibly he suspects Amali isn't dead and wants her back.' He raised steady eyes to Kade. 'You know there's only one way to find out for sure.'

'No! We can't—' Kade's hot reply was interrupted by a brisk knock on the door. He swung around, unsure how to handle her if she was really angry. He couldn't blame her. From her point of view he'd kidnapped her and was intending to give her over to a man she feared. And that had been his intent.

Days of research and introspection had changed that.

He wished he had a solution to offer her. And he wished even more that he understood his own feelings for her. All he knew was that he'd let his anger and fear push him into making stupid, hurtful decisions and Heather had every right to be bitterly angry at him.

He braced himself.

The door opened and Torin's secretary held it wide, closing it quickly behind Heather.

Kade gaped. The change was extraordinary. A few days rest and food had wrought wonders. Her short, dark hair fell in soft waves to her jaw and framed a face that, while still thin, was fuller than the last time he'd seen it. Her eyes were no longer dark-shadowed and sunken. They flashed fire in ice when they met his.

She drew herself up and looked down her nose. Without uttering a word to him, she switched her attention to Torin.

Her expression transformed, softening into wonder and tentative joy, bringing new beauty and youth.

She took a step and stopped, tears pooling on her lashes. Then she dashed forward and threw herself at Torin, wrapping her arms around his waist and burying her face in his shoulder.

'Oh! It *is* you, Torin!'

Kade froze. Jealousy strangled hope in his throat. She *did* know Tor. In the cabin…her reaction to his name hadn't been his imagination. She knew Tor—too well by the looks of it. And trusted him more than she trusted Kade.

He swore, intending to tell Torin to go to Hell. But Tor's startled confusion gave Kade pause. His partner had his hands apart, body held stiff. He patted Heather's back awkwardly.

Then he pushed her away, frowning. 'Um…'

She gulped and scrubbed at her tear-stained cheeks. 'Don't you recognise me? I'm Heather.'

Tor looked a question at Kade, who shrugged in reply, tasting bitterness at her quick revelation of her identity. He hadn't told Tor her real name. He wasn't sure why. It didn't seem appropriate. It had been a gift of trust he hadn't wanted to betray, a moment of private connection shared only between the two of them.

Torin inspected her for a few seconds. Then his fingertips on her shoulders whitened and his jaw dropped open. He sat heavily on the edge of his desk

'*Heather?*' He shut his teeth with a snap. 'But you're…they said you were…it's not possible!'

For a long moment the three of them waited in stasis, immobilised, Kade watching in angry mystification. Hope and fear warred on Heather's face.

Then Tor stood again, uttered an oath, and snatched her into his arms. She began to cry in earnest and Kade was astonished to see tears leaking from beneath his partner's closed eyelids. He'd never seen Tor cry. Not ever. Not even when his father suicided when Tor was fifteen, leaving him alone in the world. He was the coolest sonofabitch Kade had ever seen and he was crying.

Hopelessness seized Kade and he spun on his heel, heading for the door. The irony of Torin caring that much about this particular woman would, he was sure, hit him and he'd laugh about it later. Right now he needed to put some distance between them.

'Kade!' Tor's call stopped him at the door. 'Why the hell didn't you tell me who she was?' He pulled Heather against his side, smiling at her. She rested her head on his shoulder, but her attention stayed on Kade.

Kade gritted his teeth.

'It's not his fault, Tor,' she said softly. 'I didn't tell him. I wasn't sure until I saw you, so I didn't want to get my hopes up.'

'What are you on about?' Kade snapped, one hand on the doorknob so hard his fingers ached.

She smiled. 'Torin's my older brother.'

CHAPTER FOURTEEN

KADE

'So explain,' Kade crossed an ankle over his knee and folded his arms.

The three of them sat in a group of leather chairs, near the picture windows that looked out over Washington Market Park. Pale winter-sky sunlight streamed in through the window and touched red into the dark beauty of Heather's hair. She sat on a couch opposite Kade. She met his eyes briefly, flushed and wrapped her arms around her stomach, focussed on the floor.

'Mother and I left home when I was eleven.' She flicked a fearful glance at Torin. 'You were thirteen.'

'I remember,' he said, bitterness in his tone. 'I woke to find Dad passed out on the kitchen floor with blood on his knuckles and a bottle of scotch beside him. All he would say when he sobered up was that Mom had taken you and left.'

'Yes.' Heather paled and touched her left temple. When Kade observed the gesture and frowned, she hastily tucked her fingers under her thighs. 'We...had to leave.'

'But *why*?' Tor's fists clenched. 'And why did he tell me you were both dead a year later? And what the *hell* do you have to do with this?' He pointed at Kade.

'Dead!' Heather pressed her hands to her cheeks. 'I'm so sorry Torin. I had no idea. Mom wouldn't let me write you. She must have sent Dad that information to keep him from searching for us. I went to the house years later, but you'd gone and none of the neighbours knew where. I couldn't find you.'

'I'll bet I know why you left,' Kade put in, resting his elbows on his knees. He ought to leave them alone; let them thrash out their family history in private. But he and Tor were brothers in all but blood and, dammit, he was the one responsible for reuniting them. This was as much his business as Torin's. Or was it that he wanted it to be his business?

'No!' Heather put out a hand as though to stop him from speaking.

He ignored her protest. Nothing would be gained by hiding her abilities from her brother. If they were going to ever make her safe from Carleton, Tor needed to be fully in the loop. Kade thrust aside a twinge of guilt and the possibility that he was rationalising a desire to punish her, just a little. No. They needed everything in the open if they were going to work together.

'I'm guessing your father found out what you could do and that scar...' he tapped his own temple '...is why he had blood on his knuckles. Your mother left to protect you from him, didn't she?'

She wrapped her arms around herself again, shooting Kade a hurt little glare.

Torin was silent a long time. Kade waited. Tor was smart enough to see Kade's guess had hit a nerve in his sister, without having to interrogate her or make her prove it. Kade had heard enough of Tor's childhood memories to know Tor's father had become a morose alcoholic after the departure of his wife and daughter. Tor had never mentioned violence, but it wasn't unfeasible.

Finally, Torin swore and scrubbed at his face.

Heather jumped to her feet and excused herself, fleeing to the bathroom. Tor started after her but Kade held him back.

'Let her go. There's no way out of there. She doesn't want to see your reactions. She's afraid.'

'Afraid of what?' Tor gazed after his sister, doubt showing.

'Of what you'll think of her.' Kade knew Tor better than anyone and even he wasn't certain how the man would react. The man had always played his emotional cards close to his heart. 'There's a lot you don't know about her.'

Torin gave a sardonic snort and stalked over to the drinks cabinet. He cracked open two beers, passing one to Kade.

'Like that you're in love with her?' He sat and offered his bottle in a mocking toast.

Kade choked on a sip and sprayed beer on the coffee table. 'What?'

With a shrug, Tor sipped his own drink. 'I've known you since we were fifteen, Kae. Your face said it all.'

Standing, Kade rubbed at the back of his neck. 'In love? I don't know. Maybe? There's something, anyway. What, I'm not sure.' He took a few turns around the space then stopped to make sure Torin heard him clearly. 'We can't give her over to Carleton.'

'Obviously.' Tor looked again at the closed bathroom door. 'I'm not letting her near that bastard.'

Kade went for broke. Tor was well known for his rigid sense of justice. It was one of the things that made their business so well-respected. 'And we can't turn her over to the authorities, either.'

Tor paused in the act of drinking and lowered the bottle. His frown darkened. 'What about the other young women and babies who've died? Even if Amali's alive, they aren't and my sister had something to do with it. Or is there something you're not telling me?' His focus sharpened on Kade.

'Trust me.' Kade grimaced. 'If they could have been saved, Heather would have done it.' Tor opened his mouth but Kade forestalled him, adding, 'Heather only let those girls and babies go because they wouldn't have survived without medical assistance and they wouldn't go to a hospital. Illegals.'

Tor placed his beer neatly on a coaster on the table. 'I don't understand. "Let them go"? You make it sound like she had a choice—that she *decided* whether they lived or died.'

'In a way, but not as you probably think.'

Kade filled Tor in on the events of the cabin, minus a few intimate details he might take exception to in his role as brother. He tossed his phone over, complete with its photos of his scars, bruises and bloodied clothing.

Tor inspected the photos and questioned Kade closely. He didn't appear to disbelieve, but he wasn't a man easily impressed, either, so it was hard to tell what he thought. He passed the phone across the table and collected his beer.

'It's...a little hard to comprehend.' He peered blankly at the ceiling. 'But it could explain why our mother left and took Heather. She was an obstetrics and paediatrics nurse. It's most likely she had the same gift.'

'Right.' Kade pointed the beer bottle at him. 'And I think your father couldn't handle it. I think your mother saw he was freaked and took Heather with her when she went.'

'Shit.' Torin put the beer aside. He buried his forehead in the heels of his hands. 'I'll be honest. We've seen some weird stuff in this job but this freaks me out. But I don't want to make the same mistake my father did, Kade. I've lost her once. I don't want to screw this up.'

He tugged his jacket straight, giving Kade a bleak, hard look. 'And if you hurt her, man, you'll answer to me. So let's get this over with so we can concentrate on how to get Carleton to leave both her and his daughter alone.'

Kade knocked on the bathroom door and, after a long silence, it opened. Heather appeared composed when she sat on the very edge of the couch, but the way her shoulders hunched and her eyes darted between the two men spoke volumes. She expected recriminations, anger, some negative reaction.

He wanted, more than anything, to wrap her close and keep her safe, but this wasn't the time or the place. She feared and distrusted him, and why not? He'd hounded her and repaid her sacrifice by dragging her to New York against her wishes, ready to throw her to a sadistic misogynist. In that light, he didn't like himself, either.

'I want to help you, Heather,' Tor's tone was quiet and calm. 'And protect you. But I have to know the truth.'

The look Heather gave him was still fearful.

Kade observed the flicker of emotion across her face. What she'd gone through! In one night her life had changed from idyllic childhood bliss to fearful, hand-to-mouth constant running. Torn from her brother and home, afraid for her life. She'd only been a kid.

'Did Dad hit you because of this sort of thing?' Torin showed her the photos of Kade's bruising. 'Is that why you left?'

Kade tensed, ready to intervene. Tor was keeping a lid on his reactions in an effort not to frighten her but the telltale signs of pain were there: the clenching of his jaw, the working of his throat.

Heather must have felt it, for she rose and put space between them with a quick, worried glance at her brother and a hostile one for Kade. She stared out the window, her back to them.

'Yes. No.' She stroked the scar on her temple again. 'He found me in the kitchen healing our cat. She'd been injured in a fight with the big ginger tomcat from next door. I was crying over her and didn't hear him come in. He saw blood and freaked, thinking *I* was injured. Then he saw the cat, covered in blood, bolt out the door.' She turned half-toward them and Kade saw tears streaking her cheeks.

'At first he shook me and asked me all sorts of questions I didn't really understand. About Mom. I guess he must have suspected she was different, but she was careful and hid it from him. He'd guessed. He got so angry. He was screaming at me. Why had I let "her" die; why hadn't I saved "her". I didn't know who he was talking about.'

'I do,' Torin groaned. 'When you were only two, they had a daughter, Peggy. She died when she was only a few months old. Cot death. He never really got over it. Blamed himself because he'd put her to bed on her stomach. I suppose, when he found out what you and Mom could do, he transferred the blame to her and you.'

Heather murmured, 'Mom told me, years later. She couldn't have saved the baby. Peggy had been dead too long by the time they found her.' She covered a sob and wiped her cheeks. 'But that day, in the kitchen...he got so mad he slapped me.'

'Is that when Mom intervened?'

'No.' Her reply was barely audible, fresh tears shimmering on her lashes. 'That was a few minutes later. I was stunned. But when I got up I was so angry and scared I...' She stopped and covered her face with her hands, turning her back again.

Kade had to restrain himself from wrapping her in his arms. Tor rose and rubbed her back.

'Hey. It wasn't your fault. He shouldn't have hit you. I understand why Mom had to take you and go. She was afraid he would hurt you. It's ok. I'm glad we found each other again.' He held her.

She shoved hard against his chest, glaring with tear-filled eyes.

'You *don't* understand. *Neither* of you! Mom wasn't afraid he would hurt me.' She scoffed at Torin's confusion. 'Mom staged it to appear he was drunk. He wasn't. He was unconscious on the floor because *I* almost drained him, like some sort of…vampire.'

Her voice shook and she backed away from Tor.

'Don't you see? We left because she was afraid *I* would kill *him*.'

'Holy shit!' Kade clutched the back of his chair, his knees weak. Several pieces of the puzzle fell into place.

Heather uttered a broken little laugh and retreated from both men. Tor stayed where he was, staring at his sister, all stone and ice.

'That's it, Tor!' Kade strode over and yanked his partner's arm to get his attention.

Torin slowly tore his regard from his sister and looked at Kade with dumbfounded disbelief still clinging to his expression. 'What?'

Drawing him aside, Kade lowered his voice. Heather was already frightened enough without adding this to the mix.

'That's what Carleton's after.' He dug his fingers into Tor's arm, trying to get him to focus. 'It's not information about his daughter he wants. It's Heather's potential as a healer for himself and as a weapon against his enemies. You saw the reports saying he might be funding terrorism. Can you imagine what he'd use her for?'

Understanding bloomed in Tor's eyes. 'Heather, we…'

The outer door clicked softly shut.

She was gone.

CHAPTER FIFTEEN

HEATHER

Heather strode out of Torin's office with her head high, wrapping an air of purposeful, abstracted intent about herself to discourage questions by his staff. It was an impossible cloak to maintain for long; held together by frayed threads of dignity and nothing else.

She made it to the elevator. Once the doors closed, she sagged against the steel and timber wall. It was tempting to curl into a ball of depression but she couldn't. She had to get as far from Kade and Torin as possible.

Right to the last moment, she'd clung to the hope that Torin would understand and forgive her, that she would have someone to turn to; family. But his horrified, sickened expression when she'd revealed the truth had nailed that hope into a coffin. And Kade's shocked first words had been little better. In his view she'd proved herself to be exactly what he thought her: a murderer, or as good as. She'd almost killed her own father.

Both men had recoiled from her and she couldn't blame them. She hadn't stayed to hear the rest.

She'd tried hard, over the last fifteen years, to redeem that one moment of anger.

Never taken energy from anyone again. Saved thousands of lives. Always run rather than hurting anyone who suspected her gifts

But nothing would erase the fear and remorse and, even worse, the *satisfaction* of her father collapsing to the floor at her feet that night. The feeling of power and strength, the glut of energy and life thrumming through her eleven-year-old body—*that* haunted her with its seductive pull. Part of her was horrified by what she'd done, but a small part of her was empowered and wanted to do it again.

What kind of person did that make her?

The elevator doors binged open and thrust her into the real world again. She collected her bag and coat from the cloakroom of the O'Connor Inc reception desk, giving the curious receptionist a cool nod.

At the tinted glass front door, she paused and tried to quell the sudden quiver in her stomach. Outside, a chill wind whipped along the busy street, catching at scarves, hair and coats. People flipped up their collars and jammed hands deep into pockets as they hurried about their incomprehensible lives. The scent of pollution and the noise of traffic blew in every time the doors slid open. It was also the scent and sound of freedom, yet still she hesitated.

Where would she go? Her bag contained little but her old false identity papers, medical kit, a few clothes and about a hundred in cash. She couldn't get a job under those papers and, without one, couldn't afford a new identity. The stories that circulated about what happened to homeless people living on the streets of New York played in her thoughts.

But she had no other choice.

'Hey.'

Someone tapped her shoulder and she jumped. A young man faced her, smiling pleasantly. His teeth were white against olive-gold skin, his hair dark and irises a startling grey with dark rims. He couldn't be more than about twenty but dressed in a expensive trousers, polo shirt and black wool jacket suited to an older man.

'You ok?' he asked.

'I'm fine.' She backed up a step. Was this one of Carleton's people? She needed to get away.

A slender arm looped around her neck from behind, pinning her. Something stung her thigh. She cried out. Struggling did no good. Warm honey liquefied in her veins and spread lethargy through her bones. The world darkened to sepia swirls and she sank into oblivion with a groan of despair.

KADE

The door to the elevator opened. Kade and Torin launched themselves out, and almost collided with three people. One of them was Heather. Her head lolled. The other two—a well-dressed middle-aged man and woman—supported her, each with an arm wrapped around her waist.

Kade reached for the man, ready to rip his throat out. Tor stepped in the way, placing a forearm across Kade's chest and setting his feet.

'Bring her into the elevator.' He shoved Kade inside, ignoring his protests until the doors closed again and blocked out the quiet lobby and its curious occupants. Then he touched the pulse point on Heather's neck and nodded to the couple. 'Thanks. What did you give her?'

'A few mils of something designed specifically to sedate people like her,' the man replied easily. 'She'll be fine in a few minutes or so.'

'What the *hell* is going on?' Kade demanded. 'Let her go. Now.'

The woman, with a cynical shrug, relinquished Heather to Kade. He swept Heather into his arms, cradling her protectively. Her cheek fell against his shoulder and she sighed.

'Kade, this is Rowan and Logan.' Torin indicated the pair. 'I called them. Rowan was the one who told me Heather would be important to both of us.'

Kade gaped. 'Huh? You said they were practically kids.'

'What?' Tor studied them. 'They are.'

Logan cracked a laugh and Rowan rolled her eyes.

The elevator opened and they all entered Tor's office. This time Torin locked the door and pocketed the key. Kade lowered Heather onto the couch and checked her pulse again. Alive. Tension unwound in his gut.

He looked up to find Rowan standing over the couch, inspecting Heather with an expression of pity and regret, laced with a hint of interest. She brushed a lock of hair from Heather's lips.

'Leave her be.' Kade shoved at Rowan's hand. It didn't move. He latched onto her wrist. Rowan gave a wry little chortle and twisted free of his grip as though it was nothing.

Kade gaped at her. How had she done that? She strolled to the bar in the corner of Tor's office. Logan passed her a drink of something clear with ice in it.

'Tor?' Kade addressed his partner. 'Who the hell are these people, Tor?' He switched to Logan. 'And what did you mean by "designed for people like her"? Is there something wrong with Heather?' He half-expected to find her changed in some way.

Her eyes were partly-opened, but drowsy and vague. Her hand crept into his and clung weakly.

Rowan snorted. 'There's nothing wrong with her that avoiding people like Carleton won't fix. She feels inadequate, which is ironic, when you consider how superior she is.'

'Rowan.' Logan's low-voiced warning stopped her and she sighed.

'You tell it, then. I'm tired of dealing with humans like him.' She headed for the bathroom, the door slamming behind her.

'*Humans* like him?' Kade gaped at Logan. 'What the hell does *that* mean?'

Logan heaved a sigh and put his drink aside. 'Don't mind Rowan. She's stressed. We're still hunting for Finn—my father—and we've had a few…encounters. Lost a few people. She takes it hard.' He addressed Torin. 'Thanks for that latest package of information, by the way. Your call caught us on the way to the airport to follow it up.'

'I'm sorry to keep you,' Tor replied, 'but after what Rowan said at your first visit I thought I should call.'

'You did the right thing.' Logan pointed at the couch. 'Heather's coming to. I'll get Rowan.'

Kade opened his mouth.

'Wait.' Logan raised a lean hand. 'I know you have questions, but it will be easier for all concerned if we wait for Heather to wake up. As you've seen, Rowan has little patience these days. She's under a lot of pressure.'

Tor's gaze narrowed. 'What's wrong with her?'

Logan smiled with faint longing. 'Nothing. She takes a lot on her shoulders because no-one else can do what she does. Although…' He glanced at Heather. 'No. Let's sort this mess out, first.' An abstracted expression passed over his face and he gave a small nod. 'She's coming out now.'

The bathroom door opened and, before Kade could ask the new questions that had sprung to mind, astonishment stole his voice. The girl who emerged was not the same as the one who'd gone in. Well, not exactly. Basic height and build were right, but her shoulderlength, dark hair had transformed into an auburn pixie-cut that highlighted sharp cheekbones and small ears. And she seemed to be about a decade younger—no older than twenty. Most extraordinary of all, though, were her eyes. Startling light-grey, dark-rimmed colour—similar to Heather's, but not as ice-pale.

Kade looked to Logan in confusion, only to find his face changed, too—younger, more angular, his skin warm gold instead of pastey-white. What the...?

Heather stirred. Her eyes opened fully and widened. She shot upright, twisting to survey Rowan. Heather pressed her palms to her temples.

'I heard your voice in my *mind*!' she blurted. 'How did you do that? Who *are* you?'

Logan moved to stand by Rowan's side, protective, wary. She rested a cheek on his shoulder for a moment, then addressed Heather.

'We're your kin, in a way,' Rowan said. 'We are Sidhe. You and Torin are part-Sidhe.' She tilted her head to one side, examining Kade. 'I suspect you, Kade, also have a touch of fae blood. That's how you can sense Heather's emotions.'

'I haven't told anyone that.' Kade rose, ready to defend Heather. 'How the *fuck* do you know that? And how did you change your face and your hair? Him too?' He snarled at Logan then stalked toward Rowan, fists clenched.

Rowan sent him a cynical smile. 'If you honestly think you could lay a punch on me, give it a shot. I haven't broken anyone in at least three days.'

Kade started and unclenched his hands. He never reacted with violence. What was wrong with him?

'Nothing's wrong with you,' Rowan replied. 'Connecting so deeply with Heather has opened parts of your mind that have been closed off before. It's unbalanced your emotional control.' She shrugged. 'If it'll make you feel better to take a swing, go for it. I'll give you one free try.' She grinned mirthlessly.

Kade retreated. This slender kid could take him, military training and all. But how he knew that was beyond him. He sank onto the couch, gaping at Torin.

'What's going on? Who are they?' He addressed Rowan. 'How did you change your faces?'

Tor gestured to the couches and chairs and everyone sat. Rowan crossed one leg over the other and the shortening of her jeans revealed a throwing knife, tucked into her boot. She responded to Kade's frown with a wry twist of her lips.

'We cast a *glamour,*' she said, swallowing the last of her drink. 'An illusion. Torin and Heather saw through it. Being more human, you saw the illusion until we dropped it.'

'What?'

Her words still made no sense.

'Let me try.' Logan scrubbed at his jaw then reviewed Torin, Heather and Kade, one at a time. 'This can't leave your office. Is that understood? Once you hear what we have to say, if you don't agree, that's fine, we'll wipe your memory of us and you can handle Carleton without our help.' He leaned back and the chair's leather creaked. 'Up to you.'

Kade exchanged looks with Tor. Both men nodded. Heather curled into a corner of the couch, unresponsive.

'Rowan's right,' Logan continued. 'We are, all of us to varying degrees, Sidhe. The Faerie folk of legend. Really, we're a branch of homo sapiens that have additional psychic abilities—like convincing your mind you're seeing a different face—and a connection to nature that normal homo sapiens don't have.' He quirked a knowing smile. 'Although we're trying to change that.'

'What? How?' Kade raised his brows.

Logan waved the question aside. 'Beside the point. What's important here is that you, Heather, have a gift you need to learn to control in a hurry—before it kills you. Or someone you care about.'

Heather blanched at his harsh tone. Kade had to resist the urge to gather her into his arms. She had run from him a few minutes ago. Clearly she didn't want his support.

'Back off, Logan,' Tor's low voice cracked into the silence. His focus lay on Heather and her eyes widened, surprise in their crystal depths.

Logan pointed at Heather. 'What you can do is not unique. There are thousands of Sidhe in the world. All of us can heal ourselves by drawing power from nature. A few, such as you and Rowan, can heal others who have severe injuries.' He examined Rowan, whose expression was a mask, hollow and hard.

Kade inspected the young woman. What could a kid her age have seen or done to warrant such cynicism and darkness?

'And,' Rowan said quietly, indicating Heather, 'like me, you could drain people, if you want.'

Heather let out a little whimper and drew her knees up, burying her face in them.

Unable to bear her distress, Kade shifted over.

She jerked away from him. 'Don't *touch* me! Just...don't.' The flare of genuine panic in her made him waver and release her.

He glared, instead, at Rowan. 'Stop frightening her.'

Rowan's mouth twisted. 'It's not us she's frightened of. It's herself. Believe me, I understand. I'm probably the only person in the world who does. So if you want me to leave, I will. I have other things to do. But there's no-one better qualified to help.' Disgust flickered across her features. 'Especially if you want to keep her out of Andrew Carleton's hands.'

Torin started. 'How do you know about him? *What* do you know?'

She thumbed at Kade. 'Ask him. He's the one who's done the research, found the dirt. I can tell you *what* Carleton is, who he's funding and what their specialty is. But you won't like it.'

Heather let out a strangled sob.

Kade shot to his feet, unable to hide his anger from Rowan. 'How do you know all of this? About Carleton, about what I found out, about what Heather can do. Who *are* you? Why should we believe you?'

Rowan unfolded herself and rose, a few inches shorter but facing him with an arrogance that made his fist curl again.

'You've seen what Heather can do and you still don't believe?' Her look warped into scorn. 'No, you believe, but you don't want it to be true. You're scared of her.'

'Stop it,' he grated.

She chuckled, disdaining, dismissive. 'Or what?'

Kade closed the gap between them. Logan leapt up and thrust them apart. Kade staggered back, astonished by the kid's strength. His chest was bruised.

'Don't hurt Kade!' Heather appeared by his side, standing between him and Rowan.

'Rowan, chill,' Logan muttered. 'Stop hassling him.' He cast Kade and Heather a pitying smile. 'You know he's not scared *of* her, he's scared *for* her. Like I was.'

CHAPTER SIXTEEN

HEATHER

'Is that true? You're not frightened of me?' Something fluttered in Heather's stomach, hope quickening for the first time in days.

Kade cupped her jaw, searching. 'No. He's right. I'm frightened *for* you. I'm scared you'll overtax yourself again trying to save every damned kid out there. Or Carleton will take you.' His throat worked.

Honesty seeped through his touch, into her soul and she blinked back unexpected tears.

'But you...you brought me here. Why should I trust you?'

He revealed a bitterness she had no hope of understanding. 'I didn't want to believe you, Heather. Didn't want you to be a good person because of...' He waved a hand dismissively. 'It doesn't matter. The point is, the deeper I dug into Carleton's past the more I realised you aren't the problem. You never were.'

And the truth of that stabbed through his touch, into her heart. She pressed into his broad chest and buried her tears in his neck, trying not to sob like a child.

'I'm so so sorry I put you through that crap in Torin's holiday place, Heather,' Kade whispered. 'You have no idea how much I regret everything I said and did that hurt you. I was an utter idiot.'

She gave a watery chuckle. 'Not quite utter, but close.'

He groaned and stroked her back. 'I'll do whatever I can to protect you from Carleton, I promised. You're too precious. Too special. I don't think I could handle losing you.'

Another arm slid around her waist and Torin's strength engulfed both of them, protective.

'Me, either, baby sister. We're here for you. I promise,' he rumbled.

The three of them stayed that way for a good minute, until Heather's emotions settled.

'Thank you,' she said. 'You have no idea what it means to feel...accepted.'

Torin thumbed a tear from her cheek and pointed at Rowan and Logan, who waited patiently in their seats. 'Maybe we should hear what they have to say?'

Heather sent Kade a shy smile. He sheltered her within the curve of his arm. His lips brushed her cheek and she nestled against him in the corner of the couch.

Rowan relaxed in her chair, her earlier harshness vanishing beneath a chortle both rueful and genuine.

'Sorry about that. I'm not always such a bitch.' She smiled at Kade. 'Had to see how you'd both respond. She needed to know you weren't going to give her over to Carleton, and you needed to see that she cares for you.'

'You could have asked,' he said, testily.

She snorted. 'Hey, you got it better than me. My brother tested me and Logan by setting his elite strike team on us. With live bullets.'

Torin frowned but Rowan grimaced and said, 'Don't ask. I'll tell you some other time. Right now we need to teach Heather a few things about managing her skill.'

Logan tapped his watch. 'Rowan?'

She nodded. 'Logan's right. We don't have a lot of time. We postponed our flight but we have to leave today or we'll miss Finn again.'

Heather sat up. 'Did you two just talk…in your heads? That wasn't my imagination, before?'

Rowan smiled, suddenly mischievous. 'One of the many useful sidhe skills. However…' She studied her. 'I'm not sure it's one you have. You seem to have empathy but not telepathy. You're only about a quarter Sidhe, so your skills are diluted. Oh, yes.' She exposed bitterness before softening. 'You can stop worrying about killing people. I can. You can't.'

Heather covered her mouth, choking on a disbelieving cry. 'How…how do you know?'

'You have…' Rowan clenched her own fingers until they whitened '…a lesser version of the *skath sheele*—the shadow-thought—that I have in full force.'

'What does that mean, exactly?' Kade's grip tightened painfully and Heather squeezed in return. He relaxed.

With a harsh laugh, Rowan spread her hands wide. 'It means I could drain every person in this building and use the power to lay waste to half a city block if I wanted.'

Heather shuddered and shrank against Kade's side. His arm held her firm.

'Rowan, stop,' Logan said, caressing her cheek. She sighed, suddenly seeming weary beyond her years.

Logan continued. 'Rowan's ability is far stronger than yours, Heather. You don't have the capacity to hold the energy from even one person, so you can't kill anyone. But you could drain them to unconsciousness.' He pointed at her. 'Remember that if you're ever in danger. But also remember that you can't hold the power for long or it can backlash through you and cause internal damage.'

'I need another drink.' Rowan rose and strode to the bar.

'How old are you?' Torin asked mildly.

Rowan sent him a wry grin, and shared amusement with Logan. 'Old enough to drink in Australia.'

'We're in the USA,' Torin said.

She shrugged. 'Who's going to stop me?' She raised a glass of clear, sparkling liquid. 'Relax. It's soda water, so you can stop parenting me. I have enough minders already.' There was a hint of resentment in her voice and Logan shot her a quick, worried look.

'So,' Kade put in, 'what were you going to say about Carleton? All I found out was some rumours about some shady deals and possibly human trafficking. What else do you know.'

'Right,' Logan responded. 'The man we're chasing, Finn, is a member of a group called the Mors Ferrum. They've been hunting Sidhe for a thousand years and more. We're in the process of trying to disband them, but they have deep pockets and are good at hiding. We're pretty sure your man, Carleton, is one of them.'

Heather swallowed, fear rising again from her belly. Kade's arm tightened and she tried to get control of the fear so it wouldn't infect him. His touch, the security of being so close to him, was too precious to ruin. She drew a slow breath and settled her heart.

'Which means,' Logan continued, 'that Kade is right. Carleton's probably not after his daughter at all. Although...' He addressed Heather. 'I think you said Amy's husband, David, was a surgeon?'

She gave a low, nervous chuckle. 'I didn't say it out loud, but that's true. Before he quit to go into hiding with her, he was a gifted surgeon. Never lost a patient, even in emergency situations.' She sucked a gasp. 'Oh! Do you mean...'

'Probably,' Logan agreed. 'We've found that people like you, and most likely him, use their healing instinctively and don't know why it works. And you gravitate to medical jobs because that's where it's easiest to hide.' He exchanged looks with Rowan. 'So Carleton's goal could be two-fold: you *and* David.'

Heather withdrew inward, hunching her shoulders. 'But why? Why would he want us?'

'Best you don't know. It would give you nightmares.' Rowan laid a hand on Logan's shoulder and he stared at the floor.

'Is that what you meant by human trafficking?' Torin asked, his attention on Heather. 'These Mors Ferrum are taking Sidhe, specifically?'

Logan and Rowan both nodded.

'Trust me,' Rowan said bleakly. 'You *really* don't want to know what they do with them. We're trying to stop them.' She sank onto the arm of Logan's chair. 'But we can't be everywhere. If you can help with Carleton, then we can get on with finding Finn. He's the most likely candidate for re-forming the Mors's leadership core. We have to find him before he pulls them together again and they find a way to strike at us.'

Determination snaked through Heather, displacing fear. She lifted her chin. 'If it will protect Amy and David, then I'll help. What can I do?'

'No!''No!' Kade and Torin spoke simultaneously.

'You can't, Heather. He's too dangerous.' Kade grabbed her elbow. His grey eyes bored into hers, outright fear in them. 'Leave it to Torin and I. We'll find a way to make him back off.'

Rowan's mouth quirked and she eyed Heather. *Men. They can't help it, can they?* Her voice arrived in Heather's mind. *Show him, Heather. Show him you can look after yourself. You won't hurt him if you give it back immediately. I'll monitor and make sure.*

Heather studied Kade's hand, wrapped around her arm. She pulled her shoulders back and straightened her spine. 'I don't need you to protect me, Kade. You'll need me to draw Carleton in. You've told him I'm here. He'll come to see me.'

Desperation limned Kade's expression and she almost relented. No. She refused to be a victim any longer; to keep running and hiding. If Rowan was right, she had the means to protect herself.

'Heather,' Kade said brokenly, 'I—'

His eyes rolled back and he slumped across her lap.

Heather gasped.

'Kade!' Torin touched Kade's throat and glared at Rowan. 'He's got a pulse at least. What'd you do to him?'

She guffawed. 'Not me.'

Logan groaned and closed his eyes.

Heather inspected her trembling hand. 'I feel…crackly inside. Full of…sticky lightning. It tastes of…pine? Is it meant to feel like that?'

'Everyone's different.' Rowan gazed into the distance. 'For me it's like a thousand tiny needles and tastes of ozone. I can see it, too, but most can't. Orange from humans and silver-green from other Sidhe or forests.'

'Oh,' Heather said dreamily, 'now I understand. I can sort of feel it, inside, like…honey seeping through me.' She touched her throat. 'Here.'

'Good,' Rowan replied. 'That's where most Sidhe have a regulator organ that prevents them from draining themselves. You don't have it, and neither do I. Make sure you always keep one full jar of that honey in reserve and you'll be ok.' By the looks of your body, you'll only be able to hold it for a minute or two before the backlash. Best return it now.'

Heather touched Kade's sleeping face and poured the energy into him.

'Not all of yours, too,' Rowan warned. 'That's where you've gone wrong before. It's our instinct to try and heal people. Because of the *skath sheele* you give more than you should. More than other Sidhe can.'

'I always thought people were *taking* from me.'

Rowan shook her head. 'You're giving subconsciously every time you sense someone is unwell, or in pain. You can't help it. Always keep some in reserve for your own body or you'll pass out again.'

In Heather's lap, Kade twitched, blinking dazedly. He scrubbed at his temples.

'What the hell…?'

Torin sank into a chair. 'I think Heather proved a point, partner. She's not going to let us leave her out of this one, so you may as well accept it.'

Kade shakily swiped his hair. 'Don't do that again, huh?'

'Promise.' Heather smiled.

He turned to Logan. 'So what do we do now?'

'First thing,' Logan replied briskly, 'is to teach Heather and Kade how to shield thoughts and feelings. Otherwise this…' He pointed back and forth between Heather and Kade. '…will drive you both crazy. The raw emotion you're both outputting is…intense.'

Heather's cheeks warmed and Kade cleared his throat, shifting on the couch.

Torin chuckled. 'It's about time, brother.' His humour shifted into seriousness. 'Long past time.'

Heather studied Kade's haunted expression while he focussed on Torin. Clearly there was some history she wasn't aware of. Something that affected Kade and his ability to have relationships. She sat up. She really didn't know either Kade or her brother. Was she crazy to put herself in their control because Torin was her brother and she was attracted to Kade?

She'd seen the results of giving in to mutual desire too often to be seduced by its lure. Not just unwanted babies, but heartbreak, misery, abusive relationships. Everything she'd sworn never to fall into. Yet, here she was, accepting Kade at face value.

No, that wasn't true. Their connection had let her see partway into his heart. Far enough to know he was a good man. But flawed, too. And tied to his past, as she was. Was there enough commonality between them to outlast the first rush of desire and hormones? That, she had no idea about.

She found Rowan's sympathic gaze on her and flushed again. Rowan jerked a thumb at a door in the office wall.

'C'mon. Let's go into Kade's office and I'll show you how to shield. We'll leave the guys to learn from Logan.'

Heather hesitated. 'It won't stop me from doing what I do, will it?'

The bleakness of winter veiled Rowan's eyes. 'No. It won't. But you'll be able to control what you feel from others, and what Kade senses from you.'

Rising, Heather glanced at Kade, who gave steadiness back. She followed Rowan into the adjoining office.

CHAPTER SEVENTEEN

HEATHER

Where Torin's office had been heavy and masculine, with timber, leather and old world strength, Kade's was bright and open. His desk, scattered with haphazard piles of paper, was of steel and glass. The chairs and sofas were in black, with brilliant cushions the jewel-colours of the Caribbean seas. On the plain, white walls hung a Jackson Pollack print, abstract and colourful.

'Right,' Rowan said, perching on the edge of the desk. 'Let's go. I don't have long. First, tell me if you can feel the trees in the park outside this building. Here.' She touched Heather's head and an image opened in her mind: every living thing with a glow of energy pulsating through it; plants and animals, even insects. 'This is what it would look like.'

Cautiously, she opened herself. There it was. Faint and not really a colour like the image, more like a feeling of power, distant and cool.

'Sort of,' she said. 'That same honey, but a long way away. I can't see it, only feel it. Oh!' She looked at her body, half-expecting to see her skin glowing. 'I can feel it seeping from the trees into me.'

'Good. That's the *sianfath*. Can you bring more in so it's not only seeping? So you have control of it? Most fullblood can pull enough to heal themselves quickly, but I find few of the half and quarterblood sidhe have the ability.'

Heather tried but failed. The honey-lightning tendrils slipped from her grasp and she couldn't get a grip on them.

'Nothing. Sorry.'

'Damn.' Rowan scrubbed at her face. 'That would have been useful. It means you can't gain power from the *sianfath* like you can from humans you touch. At least, not beyond what normally helps to regulate and connect you.' She chewed on her lip, staring at Heather for a long moment.

Then she sighed. 'Never mind. Next we'll do shields. Then I want to teach you how to alter human DNA so they can feel the *sianfath* as well. It's helpful.' She gave a wry half-shrug. 'When they understand how important the *sianfath* is— how it keeps the environment healthy—the humans are a lot more co-operative. And less dangerous.'

'It won't hurt them?'

'Surprise them, yes. Hurt them, no.' Rowan snorted.

Heather sat, twisting her hands in her lap. It seemed odd to be taking instruction from a girl almost a decade younger than herself, but Rowan appeared confident.

'Thanks'.Rowan sent her a flicker of sardonicism. 'Y'know, we're not that different. My mother and I were on our own from when I was four, running, constantly moving. But where you were learning to help people, I was learning to kill them—to protect myself and her.' She smiled bleakly. 'You may have lost your mother, but what she taught you is a greater gift than I have, in many ways. Be grateful for that.'

'But I've had to let people die,' Heather said, her voice breaking. 'I couldn't help them. It eats at me every day.'

'How many?'

Heather swallowed. 'Ten.'

Rowan uttered a short, harsh laugh. 'Like I said: be grateful. I'm a weapon. I can't even count on ten hands how many people I've had to kill to protect the Sidhe from genocide.'

'Oh, you poor girl.' Heather's chest ached with the pain emanating from the young woman.

'Don't!' Rowan retreated, her eyes drowning. 'Don't. I can't...' She paused and cleared her throat. 'Now. To make a shield, you need to create a strong mental image of a house or a building around your thoughts. Pick a structure that makes you feel secure. Then, when it's solid, create windows to let people you know talk to you. Say, one each for Logan, me, Torin and Kade. Kade may not be a telepath, but it will let you feel his emotions when you want to.'

It took Heather several minutes to get the hang of creating a structure she felt safe in. She was practicing opening windows and creating thought-rooms when Rowan froze.

'Shit.' Rowan rose. 'Logan and I have to go. One of Torin's staff sent a message. They've spotted Finn in Orlando, Florida.' But I need to teach you the DNA alteration.' She swore. 'No time for details. Here.' She touched Heather's forehead.

A series of complex images flashed through Heather's mind, like a fast-motion film of human anatomy from her nursing school days. Then it vanished and she was left with the odd sensation that something had settled into a corner of her mind's new shield-house. She blinked.

'What did you do?'

'I Gifted you the knowledge of how to change human DNA. You appear to have some limited telekinetic abilities,' Rowan said. 'Not enough to throw a couch across the room, but possibly enough to alter DNA on a micro-scale, if you're careful. I'm sorry I don't have time to help you practice.' She leaned close and caught Heather's eyes with an intense gaze.

'But if you get a chance to use the DNA change on Carleton, do it. You just have to think about changing his DNA and my gift will take over. Teaching just one Mors Ferrum member might tip the balance in our favour.' She pressed her lips tight. 'Though I'd rather you didn't go anywhere near him, to be honest.'

After a moment's reluctance, she laid a hand on Heather's arm, tightening when Heather tried to withdraw. 'Hold still. This won't hurt.' Rowan's eyes glazed. She let go, covering her mouth with trembling fingers.

'Are you alright?' Heather asked. 'You're so pale.'

Rowan blew a thick breath. 'Yes. Just…just be careful. Stay close to Kade and don't agree to meet with Carleton or his men. Promise me? No matter what they say. Don't. If you do, there's a good chance they'll take you. And Kade.' She let out a growl and pressed her thumbs into her temples. 'I can't be sure, exactly, but play it safe.' She stalked out, the door slamming behind her.

Heather sank onto a couch, gazing blindly at the grey carpet. She touched her scalp. Had all that really happened? Had she met someone like herself and learned to alter DNA itself? Could she really shield against incoming thoughts and feelings? Could she, after all these years, live an almost normal life?

Could she touch someone without feeling what they felt?

Their pain. Their misery. Their joy.

The door to Torin's office burst open and Kade strode in. He made a beeline for her, stopped a few feet away, then edged closer, slowly.

'You ok?'

'I think so. That was pretty surreal, though. That girl, Rowan...'

'Tell me about it.' Kade checked over his shoulder. 'I thought Tor and I had seen a lot in the military. I think those two have had to grow up a lot faster than any of us. Did she show you how to shield?'

Heather rubbed her cheeks. 'Yes. And how to change human DNA so they can sense the *sianfath*. I...I'm not sure I believe it.' She wrapped her arms around her stomach. 'I mean, I don't even remember what it was like not feeling people. So many years. So much emotion swirling constantly around me.'

'And now?'

She spun to find Kade close. Maybe too close. She hadn't felt him approach. She examined his expression and was caught by the worry there. Reaching out tentatively, she touched his cheek, steeling herself.

The rasp of stubble. The warmth of his skin. The softness of his lips under her thumb.

'Nothing,' she whispered. 'Nothing at all!' She looped both arms around his neck and pressed her whole body against his, feeling only warmth and the strength of his hands around her waist.

She lifted her face. 'Kiss me.'

He held off. 'You sure?'

'Idiot,' she said, smiling. 'Yes.'

His lips brushed hers softly and she revelled in the purely-physical sensation. He paused, a few millimetres from her. She groaned and slid her fingers into his short hair, pulling his head down again. His mouth moved over hers, nipping, tasting, his tongue laving. Breathless and wanting, Heather gave a little sob and opened for him, drowning in the delicious physicality of a kiss.

'Ok, you two, get a room.' Torin's guffaw intruded and Heather broke guiltily apart from Kade.

She hesitated, then stretched a hand out to both men. They grasped her fingers and she tensed, then relaxed when nothing bled through.

'I don't know how to thank you. What Rowan taught me… I can't tell you what a relief it is to *not* feel. To touch people I care about and not be swamped by their emotions.' Laughing, she released them and whirled in a circle, arms upraised.

The room spun and she staggered, nauseated.

Kade was swift to wrap an arm around her and guide her to the couch. 'Take it easy. You're barely out of hospital, remember?'

'I'm fine.' She looked to Torin. 'Do you think Rowan's right, about Carleton? That he's hurting people? That he wants me as some sort of weapon?'

Torin crouched before her, grave. 'I see no reason to disbelieve her. Kade found out some pretty nasty stuff about Carleton and everything Rowan and Logan said about your abilities has been true, so far.' He frowned at the closed office door. 'Although I have a feeling she's not far off a breakdown, herself.'

Heather nodded. 'Yes. I agree. The poor girl has obviously been through a lot. Logan, too.'

'I warned him to keep an eye on her,' Kade added. 'He said the same about you.' He rose. 'Maybe it's time we went home and you got some rest?'

'Home?' Heather checked with Torin. 'I don't understand. I thought…'

He eyed Kade apologetically. 'When I agreed she'd stay with you, I didn't know the woman you were bringing was my sister. Maybe she should stay with me?'

'Think I have designs on her virtue, partner?'

Torin chuckled. 'I *know* you do. But that's none of my business. I meant that we have a lot of catching up to do.' He smiled at Heather.

Kade shrugged. 'Fair call.'

Heather kissed his cheek. 'I'm...not ready yet, Kade. This is all too overwhelming. I need time to think and process before I...' she waved vaguely at him '...we...you know.'

His sardonic expression faded into understanding amusement. 'Eloquent. Yes, I get it.' He held her close and kissed her forehead, murmuring, 'I'll be here when you're ready.'

A buzzer sounded from his desk and Heather jumped. Kade swore and strode over to his desk. Shoving aside some papers, he touched a button.

'Yep?'

'Is Torin with you?' A disembodied female voice asked sharply. 'Andrew Carleton is...very eager to speak with him.'

Torin leaned over the desk and spoke into the microphone. 'Cathy, tell him to call back later.'

'Er...he's here in the reception area, not on the phone.'

CHAPTER EIGHTEEN

HEATHER

Heather gasped. Only a thin wall separated her from Carleton and that wasn't nearly enough. Would he come in with men and force Torin to hand her over? Could he do that?

Torin swore and Cathy stifled a giggle.

'Give me twenty seconds,' Torin instructed his assistant. 'Then send him into my office. If he asks, Kade is not here.'

'Got it,' Cathy replied briskly.

Kade punched the button with unnecessary force. 'Slimy bastard. He was supposed to wait for our call. Does he know Heather's in New York?'

Torin scowled. 'I had no reason not to tell him, before. Apparently he called the hospital this morning, too. Blake said he heard the nurse telling him Heather would be released today into your care.'

With a whimper, Heather retreated to Kade. He held her tight.

'I won't let him take you, don't worry.'

'But you heard Rowan. He has money, resources, men.'

Kade exchanged a grim smile with Torin. 'So do we. O'Connor Inc is not short of cash and a lot of people owe us favours. We might not be billionaires, but we have enough clout to get Carleton kicked to Hell if he tries anything. Relax. We'll stay in here while Torin deals with him.'

'Record this for me, will you?' Torin murmured. He left, locking the adjoining door behind him.

Kade switched on his desk monitor and passed across a wireless earbud. Heather tucked it into her ear. He put another into his own ear and tapped at the keyboard. An image of Torin's office flicked onto the screen. There must be a camera set into the wall behind Torin's desk.

Heather wanted to speak, but Kade put a finger to his lips. He arranged two chairs close. They both sat and Heather viewed the screen, breathless.

Torin's deep voice came through the earbud. 'Mr Carleton, I was about to call you. Please, sit.'

Carleton lowered himself into a chair. His two guards took up a stance on either side. One tall, blond, with a crooked nose and ice-blue eyes with dark rims. The other stocky and beady-eyed.

'You were about to call me?' Carleton said. 'To tell me, perhaps, that you have the midwife ready for me? Where is she?'

Torin remained standing. His back was to the camera, but tension held his broad shoulders stiff. Heather clutched at Kade's wrist. He squeezed reassuringly.

'She's not here,' Torin replied evenly, leaning against his desk. 'I'll call you and set a time convenient for everyone to meet.'

Carleton heaved to his feet, his eyes glittering. His fist slammed onto the desk next to Torin's leg. 'You *lie!*' He gestured at his tall, blond bodyguard. 'Baker informs me she arrived here over two hours ago. Bring her to me. Now!'

Torin said nothing for a moment, then hitched himself off the desk and walked around behind it. He rested both hands on the surface, with his fingers pointing backward, over the edge. Carleton matched his stance on the opposite side, his cheeks reddened. The two bodyguards pushed open their jackets, guns ready. Baker's thin lips split into feral amusement. His icy eyes fixed on Torin.

Heather covered her mouth to stifle a cry.

'Wait,' Kade whispered.

Torin stiffened and inspected the two guards, his analysis lingering on Baker before switching to Carleton. 'Don't try to intimidate me. I'm not one of your staff. When she's ready, I'll tell you. This is my office and you'll wait for an appointment like anyone else.'

The door opened and six O'Connor Inc staff poured in, armed and careful. Carleton's men produced their weapons. Torin's people did the same.

Heather nibbled a thumbnail.

'For the moment,' Torin continued affably, 'you'll oblige me by returning to your motel. When I feel the woman is recovered enough to meet you, I'll send for you. Not before.'

A long silence followed, during which Carleton straightened and tugged at his dark blue jacket. His jaw worked and his heavy brows twitched together.

'Very well. But understand that I am not a patient man and you have made me wait for too long, already. I will see her in no less than two days.'

Torin folded his arms. 'Or what, Mr Carleton?'

'Or you and Mr Miller…' Carleton sneered '…will regret your actions. I have connections and the USA needs me more than they need you. I will have the President shut your pathetic little company down.'

'Thank you for making that clear,' Torin replied. He pointed to the door. 'If you will? I have your number. You're staying in the 63rd floor suite in the Mandarin Oriental, aren't you?'

'How did you—'

'I am a private investigator, Mr Carleton,' Torin replied mildly. 'It's my job to know things. Many things. About my clients, especially. Some quite interesting, actually.'

'I see.' Carleton stalked toward the door. 'I expect your call tomorrow to set an appointment.'

'You're quite welcome to expect whatever suits you, sir,' Torin said. He ushered Carleton and his men out then closed and locked the door. His eyes lifted to the camera.

'Get all that, Kade?'

'Loud and clear, Tor. We're coming in.' Kade tapped at the computer and pulled out his earbud.

Heather did the same, following him into Torin's office.

They found her brother pouring drinks. He handed each of them a clear drink with a slice of cucumber and ice floating in it. 'Not soda water. I figured we all needed a stiff gin and tonic after the last couple of hours.'

Heather sipped hers, the glass clinking against her teeth when she trembled. She sank onto the couch, clutching the drink and staring into its bubbles.

Torin rested against his desk, ankles crossed. 'If nothing else, we have him on video threatening us.' He tilted his drink. 'But we do have other evidence against him. It's all a bit tenuous, though. Probably wouldn't hold up in court.'

Downing the drink in three long swallows, Heather closed her eyes. She rarely drank. Alcohol dulled her extra senses and she'd always needed to be hyper-aware. Now, dull seemed attractive. If she didn't have these abilities, she wouldn't be in this position.

'Hey,' Kade said gently. 'It'll be ok.'

'Rowan took my wrist,' Heather said, stroking her arm. 'Then she went so pale I thought she was going to faint. She told me not to meet with Carleton, no matter what. She said if I do he'll take both of us.'

Torin frowned. 'Logan said she has precognition, but only in limited way, and only to see disasters. OK.' He straightened and put his glass aside. 'We'll take that advice and run with it. Somehow we have to avoid letting Carleton meet you. So we need to start with where you'll stay tonight.'

Kade rose and went to the window, looking down. 'I think we can assume he's got people watching the building.'

'Yes,' Torin agreed. 'And probably my apartment. And yours.'

'Can't I stay here?' Heather asked. The alcohol relaxed her shoulders. The couch did seem awfully comfortable. She hadn't slept much in the hospital.

'No,' Torin replied. 'The place is alarmed at night so any movement would set off the sirens and contact police.'

'What about the safe-house?' Kade asked. 'Anyone using it?'

Torin snapped his fingers. 'No. Good idea. But how do we get her there?'

Heather snatched up a cushion and held it like a shield. 'Please don't make me stay on my own.'

Kade hurried over. 'We won't.' He looked at Torin. 'Shell game?'

A slow smile stretched Torin's frown into amusement. 'Nice.' He buzzed his intercom. 'Cathy, can you please send in Vikki, Simone…ah…Camila, Sara, Pedro, Hans, and Luke? Oh, and contact Rosa in Wardrobe? We're going to need some clothes. A lot of clothes.'

Kade snorted. 'Like old times.'

Heather glanced between them, bewildered.

KADE

'Right,' Kade said, sweeping his co-workers with one last inspection. 'You all know what to do? Once we're in the shopping district, split into pairs, check for tails, ditch them. When you're sure you're clean, ditch the clothes and wigs and head home. Text Tor and I to let us know you're safe.'

p186

The four women and three men watched him intently.

'And,' Tor added, 'be careful. Cathy'll be here, co-ordinating. You're all on comms. Keep her informed. Carleton's people will be armed. We know of two but there may be more. Assume you're being followed. You're authorised to use force to protect yourself. But it has to be clearly in self-defence. Preferably with witnesses. And we'll be in the middle of crowds, so don't draw your weapon unless you have no other option. Everyone clear?'

They acknowledged, grim-faced.

Kade examined Heather, who stood beside him, wide-eyed, her cheeks pale. She wore a blond wig cut into a man's style, a wireless earbud, a man's black overcoat, black pants and a blue scarf—exactly the same outfit as the four O'Connor Inc female staff. He and Tor were dressed similarly and matched by the three men.

Leaving the building was risky, but unavoidable. At least this way they could possibly disable some of Carleton's men and get Heather to the safe house.

While Tor was talking to Pedro and Vikki, Kade drew Luke aside.

He pressed his apartment key into the younger man's hand. 'I need you to stay at my place tonight. I want them to think I'm home. Alone.'

Luke nodded. 'Consider it done.' He turned away.

Kade hauled at his arm. 'Tor was right, Luke. These guys are serious. Don't take risks. I'll set the perimeter alarms remotely after you're there. If they go off, call for backup. No heroics.'

'Got it, Boss,' Luke said, giving a jaunty salute and sauntering toward the door.

Heather snatched at Kade's wrist. 'You can't put these people in danger for me. It's not right. They don't know what they're getting into.'

He kissed her forehead. 'They know exactly what they're doing. Most of our people are ex-military and all of them have many years on the dojo mats. And they love a bit of excitement. Most of our work is insurance and adultery. This is fun for them.'

'Well, it's not for me. If I'd known what you were planning I wouldn't have let you. I don't want any more deaths on my conscience.'

Kade sobered. 'You're overestimating Carleton's people. He hires a lot of mercs from other countries. They'll be deported or jailed if they hurt a US citizen. It won't come to that.'

She rubbed her palms up her arms. He caught her close.

'It'll be ok. Trust me,' he murmured.

Her body trembled against his. 'Trust...it's hard. I...I've been on my own so long, Kade. I don't understand why they would help me.'

Kade kissed her softly. 'Because you're family now and every one of them would walk through fire for Tor.' He grinned. 'He has the ability to inspire that loyalty in his people. Always did. We'd all follow him anywhere.'

Heather studied her brother, brows knitted. 'That's what worries me.'

Two maxi-cabs arrived at that moment, and Kade manoeuvred her over to join the others. All ten people shuffled and milled their way through the doors and into the cabs, keeping their faces averted and collars raised. Kade, Heather, Tor, and Camila climbed into one. The rest into the other.

The cabs pulled away from the kerb and Kade checked behind. He spoke softly. 'Four tails in two vehicles behind. Any more?'

'One more vehicle ahead, sir,' Sara replied from the other cab. 'Two operatives.'

'Damn,' Kade swore and glanced at Heather's pale face. 'That's six. We have five pairs. One pair will end up with two leeches. Watch for them.'

'Roger,' replied all of the O'Connor staff, simultaneously.

'Sara,' Torin said, 'tell your driver to head for Grand Central. If you only get one car following, circle around and rejoin us at Times Square.'

'Roger, sir,' she replied. The front cab took a left turn.

Kade looked back. 'We still have two, here.'

'And our tail turned around to follow you,' Sara said.

Kade exchanged a worried grimace with Tor. He opened his mouth, but Tor flicked a warning look at Heather. So Kade resisted the urge to wonder aloud. Tor was right. No point in scaring her more, but somehow their tails knew which car she was in. How, though?

CHAPTER NINETEEN

HEATHER

They arrived at a taxi zone near Times Square and gathered into a group. Heather hesitated, looking at the grim focus of those around her.

'Right,' Torin murmured, 'I want the women in the centre, constantly changing position. These people probably have tranks, and they want Heather alive. So, until we work out how they are able to identify her, we have to keep them guessing. Men, around them and keep sharp.'

He turned to Heather and handed her a small cellphone. 'Take this, just in case we get separated unexpectedly. There are four numbers in it. Mine, Kade's, Cathy's, and Luke's. Use it if you need to find us, but stay on the line for less than 15 seconds.'

She nodded and slid the phone into her coat pocket. The thought of being separated from Torin, Kade and the others...at the mercy of Carleton's men...she swallowed hard and buttoned the pocket closed.

'Where are we going?' Kade asked, studying the surging, chattering masses.

'Into the most crowded section.' Torin pointed at the densest population. 'Then we'll split. Carmila and I will stay with Kade and Heather. The rest will change clothes and circulate until you spot them.'

'And?' Heather asked. 'Then what?'

Torin's expression turned grim. 'Take them out.'

She gasped.

He winced and held up a hand. 'Sorry. I meant out of action, not kill them. Stop them from following us. Got it?'

Nods all around.

Kade held Heather's hand. 'It'll be alright. I'll be right here.'

She swallowed. The other four women closed around her and the whole group set off into the mad, pre-Christmas crowds. With the nudge of an elbow, or a whispered word, the O'Connor Inc women guided Heather. Their moves were an intricate dance, designed to confuse anyone observing. All around people stopped, stared and pointed. Some lifted phones, or called out questions, wanting to know if they were a flash-mob or some living art display.

And always, Heather sensed, Carleton's people watched and waited. Hovering like sharks harassing a school of fish.

'This isn't working,' she muttered to Kade when he came close. 'They're still out there.'

He sent her a look of startled surprise. 'You can tell that?'

She gritted her teeth. 'I let my shield down partway. The sheer number of people is...overwhelming. But most of them are happy, or irritated. Carleton's men feel...cold; focussed.' She shivered. 'But that Baker guy has a shield so I can't sense what he's feeling.'

'Right,' he growled. 'Time to take the fight to them. Tor.' He addressed his partner. 'Heather says she can feel they're watching us. We're going to take a leaf out of Heather's book of quick-changes. Send the men and two of the women to change into normal clothes. Use the biggest bathrooms or stores with changerooms. Hopefully of Carleton's people will follow ours and can be disposed. Either way, get our team to come back asap. Time to find those six bastards and take them out.'

Torin swept the crowd shrewdly. 'You sure? That's more than half the team out of action until they get back.'

'We'll stay in the crowds. Carleton's men won't risk a big scene in this mess.' Kade indicated the surrounding bypassers.

Torin wavered then nodded and six of the team peeled off, disappearing into the chaos of noise, laughter and music. He jerked his chin at Heather and tapped his temple.

She sought the minds she'd felt. 'Still there. Somehow they know I'm here, not with the ones that left. But how?'

Torin stiffened then swore. 'Logan mentioned the Mors Ferrum were recruiting and brainwashing sidhe. He also said there was a tagging technique—I forget the name. Where a sidhe can attach a psychic tether of sorts and follow someone anywhere.'

'But how?' she asked. 'I haven't met any of Carleton's men. Or even seen them.'

'No,' Torin replied grimly, 'but I have. One of the bodyguards in my office today. Baker. The one you said had a shield. I felt the shock of recognition Logan described as a clue to meeting another sidhe. He must have tethered me. It's me they're following. They're assuming I'll stick close to you.'

'Right,' Kade said grimly. 'Then you take Carmila. I'll take Heather and Sara. If they follow you two, we know you're right.'

'And if they don't?' Torin asked.

'Meet us at the MacDonalds across the way and we'll try something else.' Kade grabbed Heather's wrist.

She wrenched free and hissed, 'Stop treating me like some stupid, helpless sidekick, Kade. I've been taking care of myself for years.'

Kade shut his teeth with a snap. Carmila snorted.

'She has a point, Kae,' Torin said. 'You are being a bit overprotective.'

Kade flushed, his eyes haunted.

Torin patted his shoulder. 'Hey. I get it. But she's not Amanda. Get Heather to the safe house. I'll send men over later to stand watch. Go.'

His jaw hard, Kade stalked away. Heather hurried after him, with Sara close behind.

'It's working,' Torin's voice sounded in Heather's ear and she jumped. She'd forgotten about the comms earpiece. 'Two are following you, Kade. The other four are still on me and Carmila. Luke and the others are splitting up to help.'

'Roger,' Kade muttered. 'We'll aim for the other end of the square and catch a cab from there. Hopefully, we'll have shaken them by the time we get to the rank.'

'We'll do our best.' That was Luke's youthful voice.

'Be careful, kid,' Kade said.

'Always.'

Kade snorted and Heather sent him a quick, questioning look. Kade waved it away.

'Sara?' He addressed the remaining O'Connor Inc staffer with them. 'When we get to that Starbucks, you peel off and see if you can draw one with you. If not, change clothes, meet with Luke, and circle back to take one out.'

'Roger that,' she acknowledged.

Heather touched the woman's arm. 'Wait. One of the people following is a woman. If you change in the women's bathroom she'll follow you. Then you can put her out of action.'

Sara sent Heather a look of shrewd interest and cocked her head at Kade, who shrugged.

'You heard her,' he said.

'Yep.' Sara shouldered her way through the crowd. Kade arched a brow at Heather.

She grimaced. 'I'm doing what I can to influence the woman's thinking. It's not easy without touching her, though.' She stopped mid-stride. Reaching through the maelstrom of minds surging around her, she poured her focus into the woman's thoughts, concentrating on one idea: the urge to follow Sara.

The woman paused, then followed Sara into the Starbucks. Heather stumbled, sagging. Kade caught her under the elbow.

'We have to keep moving,' he muttered.

'I know. It took more than I expected.' She straightened. 'Let's go.'

'Torin.' Luke's voice broke in on their comms. 'Sara's taken one out, and two more are dealt with. But there are five others. They must have called in reinforcements. Four are trailing Kade. Instructions?'

Torin swore. 'Kade, how far are you from the taxi rank?'

Kade craned over the top of the crowds. 'About eighty or ninety feet. Why?'

'You need to get out of sight, fast.'

'No.' Heather stopped again, gritting her teeth. 'That won't help. They'll keep coming and we might not see the ones who follow us to the safe house. We need to draw them out. Bring them to us, so you and the others can pick them off. I can point them out to you.'

'Too risky,' Torin argued

'Agreed,' Kade chimed in. 'If they have trank guns they'll put you down and we won't be able to stop them.'

'Not if we're the centre of attention, they won't,' she said, grimly.

Kade eyed her askance. 'What are you thinking?'

'Wondering if you can sing or juggle?' She tilted her head.

He gaped. 'What? No.'

'Right. Argument it is.' She faced him, hands on hips. '*What?* You're *sleeping* with her?' She slapped him, the sound cracking across the square and causing a hush to fall around them. People paused and a little circle of clear space expanded around them.

Kade worked his jaw. But he picked up his cue.

'Hey! You're the one who threw me out last week. Where was I supposed to go?'

'Oh!' Heather flung her arms out. 'I don't know. Maybe your *mother's* place, like you always do. But no, you had to go to my best friend! How could you?' A gasp swept through the onlookers. More people crowded in. Phones came out to video.

'Now, Torin,' Heather muttered. 'Man in the black hat and red scarf at my three o'clock. Woman in green at twelve. Man in grey with black earmuffs at ten.'

'Got them,' he replied in her earpiece.

Kade stepped closer, glowering. 'You said we were done. You said it was over. She hit on me, not the other way. Don't you lay this on me!'

Heather folded her arms. 'So you're completely unable to control yourself, are you?'

He jabbed a finger at her. 'Don't talk to me about self-control. You're the one making a scene in the middle of Times Square.'

'Two down,' Torin said. 'Closing in on the woman in green.'

Heather glanced over Kade's shoulder. 'Gun! She has a gun!'

Her cry rippled through the crowd. People screamed and ran, tripping over each other, covering their heads. A child wailed. The woman in green took a bead on Heather. Kade imposed himself between them. The woman squeezed the trigger.

Kade jerked and swore. Heather cried his name and wrapped her arms around his chest as he staggered. Torin and Luke tackled the woman and handcuffed her. The crowd dispersed, leaving Heather and Kade exposed.

Kade let out a groan and his legs folded. Heather sagged beneath his weight. She lowered him to the ground on his stomach. A dart protruded between his shoulderblades. She stripped off a glove and felt his pulse. Steady, but slow. His eyelids drooped shut.

Arms wrapped her in a bearhug from behind. She shrieked and tried to headbutt.

Missed.

She was yanked off her feet and dragged backward. Panic whited out sense. A grab at her attacker's wrist failed. Her hands were lumps, fingers unwieldy, without power or strength. All her martial arts training vanished behind a fog of fear. His grip tightened and she struggled uselessly.

Then her hand fell on bare skin and a kind of eerie calm blanketed her terror. Her assailant hauled her a few more steps, but Heather found her balance. With her palm on his arm, she sucked life from him.

The taste of pine filled her mouth. Honeyed lightning slipped under her skin and into her flesh. Her bones ached with power and her body pulsed with strength.

The man released her and folded at her feet.

Now she burned inside with sticky-lightning, needing to release it, unsure how or where.

A short, dark-haired man stalked at her, his eyes hard. He touched his ear and spoke a quiet phrase. His hand slid to his hip and the bulge under his jacket.

He grabbed Heather's elbow. 'Come quietly and your friends live.'

Heather released the energy in one pulse. Sparks skittered across her skin and his. Energy crackled through the cold air and he flew backward. He landed on the hard concrete, limp and broken. Heather swallowed bile and surveyed the comatose men. Their lives were so fragile; so feeble. She shuddered and forced herself to run to Kade's unconscious form.

Torin appeared, looming over her, questions in his eyes.

'He's alive,' she said. 'Sedated. Can we get out of here?'

His shoulders relaxed. He gestured to his people. 'Luke, you and Sara get them to the safe house. The rest of us will tidy up and see if we can track Carleton's other people. I doubt it, but we can at least make sure no-one follows you.'

Luke heaved Kade across his shoulders in a fireman's carry. He pointed at a pair of police who ran their way.

'You'd best deal with them, Boss,' he said. He gestured for Heather to join him. 'C'mon. Before they try to stop you for questioning.'

With one last glance back at her brother, Heather followed.

CHAPTER TWENTY

KADE

Kade awoke to an unfamiliar ceiling and unfamiliar sheets. The bed was too damned soft. Where was he? The room was dark and smelled faintly of cigarettes. Dim light filtered in around blockout blinds covering the windows.

Somewhere, in another room, a phone rang. Someone answered. A woman's voice.

Heather! He sat up, only to clutch at his aching skull when that echoed the beat of his heart. His mouth felt like he'd been chewing on cotton wool. He rose and stumbled to the door, wrenching it open. The tiled floor was cold under his bare feet. He was only wearing his jeans. His shirt had disappeared somewhere. Ah. There, lying over the corner of the bed.

Dressed, and squinting against too-bright lights, he emerged into a narrow hall, which led into a small kitchen-dining-lounge open plan area.

At one end of the faux-marble kitchen bench, Heather stood with an old-fashioned landline phone to her ear. She caught Kade's eye and spoke into the phone.

'He's woken up, Tor. But he doesn't look all that well. Do you want me to put him on?' She held the phone out. 'Tor wants to talk to you. I'll make you some coffee.'

He took the phone. She passed him a glass of water and flicked on the coffee machine.

'Tor,' he croaked. 'Hang on.' He downed the full glass of water then cleared his throat. 'Sorry. What happened?'

'You were sedated,' Tor replied. 'I'm at the office, cleaning up and shutting down police inquiries.'

'How many of Carleton's men did we get?' Kade scrubbed at his scalp, trying to shake off the lingering headache.

'Six. Five more got away that we know of.'

Kade swore. 'What's the blowback?'

'The six we caught are being held indefinitely under the terrorism laws,' Tor replied. 'I've had a chat with a couple of key people. Seems the FBI have been observing Carleton for a while. They're not impressed with me, though. They suspect I'm withholding information. Which I am.'

'Any danger of the phones being tapped?'

Tor laughed. 'How long have I been in this game, Kade? This line was swept and is scrambled. The one you're on was swept this morning.'

'Right. Yeah. Sorry.' He scraped stiff fingers through his hair, trying to massage intelligence back into his brain. 'Anything else I need to know?'

There was hesitation on the line.

'Tor?'

'Is Heather there with you?'

Kade resisted the urge to check on her where she fussed with the coffee cups and milk. 'Yes.'

'Did she tell you that she took out two of them?'

'How?'

'Same thing she did to you in my office. But this time she drained one and used the energy to knock out the other.' Tor sighed. 'I didn't see it, but Luke did. Said it was the coolest thing he'd ever seen. But you know him. They're both alive. Still unconscious though. Thought you should know.'

'Right. Yes.'

'Go easy on her,' Torin warned. 'She's strong but she's been through a lot the last few days.'

'Understood. Keep me posted.'

'Of course.'

Kade ended the call, considering what to say. He looked up. Heather slid a steaming cup of coffee toward him. Her eyes were huge, her cheeks pale.

'I…um…wasn't sure if you took milk or not.' She gave him the milk container, collected a packet of chocolate cookies and her own coffee, and walked into the small lounge area. She put cookies and coffee on the low table and sat, with her face down and hands folded in her lap.

Kade joined her, leaving space. They stayed in silence awhile, sipping coffee and nibbling cookies.

Finally, Kade set his cup aside and faced her. 'Want to talk about it? Tor told me what you did to protect me.'

She clutched the empty cup. Kade gently removed and placed it on the table. He took her cold fingers in his and held tighter when she murmured a protest and tried to draw free.

'Heather, talk to me. You're not on your own any more, remember?'

She nodded. 'Sorry. I'm not used to…'

'What, having someone to lean on?' Kade grimaced. 'Me either. It'll take some adjusting on both our parts. Let's start with how you feel about what's happened today.'

'Are they...' She shuddered. 'Are those two men still alive?'

'Yes,' he said, putting all the sincerity he could into thought and word. He held back the bit about them both being unconscious.

She studied him dubiously. 'I can't tell if you're lying, now. Not with the shields up.' She withdrew her hands from his and tucked them under her thighs. 'I don't know how to read people normally, I guess. I thought I was a healer, but suddenly I feel like an arm has been cut off. I can't sense when people are near, or what they're feeling, or when they're lying.'

She shuddered again. 'How do people live like this?'

He quirked a grin. 'We don't know what we're missing.'

Her responding smile was half-hearted at best. 'It was too easy, Kade. I...' she waved vaguely '...thought about sucking the life out of that man, and it happened. Then the other one grabbed me and I panicked and sort of...dumped the energy into him.' She gulped. 'The crackling sound...the smell of burnt skin. The way the first guy collapsed. It...' Her cheeks paled.

'Reminded you of your father?' he prompted.

She hunched a shoulder. Her fingers stole to the scar on her temple. 'When my father slapped me I fell and hit my head on the table. But when I cried he just...stood there. Staring at me like I was some sort of bug he wanted to squash.' She drew a slow, shaky breath. 'Suddenly he didn't love me anymore. He grabbed my arm.' She inspected her wrist. 'And yelled about throwing me out. I thought he meant off the stairs. We lived on the second storey. I thought he was going to kill me.'

'That must have been terrifying,' Kade said gently. He wanted to hold her. To tell her nothing would hurt her again, ever. But he couldn't. She needed to talk this out.

'I...' she displayed her hands '...sucked the life out of him. Like I did today. And it felt good, Kade.' She wrapped her arms around herself. 'That's what scares me most. It felt good to be so powerful. I'd always been the youngest. The smallest. Suddenly I was stronger than my father.'

Heather lifted her eyes and Kade saw fear and lingering horror in their crystal depths. 'I think, if Mother hadn't arrived, I might have killed him. She pulled the power from me. And I cried. Not because of what I'd done, but because she'd stopped me. What sort of person does that make me?'

'Ah, Heather,' Kade dragged her close, holding her, feeling her fragility, her shivering. 'When you were eleven it made you a frightened, hurt little girl desperate to regain personal power. Then you spent the next seventeen years destroying yourself trying to make up for something you didn't even do. You have to let it go. You didn't kill him.'

'But I *wanted* to,' she said, shoving at him. 'Don't you see? I would have. Like today. I didn't pause for a second when those men attacked us.'

'You didn't kill them, though,' Kade said, hoping desperately that would stay true. 'And Rowan said you wouldn't be able to. That you can't hold enough power to drain or kill anyone.'

Heather thrust his arms off hers and rose, pacing to the window. 'She's wrong. Today I worked out how I could do it.' She spun to face him. 'I can't drain someone all at once. But if I release their power into someone else—like I did today—I could still finish the job.'

Kade stilled, trying to keep calm. But she emitted a humourless laugh and turned back to the window.

'See? You hadn't even considered that. But I did. The minute the power left me, I realised what I could do.' She gave a stifled sob. 'I am what I always thought I was. I'm a killer. Some sort of monster.'

Kade rose and approached her slowly, unsure what to say. He had to get her out of this depressive spiral. Fast. He rubbed her arms.

'Hey. You're too hard on yourself. You've spent years saving lives. Almost killed yourself in the process. You're not a monster. So you could have killed that guy, today. You didn't, did you?'

She looked narrowly at him. 'Only because Torin dragged me away.'

'No. You had time. You chose not to. And you will again.'

Heather covered her face. 'I don't want to have to. I wish I'd never met you. If you hadn't dragged me here, I'd never have met Rowan. I'd never have found out what I can do.' Her voice rose. 'And Carleton wouldn't have found me.'

'And you'd never have met Torin again, either,' Kade replied, trying to keep his voice steady. Guilt dug at him. He had dragged her here against her will. He'd put her in this position. He had to get her out; to secure her freedom; to ensure Carleton never laid a hand on her.

'And now, with Torin and you in my life, I'm more vulnerable than ever.' Her shoulders sagged. 'Let me go, Kade. You can't protect me from this and I don't want Carleton hurting either of you.'

Kade caught her jaw between his palms. 'Is that what you really want, Heather? To never see me again? Or Torin? Do you want to run and keep running your whole life? Punishing yourself for something you *might* have done, but didn't?'

Tears welled; spilled onto her cheeks. His heart broke and he snatched her into his arms. She stayed still for a long moment, tense. Then she softened and her touch slipped across the bare skin of his back. She wept quietly into his shoulder, in the hopeless way people do when they've cried too much and know it does no good.

Kade held her gently, until the tears dried and she sniffed. Then he offered a tissue from a box on the counter. She wiped her cheeks and blew her nose. Crushing the tissue in her fist, she closed her eyes.

'Sorry to be so maudlin,' she murmured, a thin humourless smile pulling at her lips. 'I'm not usually like this. I'm tired. I'll be fine.'

Kade stroked back her hair. 'You're doing it again. Shutting me out. It's ok, Heather. This won't be easy, but I'm here. We'll get through this, together.'

A frown creased her brow. Now he wished he could read her thoughts.

'You hardly know me, Kade,' she said. 'You don't know the things I've had to do to survive.' Her haunted eyes flicked to his then away again. 'I'm not a good person.'

He shrugged. 'And you don't know what I've had to do, either. We're not so different. Just human.' He grinned. 'Sort of. Trying to do our best.'

He slid a hand up her smooth arm, caressed her cheek and the softness of her dusky curls. She let out a quavering sigh and, at last, met his gaze.

'Let me get to know you better?' he murmured. He kissed her neck and she quivered. Her nails dug into the thin skin on his forearms. He withdrew, searching her face for any sign of fear or rejection.

Heather hesitated then leaned in and captured his mouth with hers, warm and sweet with coffee. She swayed closer, pressing her lithe body against him. This time there was no calculation or deliberate seduction. Her hands were cool and urgent, caressing his back, stroking his chest. She fumbled at his belt buckle and Kade paused, surfacing for air.

'Hang on.' He cradled her cheeks and her skin flushed delicately. 'You sure?' he asked.

Her eyelids drooped and she gave a throaty chuckle. 'Yes, you idiot. Stop being so politically correct and take me to bed.'

Kade grinned and scooped her into his arms. 'With pleasure.'

CHAPTER TWENTY-ONE

HEATHER

Heather fitted herself into Kade's arms and stroked the angle of his jaw. He smiled and caught her fingertip gently in his teeth, suckling, licking, his gaze never leaving hers. A delicious shiver of anticipation skittered across her skin.

He manoeuvred them into the bedroom and set her on the bed. Then he stood over her just admiring for a moment.

'You're beautiful.'

'So are you,' she said. The half-light from the hall threw shadows across his lean, muscular body. She touched two round, pale scars on his right side and looked up at him in question.

He kissed her wrist. 'Another time.'

Heather stretched languidly against the cool quilt cover and scooted across, patting the bed. For the first time…ever…she anticipated sex with hunger and heat, rather than fear. Her body thrummed. She yanked off the men's business shirt she still wore from their shell-game and wriggled out of the trousers.

Kade, now wearing only his boxers, slid into bed and lay on his side with one hand propping up his head. Slowly, he caressed down the length of her body, from cheek to hip. Waves of heat and tingles of electricity followed his touch. Heather arched her back and fought the urge to close her eyes and just *feel*. To be touched. To feel physical desire and pleasure without being drained of energy. It was... almost too much.

Heat pooled between her legs. Kade nudged her onto her back and stroked a calloused palm across the flat of her stomach. His fingers dipped beneath the band of her underwear, then traced the line of her bra across her breast.

Heather whimpered. 'Oh, please, Kade. You're torturing me.'

'That's the idea,' he whispered, his breath tickling her neck.

She chuckled. 'You have no idea how different this is... to only feel touch.' She sighed and arched again. He unclipped her bra and teased it off her arms. His finger traced light circles around her breast, so close...

'That's why I want to make it feel good,' he replied. 'Tell me what you want.'

'This. I don't kno—'

He touched her nipple. Lightly.

'Oh!' The throbbing between her legs intensified and she clutched at the quilt. 'Yes.'

'Open your eyes so I can see what you're feeling,' Kade said, his voice rough.

She did, saying, 'Open your thought-window and you won't have to guess.' Would he allow it? Was he ready? Was she ready? This was all happening so fast.

His touch faltered. 'Will you be able to handle it?' He gave a strangled laugh. 'I'm holding on by a thread, here.'

She studied him. If they were going to trust each other—to believe each other—they needed to allow access to their deeper thoughts. Yes. Trust wasn't easy, but someone had to take the step.

'Yes,' she whispered. 'I know how to separate thoughts from power, now. And how to control the flow so I'm not overwhelmed.' Feeling oddly shy, she opened a window for him and felt his strength, his intelligence, his *soul* connect.

For a timeless, wonderous moment, they were suspended in what Rowan had called the *sianfath.* The connection with each other and with the Earth. Intertwined. Golden.

Heather reached for Kade and pulled him into a kiss, wanting more. His lips, soft and warm; his touch, strong and certain; his mind, brilliant and—

She tugged free and scrutinised him, desire withering and leaving cold uncertainty in its place.

'You *are* still afraid of me,' she said, slamming shut her thought-window.

Kade flinched. He scrubbed a hand over his short hair, his eyes sliding away.

She snatched up her bra and clipped it on, shaking. With loss. With burnt-out longing. With self-disgust. She had been right. Even having more control over her gifts didn't make her normal, or human.

She would never have what everyone else took for granted.

Love.

A simple connection with all the possibility of misunderstandings and hard work that made relationships so… human.

Because she wasn't human. She didn't deserve love. Not after what she'd done. What she could still do.

Behind her, Kade sighed. 'I'm not afraid at you, Heather.'

She dragged her shirt on. 'You can't lie in that thought-window connection, you know. I felt it.' She raked him with scorn. 'Oh, you *wanted* me, but you were so damned scared it was like a black fog in your brain.' Shoving her feet into her trousers, she rose and yanked at the zip, though she could barely see through tears.

'Fuck!' Kade rubbed at his temples. 'You don't understand. I—'

'Yes, I do. *I'm* afraid of me. You'd be crazy not to be. I hate myself for hoping when I should know better by now.' She snatched up her bag, then stuffed her feet into the men's shoes she'd worn. Her throat was so tight she could barely speak and her chest was leaden.

'Dammit! No. You've got it all wrong.' Kade rose from the bed and hauled his shirt and pants on.

The shirt hung unbuttoned, giving tantalising glimpses of his muscular stomach and chest. Heather gulped.

'I'm not afraid of you.' He swiped a hand across his face. 'I'm afraid of repeating past mistakes.'

She paused, wanting to believe, afraid to risk everything and be proven right again. 'What past mistakes?'

p214

He stood, his head lowered, face blank and shadowed. 'I used to be married.' He rubbed at his left ring-finger. No pale ring-mark, so it must have been a while ago. 'We met in high school. I loved her more than I thought possible. She was…a sparkler amongst candles. Brilliant. Energetic. Spontaneous.'

Reluctantly, Heather dropped her bag and sat, keeping a careful distance between them. She waited.

KADE

Kade glanced up, struck again by Heather's fierce beauty. The crystal clarity of her eyes. The poised wariness of her tension. A wild cat about to flee. If he wasn't careful he could wreck everything, right now. He paced the small, bare room twice, from the thickly-curtained window to the door and back again. He stopped by the window and twitched the curtain aside before dropping it.

'But Amanda died. Eight years ago.' He cleared his throat against a customary surge of grief and guilt. Less, now, than it had been, but still visceral; still painful.

Heather's soft mouth drooped. 'I'm sorry. What happened? That is, if you want to say…you don't have to…'

'Tor keeps telling me I should talk about it.' He smiled thinly. 'But he's not much of a role model in these things.' He tried to hold tight to the welter of emotions roiling in his gut. Returning to the window, he propped one shoulder against the wall, shifted the curtain and stared again at the busy street below. The apartment was on the third storey in a popular, expensive neighbourhood full of young families and people walking their dogs. Across the road, a young man agonised over bunches of flowers in a florist's display, inspecting first a spray of white roses, then a huge bundle of daffodils.

Amanda had loved daffodils.

Kade spoke quietly, 'I was on deployment. Clearing out terrorist cells in Afghanistan. Hadn't been home in about seven months. Took two bullets in the body.' He stroked the hard scars under his ribs.

Heather made a soft, sympathetic sound.

He didn't look around. 'My own stupid fault. We'd been warned they were using armour-piercing bullets and I got cocky. Tor got me to base and into surgery. Then I got an infection was flown to the US for better treatment.' Sighing, he closed his eyes briefly. It still hurt to remember.

'And?'

'And,' he continued, 'by the time I was lucid and healthy enough to be told, Amanda had been gone for a week.' He clenched a fist. 'I'd been less than a hundred miles away, in LA, and hadn't even known she…'

'How?' Heather asked, softly. There was a rustle and she came to his side. She fitted her warmth against his back, one hand rhythmically stroking his arm.

Kade rushed through the rest. 'She hadn't told me she was pregnant. Hadn't told anyone on the base. Wanted to surprise me.' A mirthless laugh escaped him. 'She died in childbirth. An unregistered midwife botched the delivery. Both Amanda and… my daughter…' Tears clouded the scene outside and he

p216

swore again. 'I should have been there. She shouldn't have died alone. Shouldn't have died at all! I would have made sure they were safe. They were buried before I even knew. I never saw…'

'Oh, Kade,' Heather whispered. 'I'm so sorry. Now I understand why you hated me. I'm so sorry.' Her hands pressed against his shoulders and he turned around. He buried his face in the curve of her neck, breathing in her sweet, warm smell. She rubbed his back.

He raised his head. 'I don't know if I can go through that again. *That's* what I'm afraid of. Not you. Of falling too deeply for you, then losing you. Amanda was everything to me and I haven't let anyone close, since.'

She sighed. 'People die, Kade. It's life. And I would like—one day—to have kids, so it's a risk. But I'm the least likely person to avoid proper medical treatment.' A quick frown flickered. 'Though, I don't understand…' She stopped. 'No. Never mind.'

He straightened, unease stirring in his stomach. 'What?'

'It doesn't matter.' She offered a thin, superficial smile. 'Maybe we should think about ordering dinner?' She glanced at the bed and blushed. 'I'm not sure now's the right time for anything else.'

Kade stayed where he was. 'What don't you understand, Heather?'

She disengaged from him and retreated. Her arms went across her stomach. 'I guess I don't understand why she didn't tell you. And why no-one else told you.' She raised one shoulder. 'Seemed…odd. But it's none of my business.'

He clenched his teeth. 'Like I said: she wanted to surprise me. She moved off base so none of the other partners would gossip. She knew how much I wanted kids. Can you think of a better surprise present?'

'I guess not. But I've found most married women want their husband to be part of the pregnancy as well. I just thought it was strange that she didn't.'

He returned to the window, digging his nails into his palms. She was only voicing nagging uneasiness he'd felt eight years ago and put aside, buried along with Amanda and the baby. It wasn't fair to lash out at her, no matter how much he wanted to.

'What…' her voice was soft, fearful '…what happened to the midwife?'

He grunted. 'Never caught. The police couldn't track her.' He glared, unseeing, along the street. Golden, late afternoon light sent purple shadows creeping along the tarmac. 'Her name was Miriam Johnson. Know her? It would be nice to catch up with that one.'

No reply. Kade glanced back. Heather sat on the bed, her face ashen and eyes wide. She looked down.

He frowned. 'You do know her?'

She seemed ridiculously young and vulnerable in the too-large men's clothing. Her hands clenched in her lap.

'It was one of my names. I'm Miriam Johnson,' she whispered.

Shock stole Kade's breath from frozen lungs. His body wouldn't move. All he could do was stare at her. Blood pounded in his throat and a fountain of fire burned in his stomach. He stalked toward her and she shrank away, arms raised, head turned.

'Don't!'

Kade paused, fists balled at his sides, whole body trembling with the effort of holding in eight years worth of grief and anger.

'I wasn't going to hit you,' he said, low and hard. 'I've never hit a defenceless woman in my life. But I do want an explanation.'

CHAPTER TWENTY-TWO

KADE

She slowly straightened. 'Where did she live? What was her name? Her last name. I don't remember ever seeing an Amanda Miller.'

He controlled himself ruthlessly and folded his arms. 'Camp Pendleton. She was living in San Marcos. Her maiden name was Black, but I can't imagine why—'

Heather's eyes flew to his. 'Amanda Black? I…I remember her. Blonde. Tiny. Penicillin allergy.'

'Yes.' He fought a maelstrom of emotions so wild and overwhelming he could barely name them. Adrenalin spiked through his body and he shook.

He yanked out his phone and did a quick search on Google. When he found what he wanted, he took one last view of Heather. He could barely stand to look at her, now. Not knowing what she'd done. He'd been an utter idiot for believing her lies.

'Who are you calling?' she asked, clutching a pillow over her chest. 'Kade, you have to listen. Amanda was—'

'Enough,' he growled. 'I don't want to hear your bullshit excuses this time.'

'But let me—'

'No. Her doctor, Jeff Saunders, was a close friend. He told me the medical findings; the midwife's name—*your* name.' He curled a lip. 'The birth was a month early. Mishandled and Amanda died of complications. The baby died with the cord around her neck. I don't know why Amanda called you in rather than going to the hospital, but you could have saved her and you didn't.'

Heather gasped, the colour draining from her cheeks. 'But that's not—'

'Stop,' he said. 'I'm not interested.'

She opened her mouth then closed it into a thin line. Her jaw worked, her eyes flashing.

Kade ground his teeth. She wasn't even going to defend herself. Clearly, she'd worked out there was no point. The sour taste of betrayal scorched his throat.

His thumb hovered over the dial button.

No.

He couldn't do it. He couldn't hand anyone over to Carleton, not even her. Cold and sick, he hit Cancel and rang Torin instead.

'Tor,' he said shortly, 'come and get your sister. Don't ask. Do it.' He hung up before Torin could reply and shoved the phone into his pocket. 'Get your things. We'll wait in the lobby.'

Heather gazed at him in open disbelief. 'I can't...I can't believe you did that. So much for believing and trusting me.'

'Yeah,' he said roughly, nausea twisting his stomach, 'well I can't believe I fell for your rescue-me woe-is-me crap.' He grabbed her wrist. 'Come on.'

She threw the pillow aside and rose from the bed. Her chin hardened and she looked him square in the eye.

'Let go of me, Kade Miller. Don't make me drain you, because after that stunt I will. You want to paint me as the badguy without hearing my side, then I'll prove you right. You think I'm a killer? Watch me.'

He released her. She collected her bag and coat and headed for the kitchen.

'Where do you think you're going?' he yelled, running after her.

'Away from you. I should have known I couldn't trust anyone.' She touched the scar on her temple. 'I thought I'd learned that lesson.' She yanked the front door open.

Kade threw his weight against it and slammed it shut. 'What did you mean 'your side of it'?'

'Get out of my way. I won't give you another warning.' She stopped, her eyes icy, hard, and cold as the winter winds outside.

'You can't leave.'

'You can't stop me.' She touched his arm and he felt the draw begin. Warmth drained from his body like oil. His knees buckled.

He opened the door.

She walked out of his life, head high, without looking back.

Healing Heather p223

Behind her, Kade slammed the door shut, swearing. His legs trembled and he felt like he'd run a marathon. Sickness roiled in his gut. He itched to punch something.

Anger pulsed, renewing energy through him. How could he have fallen for her crap? He knew she was a good actress. Knew she'd let mothers and babies die instead of taking them to hospital. He should have guessed she was Miriam Johnson.

But… He hesitated and straightened, staring at the gloss cream-painted door. Why would she admit to it? Why, when she could have pretended, denied knowing the midwife. He wouldn't have questioned it. If all she wanted was security and someone to protect her, then she had that with him and Torin. Why would she throw it all away by admitting who she was?

Unless…Kade covered his eyes.

What the fuck had he done?

He yanked out his phone. 'Tor? I think I've done something incredibly stupid. Send a full team around.'

'What? Why? I'm already in the car.'

'Heather and I argued,' he said, leaning on the door frame. 'She left. I'm going after her.'

'Hang on.' Tor put him on hold and made another call then returned. 'Done. I'm sure she won't go far. Ask in the local coffee shops.'

Kade focussed on the blood-red, and white tiled floor. 'You don't understand, Tor. I'll tell you later. I have to find her, now.' He hung up, dragged on his shoes and ran along the corridor, swearing at himself.

Unwilling to wait for the slow elevator, he took the stairs four at a time, leaping recklessly over the railing at the switchbacks. He emerged into the secure lobby breathless, hoping he'd beaten the lift.

No luck. Both elevators showed they were travelling to the fourth and fifth floors, so she'd already left. He pushed through the glass front door and staggered in a blast of freezing air. Dammit. He'd left his coat upstairs. Had she taken one?

Night had fallen and the streetlamps illuminated hollow patches of bright emptiness along the suburban street. Most shops were closed, barred and silent. Kade reviewed the open coffee shop next door, holding out hope. Nothing but the young man he'd seen buying flowers earlier, two morose-looking businessmen and a homeless woman cadging coins from them.

He erupted into the street. No point in yelling her name. She wasn't lost. South led toward the centre of the city. Would she have gone to Torin? That made no sense. She could have waited for him. He looked the other way. Nothing but passing cars with blinding headlights, plus a woman briskly walking her small dogs.

The young man with red roses emerged from the coffee shop. Kade paused, uneasy for no good reason.

A big, black car slid into a taxi zone and beeped.

Tor. Thank God.

Kade ran over and peered in the window. He recoiled. Something stung his arm. He yelled and plucked the dart free. He struck sluggishly at the flower-boy who lurked behind him.

The kid threw the roses aside and grabbed Kade, pinning him effortlessly. The dart fell from numb fingers and Kade slumped.

His last thought was that Tor would kill him, if Carleton didn't, first.

HEATHER

Seething, Heather stopped in the shadows and assessed her options. Anger would only carry her so far before reality imposed. Icy wind whistled down the street and tore at her coat. Her fingers and nose were frozen. She'd left her gloves and hat on the counter in the apartment.

She had hardly any money and no idea where she was. Overhead, the sky was an ugly shade of brown-orange, city lights reflecting off low clouds. A fine mist of freezing rain drifted down and she brushed it—and tears—from her face.

Where should she go?

But her mind wouldn't focus on the future. How could Kade turn on her? Not listen? Not give her a chance to explain? She thought he was different, but he wasn't. Judgmental, afraid of what he didn't understand. Like her father. Like Carleton.

She bit down, holding in an ache that dug a pit deep into her stomach. No. The ache was more than anger. The energy she'd drawn from Kade. The potential backlash. She had to get rid of the *sianfath's* power before it burned her from the inside, out.

She glanced around.

Huddled in a darkened doorway, a young man peered at her, lacklustre eyes half-hidden behind a shock of dark, unwashed hair. Maybe sick or on drugs. Certainly homeless, based on the small knapsack and sleeping bag. The city was full of homeless people and she was now one more. Perhaps he could tell her where a shelter was.

She approached cautiously and touched his shoulder. He blinked slowly. She released Kade's energy into him, clearing the fog of drugs from his blood. The young man shook himself. Awareness bloomed in him and he scowled.

She backed away. He snatched up his things, muttered something, and disappeared around the corner.

Heather slumped against the wall. Just like that, she was alone again. She checked along the street. No sign of Torin's car. She couldn't go to him, anyway. He would side with Kade. They were best friends and business partners. Her brother would trust Kade over his own sister. Of course he would, after all these years. Who wouldn't?

A scrabbling, rustling noise to her right made her jump. Was the young man back? She peered into the shadowed alley, suddenly conscious of her vulnerability.

She wrapped her coat closer.

A shadow leapt and shoved her heavily into the brick wall. Her skull smacked the hard concrete and bright lights glittered behind her eyes. She thrust out her arms to fend off her attacker but missed. Her bag was yanked off her shoulder.

And he disappeared. Nothing but light footsteps and a fleeting glimpse of dark hair and a knapsack as he fled. The boy she'd cured.

Trembling, Heather stood, numb with more than cold. Gone. That bag held everything she owned. Her medical kit. The only identity papers she had. A few dollars. She was an idiot.

'Shit. Shitshitshitshitshit!' With fingernails cutting into her palms, she vented a short, guttural scream at the uncaring, rubbish-strewn alley. It wasn't *fair*. Darkness consumed her thoughts. She sank into a crouch against the filthy wall. Tears clogged her throat and blurred the world into a bleak canvas of black and grey.

For the first time since she was a child she had family again. And someone she thought she could depend on.

Now, she had nothing, and no-one. And Carleton was still after her. He wouldn't stop until he'd hunted her down.

Helplessly, she patted at her coat pockets, hoping she'd missed something. The phone Tor had given her! She pulled out the phone, debating. If nothing else, he might lend her some money so she could start over. But he couldn't know why she was leaving, which would be difficult.

But would he tell Kade he'd seen her? Would he even speak to her if he believed Kade's story about Amanda's death?

She sighed and put the phone in her pocket. No point in splitting his loyalties. She'd been alone a long time. This was a setback, but she'd make do. Always did.

Sucking a deep breath, Heather straightened. First things first. She needed to find somewhere to stay the night or she'd freeze to death.

She rubbed at a sudden, sharp sting in her right arm, took a step toward the city and stopped. She tried to keep walking and stopped again, unable to shake the feeling something was very wrong. Changing back increased the feeling. The mugger again? There was no-one on her side of the road, or in the alley.

But across the road, someone yelled. A man. Two men seemed to be wrestling on the pavement. One trying to shove the other into a big, dark car. Three more men appeared from within the vehicle.

The fighting pair emerged into the light of a coffee shop's windows and Heather froze. She caught herself before screaming Kade's name. He wasn't resisting. His head lolled, his limbs hung limp. One of the men holstered a gun. Another of those dart guns?

There was nothing she could do. Nothing. Not with at least four of them, plus the driver. And that damned dart gun. It could only be Carleton's men. But how? How had he found the safe house?

She huddled into a shadowy nook between two shops, hidden from view. She tightened her dark coat and crouched to reduce her outline. Yanking out the phone, she photographed the car licence plate.

Within seconds, the car door closed and the vehicle accelerated smoothly from the curb. All that remained was a bunch of bright red flowers, bloody against the grey concrete.

Heather hid when the headlights swept across her position. The car growled away.

What had she done? If she hadn't stormed out in a childish fit, Kade would have been safe.

CHAPTER TWENTY-THREE

HEATHER

Tears, brittle in the sub-zero temperature, stung her eyes. After a moment's hesitation, she produced the phone and dialled Tor's number. He answered.

'How far away are you?' she said.

'About a block from the apartment. I'll be there in two minutes. Where are you? What happened?'

'Shit. That will be too long. I'll meet you at...' she squinted down the street '... the closed pet store on the west side of the street, a block closer the city.'

'What about Kade?'

'Carleton has him.'

Torin swore. 'They must have tagged him when we were in the square this afternoon. Can't believe I didn't think of that. You're safe, though? They didn't come for you?'

Heather covered her mouth for a second to hold back a cry of despair. 'Yes, I'm safe. Why didn't they tag me instead of him, though?'

'They would have only had a few seconds. He must have been the easier target. Stay where you are. I'll be there soon.'

A minute later he pulled alongside and she clambered in, grateful for the warmth of his heated SUV. Her shivering eased.

'Which way?' Torin said.

Heather pointed. He drove off without speaking, his jaw grim and fingers white on the wheel. Weaving through the traffic, he headed for the city. He barely missed a Porsche and slipped the SUV through an impossibly-small gap. Heather clung to the armrest.

'I can't see the car,' she said. 'How do you know where they're going?'

'Best guess? To Carleton's motel.'

'We can't go there!' She gripped his arm, prepared to draw power from him. 'You wouldn't turn me over to him?'

Torin frowned. 'Why the hell would I do that? We're going to see if they bring Kade in. Then we'll know what we're up against and can plan.'

'Oh.' Heather released him. Had Kade even told him what had happened? Surely not, or Torin would have said something.

Her brother swore again and narrowly missed a cyclist.

'There!' She pointed. 'That big black car ahead. Same licence plate.'

Torin eased off the accelerator, keeping the car in view. 'How many in it?'

'Four that I saw. Plus the driver.'

'Damn. Too many for me to take without risking Kade's life. They darted him I'm guessing?'

Heather winced. 'I'm sorry. It's my fault. We argued and he was chasing after me.' She twisted to see behind. 'Where are the rest of your people? Can they help?'

'I've put them on standby. We can't risk it. I need time to work out a strategy. If we stop Carleton's car his men could kill Kade or hold him hostage and that would show that we know where Kade is. At the moment they will think they have the upper hand. Think we don't know where he is.' He slapped the wheel. 'Dammit! What was he thinking? What were *you* thinking? Why did you leave?'

She examined her hands, thin and pale, in her lap. 'It doesn't matter. He lost his temper. I lost mine. We both said stupid things.' She stared out the front window, sick fear fluttering in her stomach. What would Carleton do to him? 'We have to get him back, Tor.'

'We will,' he said, grimly.

#

They followed the car all the way to The Mandarin Oriental and parked in a loading zone across the street. Carleton's men hauled Kade's unconscious body into the opulent foyer. The doorman didn't even blink, just opened the door and let them in. They vanished into the interior and Torin got his phone out.

'Luke? How far are you from the Oriental? Good man. Get over here. Observe every exit. Around the clock. Carleton has Kade and I don't want them getting out. Find out if there's a helipad. If there is, get onto our contacts at the airport and make sure we know the minute a flight plan is lodged.' He rubbed at his forehead. 'And get Cathy for me. Ask her to dig up blueprints of the motel. We need to see if there's a way in or out we can use that's not visible to cameras or staff.'

He paused, listening. 'Good. I'll take Heather to Michelle White's apartment in the tower in Time Warner for the night. She's out of town and it has a view of the Oriental at about the right level. Send a couple of people to stake out. And one of those stealth drones tech is trying out. Yes, I know. Screw the legalities. I'll pay the fine if they catch us.'

He ended the call and edged the car back into the jostling traffic.

Heather watched the hotel out of sight, fighting tears. No way could this end well, now. Carleton would offer Kade in exchange for her, and she would do it. His life was worth more than hers.

Yes, he'd jumped to the wrong conclusion about her, but he'd been carrying that burden of guilt and pain for eight years. Desperate to find someone to shift the blame onto. She should have been more understanding. Hadn't she learned that anger and judgement was *always* wrong? She stroked the scar on her temple.

She should have told him the truth. Made him listen.

But he would hate her for it; maybe even think she was lying to cover a medical mistake. So it was a lose-lose situation.

Torin drove into the Time Warner complex's private parking bays in stoic silence. Heather repressed the urge to ask him to hurry. He greeted the security and swiped a keycard for entry. In the elevator, he asked if she'd eaten. When she admitted she hadn't, he ordered takeaway she wouldn't eat. She said nothing, though, only followed him out of the elevator. Once inside the apartment's opulent living area, he locked the door, waved her at one of the grey-upholstered couches and folded his arms.

'Give. What's going on?'

Heather sank onto the couch. 'It's my fault. Kade was angry and I got scared.'

'Kade scared you? That doesn't sound like him.'

She made a dismissive gesture. 'He wasn't going to hurt me, but I thought he was. Only for a second. And I got angry and defensive and walked out.'

'What was it all about?'

Heather clenched her fingers tight in her lap. How much her hands resembled her mother's in the months before her death. Thin, blue-veined, shaking.

'Heather?' Torin's tone was gentle and he sat beside her, his expression one of concern now.

'It doesn't matter,' she said in a low voice. She couldn't tell him the truth, either. It would cause a rift between the men. A secret when they had none and trusted each other.

'Yes, it does. Kade's buttons are pretty difficult to push. If it's something that will affect how we get him free, then I need to know.'

'It's not…' She halted. 'It's…personal. Please? Don't ask me. Ask him, when he's free and I'm gone.'

'Gone? What does that mean?' He knelt before her. 'You're my little sister. I'm not letting you go.'

'You don't get to tell me what to do, Tor. Once this is done and Carleton is out of my life, I'm gone. I'll keep in touch. With you. Kade can't know where I am.'

'What the…?' He sighed. 'No. I get it. You don't want to say why. Shit.' He rose and paced, scratching at his scalp. 'I hate this, Heather.'

'Me too. I'm sorry.' She swallowed tears. 'So what do we do, now? How do we get him from Carleton.'

'We wait,' Torin replied, grim. 'For Luke's report about the building. For Cathy to send through the blueprints.' He paused. 'For Carleton to contact us about a hostage exchange.'

'You think that's what he'll do?' Her stomach sank. She'd expected it, but hoped… Stupid. Of course that was what he wanted.

'It's alright,' Torin said soothingly. 'We'll work out a way to get him without exchanging you.' His phone rang. He answered, his attention still on her. Then he rose abruptly, and paced to stand by the window, listening. His focus sharpened on the light-speckled darkness outside. Directly opposite, stood the Oriental's sharp-angled tower of glass that mirrored this building.

'You're sure?' he said. 'Right. Fall back. Get someone onto this roof with the drone and you come here with a telescope. I want eyes on the people in his suite. If he has internal security we can hack then do it. Yes. And I'll call when Carleton makes contact.'

Heather waited, every muscle tensed. He hung up and swiped at his phone's screen. Then he sank onto the couch.

'Right. Luke says the exits are all covered and the rest of the team will be here shortly. There's also no helipad, so Carleton can't get out that way.'

'But?' Heather snatched a throw cushion and squeezed it to her chest.

'But Cathy's sent me the blueprints and it doesn't seem like there's any easy way to get into his suite on the 63rd floor, either. Elevators and the fire stairs are monitored. Carleton has guards posted.'

He stared off into middle distance. 'If this were a movie or a book, we could take out the guards and overpower Carleton and his men. But we can't risk it. In real life, these things go wrong and either guards die or the hostage dies. Either of which is a bad outcome.'

Heather gulped. 'Is my skill any use? Can I help?'

'We're trying to keep you *away* from Carleton, remember?' He patted her leg. 'Don't stress. Extractions are my game. You go get some sleep. There are three bedrooms. I'll set Luke and the others up in one. You take that one.' He pointed. 'Leave Kade to me. I'll think of something.'

She opened her mouth to protest the patronising assumption that she had nothing else to contribute, then shut it and rose. No point. He was used to command. Used to running the show. Used to protecting people. He wouldn't want to hear her plan. She didn't really want to say it aloud, either. Once she did, there was no going back.

But, if he didn't have a good plan by morning, she would have to speak up.

She shivered.

CHAPTER TWENTY-FOUR

KADE

Kade swam into consciousness slowly enough to become aware of a killer headache and to remember what had happened. Taken hostage. No-brain rookie idiot! He forced himself to keep his eyes closed, his body limp, and cheeks slack. Where the hell was he? Last he remembered was the sting of the dart, the hot lethargy in his muscles, the leather-scented car interior.

Now there was only darkness and silence. The softness beneath his body could possibly be a bed. His arms and legs were not restrained. No voices or sounds to orientate from, either.

Was he a prisoner, or not? Maybe Torin had already got him free and was waiting for him to wake.

He almost moved, then decided against it. He'd stayed in Tor's spare bedroom often enough to know the smells and sounds of that apartment. These sheets smelled more like motel laundered ones. They were thick and stiff. Tucked tight into the mattress.

So not Tor's place or the safehouse.

Light played across his eyelids and he flinched.

'Ah! You're awake.' That was Carleton's urbane drawl. 'Please do join us in the living area, Mr Miller. We have good news.'

Kade swore and opened his eyes. The bedroom door swung wider, admitting a cold overhead light from the hallway outside. He squinted and flung aside the thick sheets and gold silk quilt. His feet were bare. His jeans and shirt had been replaced with a pair of white silk pyjamas emblazoned with the Mandarin Oriental hotel logo. Right. That answered one question, then.

He plucked at the top. 'My clothes?'

Carleton smiled indulgently. 'You won't need them. Not yet, anyway. Come. Dinner awaits.' He rubbed his palms together. 'Tomorrow is looking extremely promising.'

'What the hell do you want Heather for?' Kade rose. Carleton towered an inch or so taller and Kade found himself pulling his shoulders back.

Carleton's heavy eyelids drooped. 'Don't play the fool with me, Miller. You know what her…gifts are.' He cocked his head. 'But are you aware she is subhuman? A halfbreed.'

He waited. When Kade didn't react, he nodded. 'You do know and you think it doesn't bother you. It should. Her species have been trying to control humanity for thousands of years. I suspect she might have played you well. She seems to be good at getting people's sympathy.'

Kade suppressed a fresh surge of hurt at her admission to midwifing Amanda. No. He quashed the anger. He needed to think clearly. Carleton was trying to twist his emotions, to get him onside. This was a hostage situation. He had to remember that.

But perhaps, if he played along and gained Carleton's trust…

'Well, you're not wrong there,' he said, allowing bitterness to colour his comment. 'She had me tied in knots. Until she showed her true colours. But that doesn't mean I want to see anyone used in experiments, like she's some sort of animal.'

'Is that what she told you?' Carleton chuckled. 'We don't want to experiment; we want to learn. We'll take blood samples, of course, for DNA.' He leaned closer, eyes glittering. 'Can you imagine what we could do for humanity if we could isolate the genes that give these creatures their powers?'

Kade barely stopped himself from saying, *All humanity, or just a select few?* Instead, he put on a thoughtful frown.

'I'm still not comfortable with this.' He folded his arms. 'I can see the benefit, but why not ask for her co-operation instead of all this?' He indicated his room.

Carleton uttered a sharp bark of laughter. 'We tried. Many times. They won't help us. Even after their much-vaunted Council of Wisdom died off a millennia ago, they insist on separating themselves. Trying to stop humanity from progressing. Improving. Come.' He waved a negligent hand.

Kade followed him into the large, airy living space. Ten dark-clad, heavyset men were scattered around the room. Three by the door. All armed and with the stoic expressions of men well-enough paid to ignore whatever happened to a hostage.

'We tried breeding programs,' Carleton continued. 'Using captive sidhe women and selecting for specific gifts. Didn't help. The powers stay in the female offspring and weaken with each generation. Although one of our members has found a number of half-blood women here in the US with very useful gifts, so it might still come to something.'

Kade hid a shudder. Captive breeding programs? Christ.

'Anyone with the full gene complement is connected to this *sianfath* thing they go on about and seems to have trouble seeing the benefits of progress. Those with the Dark gene are fine, but a little…unstable and hard to control.'

'Dark gene? First I've heard of that.'

Carleton shrugged. 'Just the sidhe fighting amongst themselves, really. A faction that they call 'Dark' because they tend to be psychopathic and…well…dangerous. Part of why we're trying to eliminate them. But that's a conversation for another time.'

'So, what are you doing, then?' Kade sat at a huge, black marble table and helped himself to roast beef and potatoes from a silver-dome-covered dish in the centre. Seemed very ordinary fare for such an upmarket motel. Was Carleton trying to show he was a normal guy?

He cast a shrewd glance out the darkened window at the glittering cityscape outside. Was Torin holed up in one of the buildings nearby, watching? That would be protocol. Didn't his girlfriend, Michelle, own an apartment somewhere here?

'So…' Carleton sat opposite and piled his plate high with steak and potatoes and drowned it in gravy '…we aim to separate *just* the genes for the gifts. And put them into pure humans.' He spoke around a mouthful of potato and waved a fork. 'A whole new race of super-humans. With telepathy, telekinesis, healing, and a range of other useful powers.' He poured himself a glass of red wine and tilted it in a silent toast.

Kade chewed thoughtfully. 'Interesting. Where do I come in? As a hostage for Heather, or did you have something else in mind?'

Maybe he could tease out information on their grander plan. Something Rowan and Logan might find useful in their struggle against the Mors Ferrum.

Carleton pointed his fork. 'You strike me as an ambitious man. One with skills we could use. I suspect you probably find playing second fiddle to a control-freak like Torin O'Connor quite restrictive sometimes. He's very…by-the-book, isn't he?'

With an ironic guffaw, Kade reached for a cold beer from the wine bucket beside his chair. 'You can say that again. Everything legal and above-board. Makes my job damned hard sometimes.'

That was no lie, but he also didn't disagree with Torin. At least, not all the time. Laws were there for a reason, even if they were a pain in the ass sometimes.

'Excellent. Then let's see how this exchange plays out. If you have any…useful information you'd like to send my way about other sidhe you might encounter, I will see you are well-rewarded.' Carleton showed his teeth, perfect, fake. 'That will do as a beginning. Once you've proven yourself reliable, we can look at another position. Something within the organisation.'

Kade controlled a desire to punch him. 'I'll think on it.' He finished eating in silence. When he was done, he yawned. 'I'm guessing you don't need me this evening?'

'Feel free to retire.' Carleton collected a second bottle of red wine. 'The exchange will take place in the morning. Here.'

'You seem mighty confident.'

His white smile widened. 'Men like Torin Connor are predictable. His loyalty to his brother-in-arms will be his undoing. He will pretend to trade her for you, but he'll undoubtedly try some clever ruse. But, since he's not willing to break the law, it won't work. He's restricted by his moribund sense of ethics. I am not.'

He indicated the ten silent bodyguards placed around the room. 'I am also *extremely* well-protected, as you can see. I'm in no danger.'

Kade stalked to his bedroom. Two of the bodyguards followed him on silent, rubber-soled shoes. His door clicked shut behind him and their shadows darkened the gap beneath the door panel.

A swift inspection of the huge bedroom suite showed only what he'd expected. Glass windows at the top of a sheer glass wall forty or so stories above the street. The cupboards yielded nothing of use. Everything vaguely weapon-like had been removed: chairs, tables, alarm clock, hairdryer, even the pictures on the walls. The airconditioning vent was big enough for a cat, maybe. The internal walls were drywall, but no way could he cut through them without making a racket.

Kade dropped onto the bed and jammed his fingers into his hair. Shit. He was a half-witted, brainless idiot to have gotten himself into this, and now he couldn't get himself out, either.

Well, he may as well get some sleep.

Everything had been stripped from the bathroom, so he made do with rinsing his teeth and a quick, soapless shower. What they thought he could do with soap was beyond his imagination and brought a brief moment of black humour.

Finally, exhausted, he clambered into bed and slept.

Only to dream of withered corpses lying scattered at Heather's feet—including Amanda and Torin...and himself.

CHAPTER TWENTY-FIVE

HEATHER

What sleep Heather got in the massive bed was haunted by nightmares. Her mother's death. Her father's hand against her face. Carleton's sneering, arrogant inspection of her, like she was a patient without healthcare. But then his face morphed into Kade's and a shot rang out. Kade bleeding on the floor. Amanda Black bleeding and crying for her child.

And, through all of it, Heather stood, helpless, her power gone, unable to fix either Kade or Amanda. Doomed to stand by and watch as the life drained from them. As it had from her mother.

When she woke it was full dark and the bedside clock read four am. No point trying to sleep. Her stomach rumbled, reminding her she'd forgotten to eat. Eating and bathing seemed too prosaic, but both had to be done.

She showered, washed her clothing in the sink and hung it to dry, then put on a ridiculously-fluffy white bathrobe she found hanging in the huge closet.

Padding silently into the kitchen, she found, in the fridge, the takeaway Torin had ordered. Some sort of chicken kiev, perhaps. She warmed it in the microwave, cringing at the too-loud beeps. Then she worked out how to operate the barista-level coffee machine.

Seated at the huge marble table, she picked at the food, trying not to think.

'Couldn't sleep, either?'

She jumped. 'Torin. You scared me. No.' She pushed the food aside and cradled the coffee. 'Too many nightmares.'

'It'll be ok.' He busied himself getting a coffee. When he took a seat opposite, he still didn't meet her gaze. 'Luke has our gear ready in the second bedroom. Nothing much to report. They caught a brief glimpse of Kade when he and Carleton came into the living area and ate dinner. He seemed alright. A bit groggy.' He shrugged. 'Then he was taken into a back bedroom and we lost sight of him. The drone is on the roof, observing the roof exit. No other changes.'

Heather set her cup aside before she dropped it. He was alive. That was something.

'Did Carleton contact you?' She half-wanted him to say No. To say Kade had been released and it was all over.

Instead, he nodded. 'He wants you. Today. At 9am. An exchange in his room at the Oriental.'

Cold sleeted across her skin and the milky coffee soured in her stomach. 'And?' she whispered.

Torin grimaced. 'We still haven't been able to think of a way to get Kade out. At least, not one that doesn't involve someone getting injured or dying. We have no idea how many dartguns they have. Cathy's been trying to source something similar for us to use, but there's nothing readily available that doesn't require a veterinary licence and a whole lot of paperwork,'

'Rowan and Logan had some.'

'They've already left. It didn't occur to me that we'd need any. And no-one seems to know what the drug is they use. Everyone's telling us the same thing: there's no known drug that will act that fast or reliably on a human. It's obviously something developed in secret by this Mors Ferrum organisation.'

There was a long, uncomfortable silence. Heather stared blankly at the white marble table, fingertips pressed hard against the cool, unforgiving stone. She sucked a slow, shuddering breath and tried to quash the coil of queasiness in her stomach.

'I'll do it.'

A frown snapped Torin's dark brows together. 'Exchange yourself? No, you won't. I won't let you. Kade wouldn't want you to.'

She sent him a bleak smile. 'You didn't see how angry he was with me. It's my fault he's in this situation.'

'He wasn't angry when he called me, Heather,' Torin said gently. 'I heard the regret in his voice. He said he'd done something stupid. I won't let you do it.'

She rose, cold. 'I told you, it's not your decision, Torin. I've lived alone for a long time. I don't need you. Or Kade. And I won't let anyone die because of me. If you won't take me over there, I'll go by myself.'

Her brother's scowl deepened. 'You heard Rowan and Logan. She told you to stay away from Carleton. This guy is serious. The Mors Ferrum wants you for experiments.

Tortured.' He paled and clenched his teeth. 'I saw enough of that on deployment. Don't make me imagine you going through something like that. I can't lose you again.' He reached for her.

Heather retreated. 'I'm sorry, but this isn't about you. It never was. It's about me. I save people. It's what I do. Let me save Kade. And...' she swallowed '...if you can get me something...you must have access to something like...'

'What?' Puzzlement flickered through his icy eyes.

She made a helpless gesture. 'A suicide tablet. Then I have an out if it gets too bad.'

'Heather!' Torin strode around the table and snatched her into a hug so tight she struggled to breathe. 'Don't. Don't even think that. I'll get you out. Carleton won't keep you there. He'll want to move you to a holding site, or a medical facility. That will be our chance. Stay alive and we'll come for you. Do whatever he wants. Show him how your healing powers work. Whatever it takes. Hear me?'

Heather broke free. 'Show him!' She nibbled on a nail and paced the room. 'That's it, Tor!' She pressed cold hands to her heated cheeks. 'That's how we get him to leave me alone.'

Her brother folded his arms across his muscular chest. 'What the hell are you talking about? How will showing him your gifts help? Wouldn't that make him *more* determined to hang on to you?'

She firmed her chin. 'Not if we do it right.'

KADE

Kade's internal body clock roused him at what must be around oh-six-hundred. He swung out of bed, used the bathroom and checked outside. The sky was still dark, but held a hint of pre-dawn grey to the east. Far below, the morning traffic was already filling the dark streets with a steady stream of red and white lights. Manhattan music drifted up—the distant sound of honking and sirens.

A shiver glissaded over his skin. Impulsively, he opened the thought-window in his mind as Logan had taught, and sought for Heather. He concentrated on her, the unique signature that was her thought pattern. Nothing. He swore. Too much to expect it would work. Logan had said he didn't seem to have the gift of telepathy. Only empathy for Heather's feelings.

Not enough, though, apparently. If he'd listened to her; opened a window to her back in the apartment, would he have reacted the same way: like an utter jerk? Logan said you couldn't lie, mind to mind. Was it the same for pure feelings, though? Would he have been able to tell if she *was* lying about being Miriam Johnson? But why would she do that? It made even less sense than admitting to be the woman who'd killed Amanda.

He rested his forearm on the window, trying to drag his thoughts free of the unproductive downward spiral of self-blame. He'd been there before and didn't want to revisit. But there was no getting way from the fact that he'd reacted. Overreacted. He should have listened. Should have tried to understand.

But, if Heather really had been responsible for Amanda's death, what hope was there for a relationship? He'd never be able to see past it. Nor should he. She deserved prison. Didn't she?

The mental image of Heather—worn and broken, thin and dying in a prison cell—drove him to the door. Dammit, this was driving him nuts.

He had to get out of here.

The door opened and the big minion named Baker shoved a tray of food at him. No cutlery and a paper plate already soggy with bacon fat and runny egg.

Kade resisted the urge to throw it at him. Pointless waste. Once the door closed, he ate. Not much else he could do. That done, he showered, paced, and considered all the possible ways he could kill Carleton without going to jail for it. Or dying in the attempt.

Hours dragged by and the sun rose, beating in through the open curtains, flashing off glass all around. By the time the door handle rattled again, Kade had passed through anger into resigned acceptance. No way to escape this alive. All he could do was take a few with him and hope he could save Heather.

Carleton stuck his head in. His jowls sagged and his eyes were bloodshot. 'It's time. They'll be here in a few minutes. Come to the living room.'

Kade followed him out. The tiled floor was warm under his bare feet. The air smelled of cigarettes and stale red wine.

Empty wine bottles and full ashtrays lay scattered about the living space like the aftermath of a grad party.

Carleton pointed to a high-backed dining chair. 'Sit there.' One of his minions produced a ziptie.

'What the…?' Kade stayed standing. 'I thought we'd come to an agreement.'

Carleton's smile was wintry. 'Hardly, Miller. We've taken baby steps toward one, but you have to prove I can trust you. And right now they believe you're my prisoner. It's all about meeting people's expectations, I find. Helps to throw things offbalance when you subvert them, later.'

Not seeing any alternative in the face of a real pistol and a dartgun, Kade took a seat and crossed his wrists behind his back, hands fisted. 'What subversive thing are you going to do?'

His captor merely nodded to Baker, who held a ziptie. Kade's wrists were bound painfully-tight. He winced and relaxed, testing the give. Not a lot. At least they hadn't tied his ankles. But Baker waited close by, a gun trained on Kade. A real nine-mil, not a dart gun.

Kade swept a quick review of the room. Five armed guards were arrayed in a loose semi-circle around him and Carleton, facing the door. Two held sniper rifles. Five more guards stood in various locations around the room, close to cover—the bar, the stone dining table, the kitchen bench, the door to the master suite.

He ground his teeth, his heart pounding. Whatever Torin had planned, it was hard to see how it could work. Carleton held all the cards and had the tactical advantage. The hall outside the apartment was a killbox, as was the elevator. What would Torin do, bring everyone in O'Connor Inc and hope it didn't come to a firefight? Unlikely. What, then?

Kade wracked his brains, trying to think like Tor. But he'd never had the same gift for strategy, which is why Tor ran the company. Tactics, now... Kade made silent plans for taking out two or three of his closest guards, just in case.

Outside, the elevator binged softly. A knock fell on the door.

CHAPTER TWENTY-SIX

HEATHER

Heather waited, her palms slick and chest pounding so loud she could barely hear Torin's soft instructions in her ear. Carleton's door opened and she stepped inside the suite. She observed the space in a quick look and dragged her attention from Kade's horrified expression. He was surrounded by five guards and Carleton was poised well out of her reach. Torin had been right. Her plan wouldn't work here.

She would need to let herself be taken and hope they didn't dart her if she went quietly.

There were so many things that could go wrong. Her mind skittered and jumped from one to the next, trying to see, trying to work out what to do. No good. She drew a slow, steadying breath and raised her hands.

'I'm here. Let him go.'

Carleton smirked. 'Well, this is somewhat unexpected.' His men patted her down and checked the hall outside. They found the earbud and the big one named Baker ground it beneath his heel on the hard tiles.

Heather gulped. Torin had warned her it would probably be found, but she'd hoped. Her heart beat so hard the material of her white t-shirt shirt fluttered in time. Her hands were icy, her cheeks hot.

Carleton cocked his head. 'I need to be sure you're really the woman I want. I understand your real name is Heather. Last name?'

She managed to looking at avoid Kade. He hadn't told? She picked one of her aliases at random. 'O'Meara.'

'Very well.' He gestured to his men. 'Bring Miller closer.'

They dragged Kade's chair forward until he sat directly before her.

Carleton held out a palm and one of his men slapped a double-edged, serrated knife into it.

'Show me what you can do.' He thrust the dagger into Kade's right side. Kade cried out. Blood flowered across the white silk pyjama top.

Heather gasped, her knees shaking so much she could hardly stand. Carleton kicked Kade's chair over. Kade grunted, barely holding his skull off the floor when he crashed to the tiles.

'Heal him,' Carleton said coolly.

'You...you...' She glared at him.

'You're wasting time.' He inspected the knife. 'I've punctured his liver. Not his lung or intestine if my aim was good. You have time to save him from bleeding out if you hurry.' He glanced at his watch.

She sank to her knees beside Kade, struggling to hold in tears. She couldn't absorb energy from anyone else. It would give away her one, small, advantage. But did she have enough of her own to heal him? It would depend on the damage.

Getting herself together, she focussed on calming her mind and assessing her body's reserves. It would be close.

She touched Kade's side. Blood now pooled on the white tiles under him, running along the grout in straight, scarlet lines. He groaned and swore in three languages.

Heather sent out tendrils of thought, probing the wounds. Tension slipped from her shoulders. Carleton had judged it finely. Only the liver. She could fix it.

Concentrating, she pulled the sticky-honey energy from her body and delivered it into Kade's. Now she could feel it clearly, the healing process became easier. The taste of pine lingered on her tongue as she coaxed the cells to mend and knitted severed bloodvessels. Muscle and skin came next.

When she was done, she slumped to the floor, her body too heavy, strength gone. But the pulse in Kade's neck was steady. His eyes opened and fixed on her, blankly, coolly.

'Excellent,' Carleton said, clapping. He bent over Kade and examined beneath the bloodied shirt. 'Not a mark. Incredible.' He examined Heather shrewdly. 'You look like hell, though. How long does it take you to recover?'

She struggled to sit up. 'Maybe a day. If I rest and eat properly. But I was already weak from being sick.'

He tapped his lips with a thick finger. 'Right. So we need to get you somewhere secure and feed you. Got it.' He gestured to his men. 'Baker, get Miller a coat to cover the blood and his wrists. Then bring both of them. If they fight, dart them.'

'No!' Heather shoved unsteadily to her feet and stopped short when a dartgun muzzle pointed in her direction. 'You said you'd let him go.'

'I lied. He'll be useful for keeping you in line, since you clearly care what happens to him. Now turn and walk. I'd rather not have to carry you out unconscious. Money buys a lot of silence but it's easier not to have to.' Carleton waved her toward the door.

She hesitated. What choice did she have? She had to get him out of this building and somewhere Torin's men could find him. She stumbled to the elevator, ignoring Kade's slurred, angry protest. Carleton strolled alongside her, one hand beneath her elbow, behaving for all the world like a supportive friend.

#

Out on the street, a blast of cold, bitter-tasting air tossed Heather's hair into her eyes. She wrapped her coat close and concentrated on walking. Her feet dragged and her body weighed almost more than her legs could bear. She blinked against the dry chill and shook her head to clear it. She needed to think.

The group of bodyguards surrounded her, Kade, and Carleton where they waited on the sidewalk for Carleton's car. Traffic blared and growled around the traffic circle. Beyond, Central Park, revealed an oasis of greenery. Heather wished for Rowan's gift of seeing the *sianfath* and her ability to pull extra energy. She needed energy to think clearly; to save Kade.

Maybe there was another way. But should she? At the age of eleven she'd sworn not to draw power from humans again, yet what other option did she have? Or was she just rationalising? She glanced at Kade, held and at gunpoint.

No. She needed to do something. He was in this situation because of her. It was up to her to save him.

Deliberately, she stumbled and grabbed at one of Carleton's men for balance. She drew a small pool of energy from him and hoarded it in her body. He scowled and blinked. Strength oozed into her aching muscles. Not enough, though.

She would need more for what was coming. A lot more.

Maybe she could do that again?

A flash of movement. A sharp, cracking zip of sound. Carleton jerked and cried out. He jerked again and collapsed to the sidewalk on his back. A splash of scarlet stained the white shirt beneath his black overcoat. Blood?

Heather froze for a second. Then her training kicked in. She dropped to her knees. His eyelids fluttered. His breath came in rasping gasps. More blood seeped through his shirt.

But he was awake. Alive. He grabbed her wrist so hard her fingers numbed.

Carleton's men shouted instructions, drew weapons. They formed a circle, with Carleton and Heather in the middle. The men shouldered sniper rifles and scanned nearby rooftops.

Crowds of passersby scurried away. People screamed and ducked, thrusting each other out of the way in a frenzied rush for cover.

'Get him inside!' Baker said, tersely.

'No!' Heather yelled. 'Don't move him. We don't know if it's safe.'

Baker thrust Kade to the ground, a gun trained on him.

'Carleton dies, he dies,' the man snapped. 'Fix him.'

Carleton's eyes rolled up. His clutch on her arm relaxed.

'Call an ambulance, you idiot,' she managed, her voice cracking. 'And get me a cloth. I need to put pressure on this while I work.' Her body trembled so much she could hardly grip the central seam of Carleton's shirt. She ripped it open, buttons popping and pinging off the sidewalk. If the bullet was even a fraction the wrong direction…

From his position, Kade watched her, brows raised. She shook her head minutely, hoping he would understand the need to stay still. She switched her mind to clinical mode. Detached. Calm. Essential, or the terror would freeze her completely.

Steadying herself, she inspected the wounds. Two shots. Just below his ribs. Through the left side. Not immediately fatal, but he was bleeding too heavily if the pool of blood was any indication. The familiar, metallic smell settled her nerves. She could do this.

The nearby wail of an ambulance siren brought a sigh and a tiny smile.

She could do this.

CHAPTER TWENTY-SEVEN

KADE

Kade knelt on the cold concrete. With his wrists tied and a gun aimed at his skull, he was useless. He ground his teeth, observing helplessly while Heather worked on Carleton.

Carleton's blood dyed the sidewalk carmine. Her hands quaked but she stroked his bared stomach like a lovers' touch. The colour drained from her face. She slumped, her cheeks white. Carleton's eyes stayed closed, his skin pale and breath shallow.

'Why isn't he fixed?' Baker growled from behind Kade. The sharp click of a cocking mechanism sent a shiver the length of Kade's spine.

Heather sent him a frightened look. 'I tried, but one of the bullets ricocheted off a rib and nicked his atrium. He's still bleeding internally and I don't have enough energy to stop it.' Her lips pressed thin. 'If he hadn't made me fix Kade, I could.'

Baker swore. 'You're lying.'

Kade hunched his shoulders, waiting. Could he roll to one side and break Baker's knee with a kick before he pulled the trigger?

'I'm not!' Heather cried. 'I swear, if I could heal him, I would. You heard me before. It takes me a full day to recover from fixing an injury like Kade's.' She threw out a hand in supplication. 'Don't shoot him! I stabilised Carleton.' She

Healing Heather p263

pointed at an ambulance wailing down the street. 'They can get him to hospital.'

Baker barked a command to his men, who tucked away their weapons. Kade prepared to move. He needed one chance. The jittering heat of adrenalin pumped through his limbs. He shifted his weight to one knee and tucked his leg close, ready to kick. He checked Heather, who shook her head again.

He wavered. If she and Tor had some sort of plan in place, he could wreck it by doing something dumb. But what was dumb and what was smart? Dammit. Telepathy would be useful.

The ambulance doors swung open and a young man in a paramedic uniform leapt out. Kade kept his expression calm. Hopefully none of Carleton's minions had got a good glimpse of Luke during the Times Square altercations.

Kade focussed on Heather. She was carrying on an intense, medical conversation with Luke, who nodded knowledgably and asked questions using words Kade barely understood. The kid was good.

Baker and the rest of Carleton's team hovered like vultures. Baker's knee wedged itself into Kade's ribs as an unsubtle reminder of who was in charge.

Crowds milled around, forming a wall of curious faces and filming cellphones. The ambulance driver appeared. Sara. She waved the onlookers aside and hauled a gurney from the ambulance.

Luke inspected the gunshot injuries and applied some sort of bandages to the site. Kade couldn't see clearly what was happening. When Luke moved aside, there was an IV dripline in Carleton's arm. Luke jerked his chin at Sara. Together, she and Luke laid Carleton on a stretcher then heaved him onto the gurney and shoved the whole lot into the vehicle.

Luke directed a question to Heather. 'You the next of kin? Get in.'

'Yes. And that's his brother,' she said, pointing at Kade.

'Right.' Luke took Kade's arm, still hidden beneath the huge coat. 'Let me help you into the ambulance.'

Baker grabbed Kade's other arm. 'He'll follow. I'll go in the ambulance.'

Kade didn't resist when one of Baker's offsiders hauled him away from the promise of freedom. The last thing he saw was Heather's fear and Baker's gun pressing into her spine. They both climbed into the ambulance. Another of Carleton's minions clambered in after them, overriding Luke's protests with the gesture of a nine-mil.

The ambulance doors closed and the sirens wailed.

Kade watched powerlessly as the vehicle drove off.

HEATHER

Heather pressed herself into a corner of the ambulance, unable to stop shaking. Luke played the indignant paramedic to the hilt, telling Carleton's men they needed to secure their sidearms or he'd stop treating the patient.

The one named Baker snarled. 'Treat him or I'll put hole in you.'

Luke sneered. 'Yeah, because that would help. Stand down or I'll tell the driver to stop and we'll let him die.'

There was a long, tense silence. Baker's eyes narrowed but he jerked a nod at his companion and both holstered their weapons. Heather let her shoulders relax.

'What hospital are we going to?' Baker growled.

'Does he have insurance?' Luke countered, checking the heart monitor.

'Of course. The best.'

'Right.' Luke tapped on the driver's window and Sara cocked an ear his way. 'Head for the private clinic. Tell em to prep for surgery.'

'Will do.' She changed lanes.

Luke jerked his chin at Baker. 'If your friends are following, you might want to tell them to go around the corner. Emergency vehicles only at the entrance we're using.'

Baker studied Luke's guileless expression. Heather held her breath. Would he believe it? They'd had so little time to put this together. The veneer of medical competency was thin and brittle. One look by the wrong person in the wrong direction would expose the whole setup as a fraud.

Baker yanked out his phone and issued terse instructions to the vehicle following. The car that had Kade in it, bound and under guard. Heather kept her attention firmly on Carleton, trying not to let her relief show.

Now they had to take the next hurdle.

Carleton's monitor let out a long, flat beep. Luke swore and shouted to Sara to step on it. He snatched out the defibrillators paddle and elbowed Heather aside.

She gripped the second of Carleton's men as though to steady herself. She pulled as much of his energy as she could. He slumped into unconsciousness and fell across Carleton's legs. Pine and honey coursed through her veins. Almost enough. Almost. But she couldn't hold it for long.

Baker tugged at his companion's shoulder. No response.

'What'd you do to him?' Baker snapped at Heather.

'Nothing! Maybe he's sick? Ask the paramedic.'

Luke snorted. 'He probably fainted at the sight of blood. I'll measure him in a minute.' He pointed to Carleton. 'This patient is more urgent. Stay back.'

The defibrillator whined into readiness. Luke ripped open Carleton's shirt and placed two pads on his chest.

Baker yanked out his gun and trained it on Heather. 'Don't give me that shit. You did something.'

'Clear!' Luke yelled. Baker's attention switched to Carleton for a second. Luke spun and slapped the defibrillator paddles onto Baker's thigh and chest and pushed the button.

Heather ducked. Baker stiffened and gargled a cry. His muscles contracted. A shot rang out, deafening in the confines. The bullet whined over Heather's shoulder and cracked through the ambulance's skin.

Luke dropped the paddles, He snatched out a hypodermic filled with yellow liquid. Baker took a couple of shuddering, shallow breaths. Heather wrenched his pistol free and pointed it at him, trembling.

Luke jabbed the needle into Baker's thigh and depressed the plunger. The bodyguard flailed feebly at him but Luke tugged free and patted the big man's leg.

'Sleep good, dude.'

Baker slumped into the corner, his movements sloppy and slow. His eyes closed and he started snoring. Heather let out a shaky sigh. Luke had taken a big risk. Defibs could kill someone whose heart was functioning normally.

Luke jerked his chin at her. 'Better give me the gun.'

She passed it over without protesting. What did she know about guns? She was shaking so much she was more likely to shoot Luke than Baker, anyway.

He pointed at Carleton. 'If you've got any of that juice you took from our other sleeping beauty next to you, best use it on Carleton now or we're screwed.'

She gasped and checked the monitor. Still flat. 'It's real? I thought you'd rigged it to distract Baker. Oh, God!' She tasted the pine sticky-honey energy stockpiled inside. The sharp beginnings of disintegration ate at her body. Hastily, she laid hands on Carleton's chest.

Once more she trickled power into him, fighting the urge to pour it in and rid herself of the threat. Steadily, she twined the energy into his cells, fixing the worst of the internal bleeding.

But there was no time and not enough energy to cure him completely. She couldn't let his heart remain silent for much longer. She delivered the rest as a small shock, straight to his atrium superior node. The monitor beeped again, regular and strong.

Heather sagged against the wall, her eyes heavy.

'Heather?' That was Luke's anxious voice. 'Stay with me! Shit.'

The world faded into blackness.

CHAPTER TWENTY-EIGHT

KADE

Kade sat in the back seat of a black limo, fuming, wrists still tied. Facing him were two of Carleton's goons. Guns resting on their laps, muzzles square on his stomach, fingers light alongside the triggers. They wore dark glasses, but their easy, relaxed postures revealed their level of skill and experience. He was dealing with professionals.

To make matters worse, his hands were numb and his wrists cramped. Even if he could get free of the ziptie, he wouldn't be able to use his hands effectively.

The car took a sharp left and he tipped over on the seat, cracking his head on the door handle. Swearing, he struggled upright. The two guards watched, the shorter, blond one giving a small smirk. The taller, with buzzcut dark hair, with disinterest. Kade clenched his teeth.

Up front, the smoked-glass divider opened and the driver called, 'We're almost there. Private hospital. Ambulance is going to the emergency vehicle entrance.'

The car took another turn. This time Kade managed to stay upright. He caught a glimpse out the front windscreen. Enough to see they were angling into a narrow side street while the ambulance kept going straight.

'Where are we going?' he asked.

Buzzcut shrugged. 'You heard. Private hospital. Once the boss is stable he'll decide what to do with you. Until then, you'll stay here under guard.' He pointed at the floor with the gun.

Kade considered his options. He now knew what Torin's game was. The brief view out the window told him. No private hospital existed in this area. Which meant Tor'd hired a building and thrown money at superficially creating a clinic. Which also meant that all the staff would be O'Connor Inc people ready to help.

So all he had to do was get inside the building.

'Gotta use the men's room,' he said, diffidently. 'I mean, I'd piss here, but I'm not sure Carleton would be impressed when he gets out.'

Buzzcut swore.

The limo glided to a halt and the window slid down again.

'Entrance is there,' the driver said. 'Two other teams are securing the exits and covering the emergency vehicle entrance. The ambulance has arrived.'

Kade toed Buzzcut's leg. 'Really gotta go, dude.' If he was right about what was happening in that ambulance, the two men who'd gone with Carleton were now either dead or unconscious. He wanted to be out of this killbox and in the building before the driver heard that tidbit.

'Fine!' Buzz threw open the door and got out. 'Hurry it.' He half-hauled Kade out of the limo and shoved him across the road.

Kade staggered, regained his feet, and dodged a taxi that blared its horn and swerved to miss him. The coat that covered his bound wrists and bloodied shirt slipped off and fell to the street. He didn't bother stopping and nor did his escort. Buzzcut grunted and elbowed him again. Blondie joined them, buttoning the front of his black jacket.

The clinic entrance glass door opened to reveal a room that appeared suspiciously like an office reception, rather than a nurse's station. Dark grey desks. Potted plants. A few chairs plushly upholstered in grey leather. Expensive abstract art on the walls.

Behind the desk waited a smoothly-coiffured middle-aged woman in a pale grey uniform-type dress. She arched sculpted brows. Kade kept a poker-face with difficulty.

'May I help you?' She rose, all polite efficiency. 'You're injured!' She tapped a button and spoke. 'I need a team to reception, stat! We have a bleeder. Doctor Blake, please attend.'

'No, lady,' Buzzcut said. He had tucked his gun into the holster beneath his arm. 'He's fine. It's not his blood. He's not hurt. Just needs the bathroom.'

Cathy, Torin's secretary, raked Buzzcut with a cool look, reminding Kade forcibly of his most terrifying elementary school teacher. 'I think we should let the doctor judge that.' She gestured to Kade and emerged from behind the desk. 'Come here and we'll put you in the examination room, sir.'

Buzzcut produced his gun and aimed it at Cathy's chest. 'Shut it, bitch, and get behind your desk. Tell me where the damned men's room is.'

Her hands flashed out. One smacked the inside of his wrist. The other twisted the gun free. She backed up, the gun safely in her hold, muzzle pointed at Buzzcut's head.

Kade lashed out with a short side-kick at Blondie's knee. The joint cracked audibly. Blondie screamed and collapsed, grabbing at his leg. Kade kicked his temple and the bodyguard's eyes rolled up.

Buzzcut shouted and lunged at Cathy. She lowered the gun and pulled the trigger. The shot cracked loud in the small space, even with the suppressor. Chips of tile and blood sprayed across the floor. Buzzcut yelled and grabbed at his arm. Blood oozed between his fingers.

He gaped at her. 'What the fu—'

'On the floor.' Cathy aimed the gun again. 'On your face or the next one will go into your thick skull.'

Visibly shaken, Buzzcut lay down and laced his fingers behind his neck.

Kade chuckled. He wormed his arms under himself until they were out in front. Raising his arms high, he brought his wrists down across one knee. The ziptie snapped and flicked across the room to skitter over the white tiled floor. Blood and pain flooded into his hands and he groaned, flexing them.

'You ok?' Cathy asked, the gun still trained on the two men.

'Will be in a minute. Nice work, Cath. Thanks.'

She threw him a casual salute. 'Any time. Tor's upstairs. The others are securing the two cars outside. Once we have all of his men—'

'Two cars? Where's the third? There must be at least two or three men unaccounted for in that vehicle. Tell Tor.'

She tapped her ear. 'Tor—'

'Look out!' Kade dove and tackled her to the ground. Glass shattered. The sliding door cascaded in glittering fragments to the floor.

Buzzcut scrambled to his knees and snatched at Cathy's gun. From her position under Kade, she squeezed the trigger. Buzzcut's leg folded. Blood blossomed dark beneath his shattered knee. Kade lashed a kick at his head and the big man joined his mate in lala land.

Rolling off Cathy, Kade hauled her behind the reception desk. Another shot from outside ricocheted off the tiles where they had lain.

'They're serious,' she panted.

'You hurt?'

'Just my pride.' She patted her ass. 'You? Hard to tell with all that blood on those nice silk pyjamas.'

'Nothing bad.' He ignored the sting in his left arm. Something warm dripped off his fingertips. He pointed at the door behind the desk. 'Exit?'

She agreed. Another shot zipped through the broken door. This time it pierced the melamine and timber desk above where they hid. Kade grunted.

'High-powered. Must be the guys with the sniper rifles. Let's go. We need more walls between us and them. Get me to the ambulance.'

Cathy began crawling. 'If you want to get to Heather, then we need to go up. Luke has her. Along with Carleton and his two goons. Upstairs with Tor.' She glanced over her shoulder. 'But Heather's unconscious and they can't wake her up. And Carleton's still bleeding internally. Luke's trying his best but he's an army medic, not a doctor.'

Grimly, Kade swore shoved the door open. He threw himself through and rolled to one side. Two more shots hit the wall nearby. Cathy lunged through and closed the door. Together, they ran for the next exit.

In the reception, footsteps crunched on broken glass.

CHAPTER TWENTY-NINE

KADE

Kade followed Cathy to a corner office on the third floor. He checked behind then shut and locked the door. Unusually for a corner room, only one wall was windowed. The adjoining appeared to be solid concrete, with some whitewash and a couple of uninspired abstracts.

The other two walls were drywall—no stopping power against high-cal bullets. And the room, itself, held only the usual office furniture. A decent oak desk, a few chairs, a couch in a revolting shade of yellow.

'Where're Tor and the others?' He gripped Cath's arm. 'Where's Heather?'

Cath smiled and tapped on the concrete wall. It swung open and Torin stuck his head around.

'Nice work, Cath. Get in here.'

Gaping, Kade entered a room half the size of the office outside but far more interesting. All four walls were concrete and lined with shelves. Each shelf was stocked with either food, water, or some sort of essential survival supplies.

Several had been disturbed. Bundles of bandages lay tumbled on the bare floor and a cabinet of drugs hung open. Another wall held racks of weapons. Knives, assault rifles, pistols. Even a crossbow.

'Where the hell are we?'

'Friend's place,' Tor replied. 'He had it built after nine-eleven. Complete with panic room.' He shoved aside a grey futon-couch and pointed to a square in the floor. 'And escape hatch. Leads to a fireman's pole to the basement. That connects to a tunnel that comes out a block away in a subway station.'

'Paranoid, much?'

Tor laughed. He gave Kade a rough hug then inspected him. 'Seen you look better.'

'And worse.'

'You ok? What's the blood on your shirt?'

'Carleton stabbed me and made Heather heal me to prove she could.'

Torin swore. 'I know we can't kill him, but there are moments when I *really* want to.'

'You and me, both.'

'What about the arm?' Tor pointed at Kade's left arm.

Kade checked. The white silk sleeve was scarlet. 'Minor graze. Just bled a lot.'

'Hold still.' Tor wound a bandage around it, tying it off with untidy efficiency.

'It's not bad,' Kade complained.

'That's not the problem.' Tor pointed at the floor. A trail of blood drops led from the closed hidden door to where he stood.

'Crap.' Kade scrubbed at his scalp. 'It'll lead them right to us.'

Heather lay unconscious on the floor, her cheeks pale, her chest rising and falling almost imperceptibly. Next to her lay Carleton, asleep or sedated. Baker and another goon were stretched out along the far wall, also out to it.

Luke watched over all of them. He kept checking Carleton's pulse and the bag of blood hooked to a portable IV unit.

'Is she ok?' Kade asked, absorbing guilt. He was a fool. If she had overstretched herself trying to save Carleton...trying to save *him*...then it was his fault. If she died, it would be his fault. But if she really was the midwife who'd killed Amanda then her death was his own wish-fulfillment, wasn't it?

So why did his chest ache at the thought of even causing her this much pain and fear?

Luke, kneeling beside Heather, measured her pulse again. 'She's asleep, I think. She took some energy from that dude.' He pointed. 'Used it to bring Carleton back to life. Overdid it. She should recover, soon.'

Kade took a step toward her and stopped. She had made it pretty clear that she wanted nothing more to do with him. Yes, she'd cured him of the knife injury, but she would do the same for anyone. That's who she was: a healer.

Of course she was.

He groaned and buried his head in his hands. How had he thought, even for a second, that Amanda's death was her fault? Hadn't Heather saved his life twice now, when she didn't have to? When it gave her no benefit at all? The first time saving him had almost killed her. Even apart from everything else he'd learned about her, that should have told him everything he needed to know.

She would never have let Amanda die if she could have stopped it. And, given Amanda had health insurance, if Heather couldn't save her, she would have called for an ambulance.

Which meant Heather either hadn't been there at all, or he didn't know the whole story.

And he needed to know.

He needed her to tell him. To trust him, even though he didn't deserve it.

But first he had to save her from Carleton.

'I should go,' he said to Torin. 'I can clear the blood trail that leads here and run to a different part of the building. Lead them away.'

Tor shook his head. 'I think we have another option. We'll use our unconscious friends here as decoys.'

'I don't see any injuries on them. No blood trail.'

'That can be remedied,' Tor said, grimly. 'But first we need to wake Heather. We can't carry her down the pole. Space is too narrow. And she needs energy to heal Carleton. She can draw it from his men, first.'

'What? You're still going to heal him?' Kade stared at him. 'Why?'

'We don't kill, Kade.' Tor's blue eyes hardened. 'We both had enough of that, remember. I know you've got a personal stake in this. Believe me, I do, too. But for Heather's peace of mind and our own, we need Carleton alive.'

'What's to stop him from coming after her again?'

Tor sighed. 'Heather had a plan. She wouldn't tell me exactly what, but she thought she could convince him to leave her alone. Once she healed him.'

'And I thought I was the optimist,' Kade growled.

Luke touched Carleton's neck. 'Cathy? Kade? Either of you A Positive blood type? Or O positive? I've taken blood from sleeping beauty number one—he was carrying a donor card. That Baker guy has been sedated so I can't use his blood for Carleton. No-one else is compatible.'

His expression became grim. 'His pulse is weak. If we don't get him to a hospital soon, he'll die.'

Both Cathy and Kade admitted they had the wrong blood type.

Tor swiped a hand over his face. 'Right. We definitely need to wake up Heather, then. And fast. Cath, use a knife and put a small hole in our unknown sleeping friend there. Something that will justify the blood trail. Observe him, though.' He pointed at Luke. 'You drag him outside and give him a lump on the head to explain why he's unconscious. Kade? Think you can wake up Heather?'

Kade felt his face heat, remembering what he'd done in that snowy mountain cabin. The feel of her body against his. The way she'd almost slipped away. Could he go through that again?

What if he failed and she died? Or, what if he saved her, now, only to lose her later when she rejected him. Or, even worse, if she forgave him and something happened to her, further down the track in their lives.

Could he handle that?

Aware of Tor's expectant gaze, he drew on his military training and thrust aside emotion. Right here, right now, she was just a battle-comrade who needed help to survive. That was all he had to focus on. No space for anything else.

Now, or in the future.

She deserved better. She deserved someone who could commit their heart to her.

Someone else. Not him.

He joined Tor at her side. 'Are there any sugary drinks here?' He lifted her, ignoring the urge to kiss her pale lips and breathe in the scent of her hair.

Tor produced a warm box of long-life orange juice. Together they managed to get a few mouthfuls into her. She swallowed, coughed and swallowed more. Her eyelids fluttered and opened, vacant.

'Put her hand on your arm,' Kade said to Torin, low. 'She'll probably find contact with you easier than me at the moment. Brace yourself, though. It feels a bit like having your soul sucked out.'

Tor offered his arm. 'Heather? Go ahead. Take energy from me.'

'I…can't,' she protested. 'Can't control…might kill...'

He pushed his arm inside her curled fingers. Her grip tightened convulsively.

'I trust you, Heather,' Tor whispered. 'Do it.'

A long silence. Kade held his breath.

Then Tor stiffened. He slumped, half-collapsing onto the floor.

Heather's eyes snapped open. She wrenched free, shuffling across the concrete until her back was against the wall

CHAPTER THIRTY

HEATHER

Heather took in the familiar faces and released the breath she'd been holding as an exhalation instead of a scream. Torin raised his head and she covered a gasp. His skin was grey, his eyes lacklustre. His energy thrummed in her body, sharp, crackling like caged lightning.

She stretched toward him. 'I'm sorry! Let me give some back.'

He waved her off and, instead, gulped several large mouthfuls of orange juice from a box on the floor. Wiping his mouth, he pointed at Carleton, lying nearby.

'Use it on him, instead. Luke says he doesn't have long.' Torin shot her a straight look. 'If you don't save him, then we have to get him to a hospital and all the questions that entails. If he dies, it gets worse.'

She pressed her palms to her cold cheeks. Did she have enough energy?

Kade eased himself down next to her, not touching. 'Don't pressure her, Tor. She'll do the right thing. She always does.'

Heather snuck a glance sideways. What did that mean?

Luke and Cath appeared in the doorway.

'Sleeping beauty has been laid out for the minions to discover.' Luke locked the heavy door. 'Carleton's men are searching the building. Heard their voices close by. They've found the blood trail.' He chortled. 'With any luck they'll find sleeping beauty and think it came from him.' He crouched beside Carleton and confirmed a pulse, but his jaunty grin faded. 'If you're going to help him, better be now.'

Heather crawled over. She could do this. It was like fixing anyone else. No, not quite. She frowned. To do it right, she would have to go beyond mere fixing.

She would need to change his DNA on a fundamental level, as Rowan had explained. Combined with Rowan's Gifted knowledge, Heather understood what to do. Her medical background gave her a solid grounding in genetics and she'd always tried to keep up with the latest information.

But fixing the damage to his body *and* changing his DNA with her small store of energy was impossible.

She laid her palms on his chest. Yes, he was still bleeding internally. The blood was pooling in his abdominal cavity. One lung had been nicked by the bullet. She'd missed that before. Blood was slowly filling it up. Even if she cured him, he would need observation and possibly surgery. And he desperately needed more blood.

Luke was right. She had very little time left.

'I need more energy.' Her voice quaked. 'I don't have anywhere near enough to fix him and do what Rowan said.'

Kade, Torin and the others exchanged looks. Muffled voices sounded outside and everyone froze. Carleton uttered a gargling cough, blood spattering his lips and cheeks.

'Take some from me,' Cath whispered, sitting beside her. 'You already drew from Tor. Kade's a better fighter than me and Luke's a medic.' She glared at the men. 'Make sure you take care of me or my husband will *not* be happy.'

'You sure?' Heather said. 'You trust me?'

'You were willing to sacrifice yourself for Kade. That makes you trustworthy to me.'

Heather's cheeks burned and she carefully didn't catch Kade's gaze. She took Cathy's offered arm and withdrew as much power as she dared. The woman sagged into sleep.

Luke checked her. 'She's fine.'

Laying her hands on Carleton again, Heather let the power burrow into his cells and organs, healing, repairing, knitting bone and muscle. He stirred and she used a skerrick of power to suppress the parts of his brain that were firing into wakefulness. Not yet.

Sagging, she barely remembered to keep enough power tucked aside for herself, this time.

The voices outside grew louder. Sounding surprised, now. Calling a name.

'You alright?' Kade's soft whisper barely reached her.

'Fine,' she muttered. 'Stop fussing. Carleton's alive. He'll still need more blood and hospitalisation to get rid of the fluid in his lung, though.'

'So it's all good? We can get out of here?'

'No.' She swallowed. 'I have to…to *change* him. And to do that I need more power. A lot more.'

He nodded at the sleeping Baker lying against the rear wall. 'What about him?'

'Even if I took from him, you, and Luke, it still wouldn't be enough,' she whispered. 'I need at least four people. Total, that is. Not plus you. I'd rather not draw from you because that would leave all of us vulnerable.'

Kade swore and scrubbed at his scalp. 'Tor? Your call. What was the plan? What's this *change* she's talking about?'

Heather explained. 'Rowan taught me how to unfold certain human DNA. So they can sense the *sianfath* the way most sidhe can. Apparently it makes them more…empathetic to the sidhe cause. Then Carleton won't come after me. Or any sidhe.'

Kade arched a brow. 'And what, exactly, is the sidhe cause—apart from trying not to be annihilated or used as human guineapigs?'

'They're trying to change enough key humans to help stop those things, and to help slow the rate of environmental destruction. The sidhe, humans, the forests, the *sianfath*…we're all one system. We just need the humans to see that.'

'Lofty ambitions.' He sat on his haunches and reviewed Carleton. 'So you're saying that, if we can get you a few more people, you'll have enough energy to make this asswipe into a better person and convince him to let you go?'

She shrugged. 'I hope so. Otherwise this has all been a complete waste of time. Without it, once he recovers, he'll never stop chasing me.' She gazed at Carleton, emptiness aching in her chest. 'I know it, now. I'll be running forever.' She managed a broken laugh and murmured to herself, 'But maybe that's what I'm destined to do. All I'm worth to anyone.'

Kade gripped her shoulders and forced her to meet his fierce gaze. 'Don't say that. You're worth more than all of us combined. What you have. Your gift... It's incredible. You deserve to be safe and have the chance to help people without being afraid. So do all the sidhe.'

Heather's heart sank. Whatever human feelings he'd felt for her were dead. Killed by the awareness of what she was. She'd been naïve to think understanding who she was would somehow make her more acceptable to him.

Nothing she could do would make her normal...or worthy of love. That little speech he'd just given proved it.

But, at least she could protect him and Torin from this one threat before she moved on.

'Yes. My gift is...incredible.' She shivered. 'Well, if you want me to do this, you'd best get me some more...' she smiled thinly '...victims. Once I start, I can't stop partway, so I need all of them here at once.'

Kade whistled soundlessly. He, Torin and Luke exchanged glances.

As one, they turned to survey the rack of weapons hanging on the wall.

CHAPTER THIRTY-ONE

KADE

'Non-lethal, right?' Kade studied the weapons array. He cocked an ear. The voices were retreating. 'And quiet.'

Torin scratched at his jaw. 'We don't want to give Heather more people to heal.'

Kade pointed. 'Think that's a stack of tear-gas grenades? Which would go very nicely into an elevator.'

'Yep. And there are three tasers,' Luke added. 'And gasmasks. Shall we, gentlemen?'

They armed themselves, adding bulletproof vests Tor discovered.

Kade finished putting his on and found Heather standing close by, her expression half wary, half fearful. For him or of him? Dammit! Why had he been such an ass? She didn't deserve it after all she'd been through.

But he had no idea how to redeem himself. Or even if he should. It was clear he wasn't ready to move on; to risk losing someone again. They were both best off if he left well enough alone. Left her alone.

'You'll be ok,' he said, more roughly than he intended. He pressed a gun into her hands. 'Rubber bullets. Use it if anyone comes in that shouldn't. We'll be back.'

She held the weapon in two fingers. Her eyes were huge. He wanted to hold her, to kiss her, to tell her he would never leave. But he couldn't. Even if she would let him, which he doubted.

So he held back when Tor wrapped her in a quick hug.

Tor stroked her cheek. 'We'll knock like this.' He rapped his knuckles on the wall nearby.

She nodded. Luke cracked open the door and peered out. He gestured and Kade and Torin followed. Kade glanced back as he closed the door. Heather had retreated into a corner, the gun held close to her chest. He closed the door.

'Right.' Kade adjusted his mask. 'Let's get three of these bastards here asap. I want to make sure Carleton lives to get his people off her case.'

'Their turn to be guineapigs.' Tor hefted a tear gas grenade and pulled down his mask.

Luke opened the outer office door. Voices echoed in the corridor and the elevator *pinged*. Its doors slid open. Three of Carleton's men vanished into its gaping maw. Luke sprinted past and lobbed in a grenade before the doors closed. Torin and Kade took positions on either side.

Inside the box, yells and coughing. The doors re-opened and gas poured into the hallway. Two men staggered out, squinting, choking.

Kade tasered one, who collapsed, legs jerking. Tor did the same with the other. Luke dragged Tor's man along the corridor, whistling jauntily through his mask.

Where was the third? Had he managed to escape through the access hatch in the elevator roof?

The third man leapt out, short and muscular. His eyes were tight-shut, his mouth clamped into a thin line. He dropped to the ground, beneath the gas layer, and opened his eyes. His attention fixed on Kade and he snarled.

Kade lunged for him, taser ready. Shortass rolled over one shoulder and got to his feet. He lashed a kick at Kade's skull. Kade managed to dodge and missed the chance to trap the leg.

The teargas dissipated and Kade stripped off the mask to see better. Tor approached the guy from behind and got a foot in the stomach for his trouble. He was quick!

Shortass shifted sideways so he could keep them both in view. Kade caught Tor's attention and gave a thumbs up. They'd double-teamed so often in the past they didn't need words.

Tor lunged with a fake attempt to punch. Kade used the moment of distraction and closed the gap. He landed one good kick to the thigh nerve and wore a quick strike to the jaw that flashed stars in his skull. But Tor swarmed in and got a sleeper hold on.

Kade ankle-tapped the fighter. Tor dropped with him, tightening the hold. Carleton's man clawed at Tor but his actions grew feeble. After about ten seconds Torin released him.

Kade tasered the minion, just in case, then checked the hall to make sure they were still alone.

He grabbed the unconscious man's feet and hauled him to the office where Heather waited.

HEATHER

Heather crouched in the corner, the pistol resting on her knees. Inside the concrete bunker was nothing but heavy silence and deep breathing from Cathy, Baker, and Carleton. She strained, trying to hear beyond the walls. Was Torin alright? And Kade? Had they been taken prisoner? Was she stuck here, alone?

Would they return?

She'd been alone so long. It was terrifying to realise how quickly she'd given over her independence; allowed Torin and Kade to run things. But that was a slippery slope. She couldn't afford to rely on them. They barely knew her. Didn't really care for her, as a person. Only the idea of a sister and a lover.

If they knew her... Once they truly had time to think about what she could do and how she could affect their lives, their bodies, their minds. Then the truth would dawn on them and they would leave. It was only a matter of time until she was alone again.

A kind of resigned acceptance seeped into her tense shoulders and she relaxed.

Yes. She knew what to do, now.

What had to be done to protect Torin and Kade. Protect them not only from the Mors Ferrum, but from her as well.

She paused, listening. Something was different. Was that a noise outside?

Someone ripped the gun from her hands. An elbow pressed into her jaw, shoving her against the wall. Sparks of pain shot through her neck and she whimpered.

'Tell me how to get out of here, girl, or I'll blow your damned head off,' Baker's deep voice growled in her ear. The pistol cocked, next to her temple.

Heather smothered a cry. Her heartrate tripled and her stomach heaved. The bullets might only be rubber, but from that distance the concussive force would still kill her.

'Door,' she managed, pointing at the semi-concealed exit. If he left that way, maybe he'd meet Kade and the others returning.

He hauled her to her feet, the muzzle pressed against her skull. 'You're coming, too. I'll trade you for Carleton, later. Maybe.'

Could she drain him? No. It took a few seconds. More than enough for him to fire the trigger.

'Open the door,' he ordered.

Trembling, she unhooked the latch. A knock sounded faintly on the concrete.

Torin's knock! They'd come for her. Heather covered a cry of relief.

Baker swore and dragged her backward, into a corner, using her as a shield.

Luke entered first, lugging a body. He dropped it next to Carleton and straightened. Then he turned and froze, swearing. Kade and Torin followed, each bearing a comatose man in a fireman's carry. They both stopped, then lowered their burdens to the floor and raised their hands.

Kade's mouth pressed into a hard line. He took a half-step forward. Baker's arm tightened around Heather's waist and he retreated.

'Wait, Kae,' Torin warned.

After a moment's hesitation, Kade obeyed. But the hardness in him spoke volumes.

'Don't be a moron, Baker,' he growled. 'We're trying to help Carleton.' He pointed at Heather. 'She needed more...time to be able to recover enough to heal him. These guys are just unconscious. We're not intending to kill anyone. So put the gun down and let her help.'

'Please,' Heather said. She tried to catch Baker's eye but his attention was fixed on Kade and Torin. 'He'll drown in his own blood soon if you don't let me help.' On cue, Carleton coughed and blood sprayed from his lips. He groaned, twitching. She needed to put him under before he became lucid enough to realise his pain was gone.

A long silence followed. Baker's arteries pounded against Heather's spine. Finally, he shoved her at Carleton.

'Do it, then. But make it fast. Otherwise I'll shoot all three of you.'

CHAPTER THIRTY-TWO

HEATHER

She paused. 'I could use your help. When he comes around, if he sees my friends he'll be worried. Can you help me sit him up?'

Baker hesitated then gestured with the gun to Kade. 'You three…up against the other wall. Keep your distance.' They complied and Heather tried to keep her anxiety from showing. She wiped sweating palms on her thighs and sat beside Carleton.

Slipping one arm under his shoulders, she pretended to try and lift him. Baker knelt opposite and worked a hand under Carleton's back. His fingers touched hers.

That was all she needed.

Focussing everything she had on him, she drew half Baker's energy into herself. He gave a groan. The whites of his eyes showed and he collapsed sideways, half-across Carleton's chest

Now she was full of sticky-honey, conifer-tasting power. Too full. She needed to get rid of it, fast.

She ordered the others, 'Help. Bring the other men close and get him out of the way. I need a continuous supply.'

Kade reached for her wrist but she snatched free of his grasp. 'Don't touch me! I can't lose this and I can't hold it for long.'

Ignoring him, she focussed on Carleton and touched his chest again. Now came the tricky part. Rowan had shown her a mental image of how it worked. Of what the DNA should look like before and after. This had to work, or... no. It didn't even bear thinking about. It had to work. This was her only chance at freedom.

Even if it meant a life on the road again.

She quashed a flicker of hurt and dove into Carleton's bone-marrow.

KADE

Kade and Torin arranged the unconscious men, while Luke bound and gagged Baker in one corner of the small room. Then Luke attached the heart monitor to Carleton again and gave Heather the thumbs up. The regular beeps were loud and irritating. Kade hovered over her. The pallor of her skin worsened and sweat sheened her forehead.

'More,' she whispered. Tor thrust one man's limp arm within contact. She absorbed power and straightened, colour in her cheeks. But it faded once she transferred energy to Carleton.

Kade ground his teeth, resisting the urge to stop her. She knew her own limits...didn't she?

A minute later she repeated the demand, her voice barely a whisper. After completing the transfer to Carleton she didn't straighten and her colour didn't recover.

When she asked a third time, Kade growled.

'Stop, Heather. It's not worth it. He's not worth it. It's taking too much out of you.'

'Shut *up!*' she snapped. 'I'm close, now. Get me the last one.'

Tor complied and she took the power. Tears trickled from beneath her closed lids and she emitted a broken whimper.

Kade reached for her, but Tor held him back, saying, 'Give her a chance.'

'She'll kill herself!'

Tor hauled him away from Heather. 'Get a grip, Kade. She's been doing this her whole life. She knows what she's doing. You can't protect her from everything.'

Kade broke free, scrubbing at his hair. 'You don't get it! This is my fault. If I hadn't overreacted back at the apartment, we wouldn't be here. She wouldn't be risking her life for this asshole.' He sat on a stool, staring at the floor. 'I screwed up, Tor. Big time. Now she's paying the price.'

'What happened? What did you two argue about?'

'I told her…' Kade swiped at his mouth '…how Amanda died. Heather admitted she was the midwife.'

Tor's eyes widened, his jaw dropping. 'What the… jeezus, Kade. That's why she thought I was going to hand her over to Carleton when I picked her up?' He hesitated. 'But why would she admit to letting Amanda die? That makes no sense.'

With a short laugh, Kade shook his head. 'I asked myself the same thing. But way too late. She had already left by the time I came down from my righteous anger and thought it through.' He groaned. 'And I walked right into Carleton's arms like some utter rookie.'

'Uh…' Luke's worried interjection broke into whatever Torin had been about to say. Heather gulped a shuddering sob and slumped. The younger man leapt over Carleton's body in time to catch her.

She sagged into his arms, limp and pale.

Kade and Tor hurried over. Kade snatched her from Luke and cradled her close. He felt her pulse and swore. Thready and skipping. Same as before, in the cabin, when she'd overdone it. A sigh fluttered from between blue lips and she sagged.

'Luke! Tell me you've got something in that medical kit.' Kade touched her neck again. 'I've got no pulse.'

The younger man stripped open a hypodermic and jammed it into her thigh. 'Adrenalin,' he said, then thrust Kade aside, laid her down and began CPR.

Kade sat by, helpless, knowing it wasn't the one thing she needed. She'd depleted herself of the *sianfath's* energy and only more of that would save her. But she had to be alive to draw it. Catch-22.

Luke paused and felt her throat. 'Got a faint pulse, but we should get her to hospital.'

'Wait,' Kade said. 'Take Carleton, Baker, and the others and put them into the elevator. Send them downstairs. Put a note on Carleton so they know to take him to the hospital. I know what to do for Heather. Give me a few minutes.'

Torin wavered. 'You sure? I can help.'

'Get them out of here,' Kade growled. 'Call for backup to get all of us out through the tunnel. I'll bring her back, I promise.'

With Heather's faint pulse beating beneath his touch, he waited until Tor and Luke had gone, taking Carleton and his men with them. Only Cathy remained, sleeping in one corner. Kade rose and locked the door.

He hauled Heather into his arms. Stroking aside her sweat-damp hair, he kissed her forehead.

'I'm sorry, Alanna. I'm sorry I didn't listen. Sorry I jumped to conclusions. Sorry I was too scared to let you close. I couldn't save Amanda, but maybe I can save you. Maybe you can live the life you deserve, with someone who'll appreciate who you are and how incredible you are. Here.'

He kissed her cool lips and splayed one hand across her cheek. Then he imagined opening a thought-window to her. Nothing. No sense of her mind or emotions. Empty blankness where her vibrancy used to live. Her body clung to life, barely.

But she had quit living.

He couldn't let her die. Not this way. Not giving her life for some bastard who didn't deserve to share the same air. Drawing a steadying breath, he envisaged pouring his energy into her frail, slight body. It was the least he could do. It had to work!

Nothing changed.

Kade groaned, tears trickling down his cheeks. 'Come *on!* Please?' He focussed all his mind, his body, his heart on her and *willed* himself into her; *willed* his strength into her; *willed* her to stay.

Still nothing. Her body remained limp and soft in his arms.

'Please, Heather,' he murmured. 'Please don't give up. I need you. Come back.'

Was that warmth in her skin? He pressed his cheek to hers.

Yes! And her pulse beat still beneath his fingers. She stirred under his touch. A thread connected them, growing thicker as she drew from him; as she pulled *something* thick from deep in his body. His fingers grew numb, his arms heavy and cold.

He laid her gently on the ground and fitted himself alongside, pillowing his cheek on her shoulder. Her breast rose and fell. But still, she didn't wake and he couldn't feel her emotions.

'Come on, Alanna,' he whispered. 'Come back. I…I love you.'

He opened his heart.

Opened his mind, shields lowered.

Opened everything he had held behind closed doors and gave it all to her.

CHAPTER THIRTY-THREE

HEATHER

Heather woke with a gasp. Above was the bunker's dark grey concrete ceiling. Below felt like more concrete, cold and hard. Something heavy lay on her shoulder and draped across her chest. No... some*one*. She pushed the arm off and scrambled away.

Then she returned. Kade lay there, eyes closed, face slack, body limp. Was he even breathing? She touched his lips and felt nothing. No pulse in his neck, either. But there were no marks on him.

She looked around, panicked. Where were Torin and Luke? Where were all the men? And Carleton. Only Cathy was left and she was still unconscious. What had happened? Last she remembered was...

Oh, no!

She had poured everything into Carleton and the DNA alteration had worked. She was sure of it. He would be aware of the *sianfath,* but the effort had taken everything from her.

Now her body thrummed with sticky-honey power again. And the one person around was Kade. What had he done?

She touched him and sparks crackled off her fingertips, coruscating across his skin.

Why? Why had he given so much? He must have known he didn't need to. He'd helped before and knew she could recover on far less than he'd given.

So why?

She stroked his jaw. Could she really be that important to him? So important he was willing to die for her?

Tears blurred his image and she leaned close.

'Idiot,' she whispered, and kissed him, transferring power.

His heart jumped and beat steadily. His eyes fluttered open. He groaned, his arms sliding around her until their bodies were entangled. He gathered her close, his lips warming and parting beneath hers.

Finally, he let go and studied her with an anxious question in those grey eyes.

'I'm ok,' she murmured. 'You?'

'Honestly? I wasn't expecting to be alive. You weren't waking up. Then it all went black.' He struggled up. 'I've felt better. I feel like I haven't slept for a week and everything aches.' He examined her face. 'You sure you're alright?'

She frowned. 'So you knew what you were doing? You did it on purpose? Why?'

He flushed and took her hand, one thumb rubbing across the back. 'Because I'd been a fool. I overreacted and drove you away. You almost died because I got you into this. You deserve to live and be happy. I wanted you to have that chance.'

Heather recoiled and yanked free. 'You did it out of guilt?'

'What? No!' Kade hesitated. 'Well, partly, I suppose.'

p306

Her heart solidified into stone and she rose on shaky legs. She was the idiot. Of course he hadn't made some noble sacrifice because he loved her. 'Thank you for saving me. The procedure was successful on Carleton so perhaps you and Torin can convince him to leave me alone, now.'

She went for the door. 'I'll go...' Where would she go? She still had no money, no identification, no medical gear. She covered her mouth to hold in a sob of despair.

'Do you...' Kade cleared his throat '...do you really want to go? I mean...you could stay. Tor would want you to stay.'

She said nothing, unable to speak through a throat tightening around tears.

'What if I...' He faltered then spoke in a rush. 'What if I don't want you to go? I screwed up. I should have listened to you. I just...Amanda...' He sighed. 'No, there's no excuses. I'm sorry. I'll work on it. Try to listen first instead of jumping to conclusions. You tried to tell me something about her. What was it?'

She edged away, afraid to say what she'd wanted to throw at him in anger before. Afraid to be trapped in this small, lethal room with a man who might take out his hurt reaction on whoever was close. She rubbed at the scar on her temple.

Hesitating, she straightened and lifted her chin. She'd been running from angry men her whole life. First her father, sometimes boyfriends, or husbands of women she'd midwifed for. Then Carleton.

Was that going to be her whole life? Running from men because she was afraid of what she might do to them? She inspected her hands. Today she had saved Carleton. And Kade. So, perhaps, her mother had been right. Perhaps the time had come. Perhaps she could be more than just a midwife. More than just a frightened girl, running and hiding. More than a martyr, sacrificing her life for others.

Glancing up, she caught Kade's apprehensive stare. And perhaps the right man had come along as well. One who could feel what she felt and not be overwhelmed. Who was willing to learn and grow.

But would he accept her, wholly?

And could he really let go of his past, and her part in it?

Only one way to find out.

She lifted her chin. 'Are you sure you want to hear the truth about Amanda?'

'Yes.' He drove his fingers into his hair. 'No. I don't know. But I think I need to.'

'And what if it turns out I did have a part in her death?' Heather folded her arms. 'What then?'

Kade's jaw clenched, his fists too. Then he relaxed.

'I wouldn't believe it. It took me awhile. Too long. But I finally saw who you are.' He stepped closer. 'You're the sort of person who will drive into the middle of nowhere to help a terrified illegal girl. Who'll save an absolute stranger, even at the risk of your own life. Even when it might mean losing your freedom. The sort of person who would save the life of her worst enemy if it was the right thing to do. No way did you kill Amanda. I know that, now.'

He stared into her eyes, mesmerising. 'Tell me.'

Heather suppressed the urge to retreat. 'Amanda Black died of complications from a home abortion. I was called in too late. Her *doctor* was her lover. *He* botched the abortion. She was only three months pregnant. The child wasn't yours. They were trying to hide the evidence of their affair.'

Kade stilled.

She retreated, observing him.

'Hell.' His word emerged broken. 'Jeff Saunders was the father?' With a cracked laugh wiped at his face. 'That explains a lot. He was one of my best friends. I wondered why he left town suddenly. I thought he felt guilty for not saving her.'

He buried his forehead in his palms and slid down the wall. 'Christ. Everyone at the base knew. The looks they gave me when I went to the base.' He looked up, eyes haunted and shadowed. 'Why didn't anyone tell me?'

Her heart broke for him and her fear dissolved. Heather eased herself alongside him and tucked an arm through his.

'Because you're a good person, Kade Miller. You were barely out of hospital. You'd lost your wife and child. No-one wanted to hurt you. I'm sorry I had to. Truly.'

He sighed. 'You didn't.' His lips pressed warm against her forehead. 'You set me free.'

He rose and drew her to her feet. His arms wound around her waist and he held her close. Heather rested her head on his shoulder and, for the first time in her life, allowed herself to relax in a man's arms.

She opened her mental shields to him. Kade smiled, traced the line of her cheek with one finger, and kissed her. She felt the moment he dropped his own shields. His fear was gone. All that remained was the spark of wonder and hope, the smouldering heat of desire, the solid foundation of belief and trust.

Belief and trust in her.

Wonder and hope for their future.

Desire to understand and love her. All of her.

With a sobbing laugh, she threw her arms around his neck and kissed him,

'I love you, Kade Miller,' she whispered.

'I love you, too, Heather O'Connor.' His lips softened against hers.

She surrendered the last of her fears to the honesty of that love.

#

END

I hope you enjoyed this fourth in the Shadows series – part of the Ruadhan Sidhe series. If so, please do leave reviews on your favourite retail sites and review sites. Reviews help other readers find authors they love and helps to prevent hardworking authors from starving.

Discover other titles by Aiki Flinthart
at: **www.aikiflinthart.com**
Including:

The Blackbirds Novels (Historical Fantasy)
Blackbirds Sing (#1)

The Ruadhan Sidhe Novels (YA Urban Fantasy)
Shadows Wake (#1)
Shadows Bane (#2)
Shadows Fate (#3)

The Kalima Chronicles (YA Adventure/Fantasy)
IRON (#1)
FIRE (#2)
STEEL (#3)
A Future, Forged (prequel)

The 80AD series (YA Adventure/Fantasy)
80AD Book 1: *The Jewel of Asgard*
80AD Book 2: *The Hammer of Thor*

Healing Heather p311

80AD Book 3: *The Tekhen of Anuket*
80AD Book 4: *The Sudarshana*
80AD Book 5: *The Yu Dragon*

Sold! (Contemporary Romance/Adventure)

Short Story Anthologies
The Zookeeper's Tales of Interstellar Oddities
Return
Elemental
Rogues' Gallery